FLIGHTS OF FANCY

Flights of Fancy

Cheryl Mildenhall

HEADLINE
Liaison

First published in 1996
by HEADLINE BOOK PUBLISHING

A HEADLINE LIAISON paperback

10 9 8 7 6 5 4 3 2 1

ISBN 0 7472 5215 7

Typeset at The Spartan Press Ltd,
Lymington, Hants

Printed and bound in Great Britain by
Cox & Wyman Ltd, Reading, Berks

HEADLINE BOOK PUBLISHING
A division of Hodder Headline PLC
338 Euston Road
London NW1 3BH

Flights
of Fancy

Chapter One

Lisa felt her left ankle give a little as she swung around and hit the wooden blocks with her right foot. Wobbling unsteadily, her foot still poised in midair, she glared at the sandy-haired teenager who was holding the blocks and desperately trying not to snigger.

'What do you call that?' he said, unable to contain himself. 'A kick like that wouldn't chop a mosquito in half.'

She glared even harder at her partner before remembering she was a good twelve or thirteen years older than him. Composing herself, she forced an air of nonchalance.

'My ankle went, that's all,' she explained. Bending down, she rubbed it and then straightened up. 'Tell you what, Sam. Let's try that again.'

The second kick was much harder and she watched with satisfaction as young Sam rocked on his heels. He nodded approvingly and Lisa forced herself not to look too pleased. Praise from someone as young as him was almost as irritating as scorn.

Mrs Swift, Lisa's mother, had said countless times that her daughter's pride would get the better of her one day. Her words had not been intended to be prophetic, more a

1

caution to anyone who happened to be within hearing distance. But as Lisa grew older so the warning began to sound as though it might actually come true. Lisa was proud of herself and her abilities. Sometimes she felt as though she could conquer the world. Or at least the part of the world that she occupied.

At work she was a high-flyer, literally. As a member of the cabin crew for British Airways she rarely kept her feet on the ground and had aspirations of climbing the corporate ladder as far as she could go. If there was a glass ceiling, as so many of the female employees within the industry claimed, she would make sure she was the first to shatter it to smithereens.

Having such ambitions were okay and would be more than enough for any normal woman, but what she really aspired to was so far beyond her grasp – and even beyond the realms of reality – that she couldn't ever envisage it happening. Flights of Fancy, as she dubbed her concept, would probably remain just that – an impossible dream.

'Lisa!' The shout from her instructor, Jack, brought her out of her reverie. 'You will please demonstrate for us the elementary *Pinans*.'

Lisa sighed. *Not again*. At the end of every second lesson, it seemed, she was called upon to execute the five basic *kata*, or karate moves, for the benefit of any visitors present. These were usually doting parents, or other relatives of her classmates.

At twenty-eight, she was by far the oldest person there still to be sporting a yellow belt. Even the youngest, ten-year-old Kazuo, was already two belts ahead of her on green. She sighed again. Sometimes, like today, she hated having a job with such irregular hours. It meant she couldn't even keep up with a simple karate class.

Trying not to look as unenthusiastic as she felt, she walked into the centre of the room where a huge space awaited her. As she stepped forward she glanced around. The rest of the class encircled her, white suited figures of various heights and builds all seated cross-legged and waiting patiently. A brief smile flickered across her face as her opponent rose from the circle and walked forward to meet her. Kazuo, of course, how fitting that she should have to suffer the ultimate humiliation.

It was then she noticed *him*. The inscrutable oriental man dressed entirely in black. He looked like a raven standing there just slightly apart from the others. Or a panther. Something predatory at any rate. A strange rhythmic beat seemed to build in tenor and surround her – as though she could hear and feel the vibration of his heartbeat from where she stood – and for some inexplicable reason she felt drawn to him. The rest of the class seemed to recede, fading into the background until the only people left were herself and the man. In the next moment a loud rushing sound filled her ears, her eyes widened as though she suddenly realised what was happening to her and then she swooned.

'You a'right, Lisa?' Young Kazuo had caught her by the arm and for a few seconds it was only his weight that supported her.

Feeling stunned, Lisa glanced down into his silky black eyes and nodded. 'Yes, I just felt a bit funny for a minute,' she said, 'but I'm okay now. Thank you.'

An uncertain smile crossed her face as she flicked a

stray tendril of curly dark hair away from her eyes, dusted her palms together briskly and assumed the appropriate stance to demonstrate the first of the *kata*, the *Kanku sho*.

Kazuo followed suit, mirroring her every move but, it seemed to her, with a lot more agility and finesse. What did that boy have that she didn't – apart from Japanese blood running through his veins?

At the end of the five *kata* she found her pride was to be tested even further. In an authoritarian voice that brooked no argument, Jack ordered a practical demonstration of sparring. 'No actual contact,' he warned, 'just the moves.'

Kazuo and Lisa nodded and bowed respectfully to him from the waist. Then they turned and bowed to each other before taking up the 'ready stance'. There was a momentary hush, then a split second later it was like being surrounded by a human tornado. Kazuo was everywhere, feet and fists flying so fast they were a blur, while all she could do was attempt a few ineffectual blocking movements.

God, it was embarrassing to be shown up by a child, even one as talented as her current partner. The humiliation seemed to go on and on and, to make matters worse, on several occasions Lisa caught the Japanese man watching her as she sidestepped Kazuo. He should have been watching his son but for some reason she felt certain his dark, narrowed eyes were directed only at her. It was weird but she didn't have time to think about it.

Lisa forced herself to concentrate on the demonstration. At last Kazuo seemed to be starting to lose his impetus and now she felt ready to show what she could do.

With only a moment's hesitation she lifted her right foot, brought the knee up to her side, spun on her left leg and delivered a roundhouse kick to the boy's head. *Thud!* She felt her foot connect with his skull and she dropped her foot immediately as Kazuo fell to the floor.

Shit! He wasn't supposed to do that. He should have deflected the kick. He should have blocked her. He should—

'I'm sorry. I'm sorry,' she repeated over and over in desperation as the rest of the class crowded around them.

Jack pushed his way through the buzzing throng and told Kazuo to lie still where he was. 'I am going to call for an ambulance just to be on the safe side,' he said to no one in particular, although his searching gaze finally found the troubled face of the Japanese man. 'Ah, Mr Tanaka. I assure you your son will be okay. It was just a minor accident. The ambulance is only a precaution.'

Lisa glanced at Jack and then at Kazuo's father.

'I am not the boy's father,' he said, 'I am his uncle.' His glance fell on Lisa. 'Do not trouble yourself, young lady. He has taken much harder knocks than this in his time.' To her surprise, his face softened into a smile.

She could feel her insides melting. 'I am really sorry,' she said faintly. 'Please, can I come to the hospital with you?'

His smile continued, creasing his finely chiselled face, long lines running from the outer edges of his lips to the uptilted corners of his dark, almond eyes. He nodded. 'Of course, although I do not think hospitalisation will be necessary. As I said, the boy has taken much harder knocks. He has a skull of steel, just like his uncle.'

Lisa stared at him and his gaze and smile were unwavering. Eventually she was forced to look away. The thread that seemed to hold the two of them spellbound was unceremoniously broken by the arrival of the paramedics. One, a no-nonsense character in green overalls, cleared everyone out of the way with a few stern words and proceeded to pronounce Kazuo fit and well.

'He'll probably have a headache for the rest of the evening,' the man said, 'but nothing a couple of paracetamol won't cure.'

'Can I still go to school tomorrow?' Kazuo asked, sounding and looking anxious.

Lisa was amazed. Since when did kids worry about taking a day off?

The paramedic nodded. 'Don't see why not,' he said, gratified to see the relief on the boy's face and to know he was responsible. Godlike moments such as this went some way to compensate for all the financial and marital suffering that his job caused him.

Mr Tanaka helped his nephew to his feet as Jack saw the paramedics to the door. While all the drama had been taking place the rest of the class had changed out of their karate suits yet were still waiting patiently in rows for Jack to go through the usual home-time ritual. They stood, they bowed, they mumbled in Japanese and then they were streaming out of the door and into the early-evening air.

'Would you care to join us for refreshment before you leave, Miss— Er?'

Lisa turned, it was Kazuo's uncle talking to her. Without realising what she was doing, she nodded dumbly.

'Your name?' he prompted gently.

Feeling unaccountably flustered, she fumbled for her powers of speech. 'Oh, er, Lisa,' she said, 'Lisa Swift.' She held out her hand. 'Pleased to meet you, Mr Tanaka.'

Kazuo's uncle had resumed his inscrutable expression but his black eyes seemed to twinkle as he grasped her hand and shook it. 'I am also very pleased to meet *you*, Lisa,' he assured her, hesitating over her name for just a second. 'And call me Akira, if you please. To hear you call me Mr Tanaka is too formal even for my sensibilities.'

He watched, amused, as Lisa blinked. It was obvious that the young woman was confused by the way he spoke. And she seemed nervous. She could hardly look him in the eye and blushed nearly all the time. Entertaining though her reactions might be, they were also very attractive.

He stopped at one of the white melamine tables that populated the cafe area of the sports centre and indicated that she should sit down. Kazuo made it clear he wanted to sit next to her, so Lisa slid across to the seat opposite Akira. She could hardly bear to look up at him but when she did she was relieved to see that he was engrossed in the menu.

Susan, her favourite waitress, came over to their table, pad and pencil poised, to take their order. Having asked Akira what he would like, she winked surreptitiously at Lisa. Lisa grinned. Susan obviously thought there was romance afoot. Equally surreptitiously, Lisa glanced at Akira and then shook her head.

'Just coffee please.' Akira's voice made the two women jump guiltily. 'What about you, Kazuo?'

Obviously feeling much better, the young boy confidently ordered a serving of French fries and a glass of cola, with chocolate ice cream to follow. Lisa smiled and added another coffee to the list.

As Susan melted into the background again and Kazuo got up to play on an arcade game on the far side of the room, Lisa felt herself drawn by the force of Akira's gaze. Her head felt heavy as she raised her chin and felt her eyes focus on his face. Unwilling to look completely at him, she concentrated on his nose instead. It was a nice nose, straight and neat, with just the slightest bump halfway down the bridge.

'Why can you not bring yourself to look at me?' Akira's words came to her softly, floating into her ears like wisps of smoke.

Lisa's voice was hoarse as she forced herself to reply. When she did, it wasn't what she meant to say. 'You frighten me,' she said.

At last she dared to look into Akira's eyes and felt a powerful warmth creep up on her. Starting at the tips of her toes, it spread like wildfire throughout her whole body.

'How do I frighten you?' he asked in an amused tone. 'Am I fierce. Do I threaten you with harm. Tell me how?'

'I don't know,' Lisa replied softly, shaking her head in confusion. 'You just do that's all. It's – it's the way you look at me I suppose.'

She was unable to qualify her feelings any further. The heat in her body hadn't abated. In fact, if anything, it was growing stronger, licking at her fingertips and the soles of her feet, setting her hair alight until she felt as though she had a glowing halo around her head. Keenest of all, she felt the fire inflame her womb.

Pinned by Akira's steady gaze, she felt her body weakening, melting into the chair where she sat. Her juices were running freely now, soaking the crotch of her knickers and seeping into the thick cotton of her trousers. The insistent trickling sensation made her itch. It made her sex itch so badly that she squirmed on the seat in an effort to alleviate it.

'Don't do this to me,' she whispered, conscious only of his eyes upon her. Everything else around her meant nothing. Nothing else existed. Only herself and Akira.

'Don't do what?' He laughed lightly although his expression didn't alter. He narrowed his eyes still further. 'Do you know I can see into your soul?'

Able for a moment to escape the clutches of his gaze, Lisa's eyes roamed wildly. What the hell was happening here – why couldn't anyone see that this man was the devil himself?

'You love sex, don't you, Lisa?' he continued in the same low tone, his questioning as remorseless as his piercing stare. 'If you could, you would devote your whole life to pleasure.'

'I don't know what you mean.' Lisa felt her voice growing hoarse. It hurt to speak, to deny his claim. It was true she liked sex. She was a normal, healthy, red-blooded young woman, why shouldn't she enjoy it?

His gaze made her feel guilty. Of course she knew what he meant. If she could afford it she would stop work tomorrow and simply become a hedonist. But then after a few weeks she would become bored. Her mind was too active for indolence. She needed a challenge. The perfect combination of sex and work would be Flights of Fancy but, as she'd already come to accept, that could only ever be a dream.

'I am going to allow you to come now,' he said quietly.

'What?'

Lisa gazed even harder at him, her eyes widening. Something was happening to her. The itching in her sex had turned to a dull pulsing that grew in intensity with each passing second. Her knickers were soaked with her own juices and the crotch of her trousers was similarly sodden. There was so much moisture she could smell it. The heady, musky scent filled her nostrils, making her feel light-headed.

Akira wrinkled his nose and nodded confidently.

Dear God, he could smell her arousal too!

Lisa gripped the edge of the table for support. Her cheeks flamed and she had to fight to control her breathing. She had never, ever felt as embarrassed or as out of her depth as she did right at that moment. Her lungs were tight, as though they were being squeezed, and there was a blockage in her throat.

Beneath her jacket, she could imagine the sight of her full, rounded breasts heaving with the effort of each breath. She couldn't see them, couldn't tear her gaze away from his, yet she knew the gaping neckline of her jacket put the upper swell of her breasts on show. And even though his eyes concentrated on hers, she didn't doubt for one moment that he could also see other parts of her body.

An awfully long time seemed to have passed and yet

Susan had not returned with their order and Kazuo was still playing with the arcade machines on the other side of the cafe. Lisa licked her lips. She was perspiring heavily now; it trickled down her face in salty rivulets and pooled in the hollows of her collarbones and in the dip at the base of her throat.

However damp the top half of her body might be, it could not match the wetness between her legs. She shifted in her chair slightly, trying to ease the uncomfortable sensation, but the movement set her sex pulsing anew. This time she literally felt her clitoris swell. She could feel it forcing apart her inner labia and nudging its way between her puffy outer lips. The seam of her trousers rubbed against the tormented flesh as she moved, arousing her even more.

She crossed her legs and rocked gently back and forth. The stimulation was bliss. Sweet, erotic bliss that carried her away on a wave of sensuality. Tighter and tighter she gripped her thighs together and rocked, harder and harder. She could feel her breath coming in short, sharp gasps. Perhaps people could hear her and see her. By now it hardly mattered. So what? She had very nearly reached nirvana. What did it matter if others were there to witness her transition?

Her cry was hoarse and cracked. To her ears it sounded as loud and as shrill as the wail of a banshee, but in reality it was nothing more than a muffled groan. Slumping over the table, she lay her burning cheek on the cool melamine and waited for her rapid breathing to subside. A cool draught dried the perspiration on her face and neck. To her surprise she realised that her hands were no longer

11

gripping the table but were tightly clasped between her thighs. Slowly, the realisation hit her. She had been masturbating in public. In full view of everyone. *Oh, God!*

For a long while she kept her eyes closed and her face resting on the table top. Finally Susan slammed down a cup and saucer in front of her and she was forced to open her eyes.

'This isn't a motel you know,' the waitress said tersely.

Oh, dear God! Lisa thought again. *She watched me. She knows.*

'Go home if you want to sleep.'

With a sigh of relief, Lisa realised that Susan hadn't seen her masturbate at all. In fact, a hasty glance around told her that no one was paying any attention to her whatsoever. Did that mean she hadn't really masturbated – or simply that she had but that no one had noticed? *If a tree falls down in the forest and there is no one there to witness it, does that mean the tree never fell at all?*

Lisa picked up her coffee cup and, with trembling fingers, brought it to her lips. At that moment Kazuo returned and instantly began tucking into his plate of fries. By the time the boy had finished his ice cream, Akira and Lisa were both on a second cup of coffee.

She glanced at her watch. 'It's getting late,' she said. 'I didn't realise.'

Akira nodded and laid a ten-pound note down on the table. 'Yes, it is time for us to go.'

Lisa hesitated. All at once she dreaded being parted from this man – this strange, enigmatic man who seemed to know the workings of her body. He had said he could see into her soul and she believed him.

'Come.' As he stood up he held out his hand to her.

Lisa ignored his outstretched hand but rose to her feet anyway. 'Do you mean you want me to come with you?' she asked hesitantly.

Again he nodded, a smile touching the corners of his mouth. 'I do.' He glanced at Kazuo. 'We will drop the boy off at my brother's house and then I will take you to my apartment.'

She felt as though something momentous were happening to her. Her car was in the car park but it would be quite safe. She wasn't due back on duty for another two days so she had plenty of time to kill.

'Okay,' she said. 'I'd like that.'

The understated opulence of Akira's apartment came as no surprise to her. It was stark in its simplicity, with plain black walls and parchment screens dotted about everywhere. The furniture was low and black, nothing above waist height, not even a cupboard. It was very Japanese and yet modern too.

The paintings that decorated the walls at odd intervals were an eclectic mixture of old and new. A Picasso hung next to a similar contemporary work by an artist whose name had appeared frequently in the Sunday supplements. Pieces of blue and white porcelain were interspersed by tall, straight-sided vases of opaque black glass. The modern vessels held arrangements of ikebana – fresh flowers and twigs arranged with precise artistry.

Suddenly, at the far side of the vast living room a door opened. Painted matt black like the wall, the door was a piece of visual trickery. One moment the room contained only the two of them and then there was a third.

The interloper was a young Japanese woman, no older than her early twenties. She was tiny and perfectly formed, like a little bird. Her body seemed so fragile, her limbs as straight and as neat as the ikebana twigs.

'Tanaka San, you are much later than I expected.' The young woman's voice danced lightly across the space that divided them. It was a musical voice, sweet and pure.

Akira smiled and held out his hand to the young woman who rushed to his side immediately. 'Michiko, I would like you to meet Lisa—?' he broke off and looked at Lisa inquiringly.

'Oh, I thought I told you. It's Swift,' she said hastily. 'Lisa Swift.'

'Swift,' Akira repeated looking firstly at the Japanese woman and then at Lisa herself.

The melting sensation started up again and she sat down hastily without waiting to be asked.

'You will want the bathroom,' Michiko said to her. It was a statement rather than a question and to her surprise Lisa found herself nodding enthusiastically. She did want to use the bathroom. Now she came to think about it, she was desperate to empty her bladder.

She followed Michiko across the room to another trompe l'oeil door. Like the rest of the apartment, the bathroom had a monochrome colour scheme, with a precisely patterned mosaic of tiles covering all four walls from floor to ceiling. The fittings, including a bidet and huge sunken bath, were of black marble and all the towels looked as thick and inviting as clotted cream.

Relieving herself quickly, she moved to the basin and

began to wash her hands. As the warm water played over her fingers, she found that she was gazing at herself. Or rather, her reflection. But she hardly recognised the young woman who stared back.

It seemed her usually pale complexion was bright pink, almost crimson in places, especially on the rounded contours of her high cheekbones. She realised that with the deeper skin tone, she had quite an oriental look about her.

Her eyes were almond-shaped, although much less narrow and more elongated than those belonging to Michiko or Akira. Her nose was small and perfectly proportioned, whereas her mouth was wide, with full, generous lips. Leaning forward over the basin she peered closely at her lips. They seemed swollen, she realised, as though she had just received the bruising kisses of an ardent lover. And despite the fact that she wore no lipstick, their colour was a deep, plummy red.

Regardless of her individual features, it was her hair that seemed the most oriental. Thick and curly, the dark, almost jet black tendrils had worked themselves free of the pins that had been holding them and now fell freely, surrounding her face with a dusky cloud.

'Lisa, you are alright?' Michiko's voice came to her through the locked door and she straightened up.

Turning off the taps, she dried her hands quickly and walked back across the bathroom, opened the door and stepped once again into Akira's lair.

He was waiting for her with a glass of champagne in each hand. Thrusting one crystal flute towards her, he smiled and invited her to sit down. Lisa glanced around. Michiko had disappeared.

'She has gone to bed now,' Akira said in answer to her unspoken question.

Lisa nodded. 'I assume Michiko is your wife?'

'Then you assume wrong.' Akira sat down at the other end of the three-seater leather sofa.

'Sister?' Lisa asked. 'Girlfriend?'

Infuriatingly, Akira shook his head. Then after a few moments of silence had passed between them he relented. 'She is my assistant,' he said. 'A sort of secretary cum personal valet.'

Now it was Lisa's turn to nod, pretending that she understood when she didn't. Was it normal for employees to live with their bosses?

Feeling as though she was out of her depth, she decided to change the subject. 'This is lovely champagne,' she murmured as she raised her glass to take another sip of the delightfully effervescent liquid. Hundreds of bubbles exploded on her tongue and at the back of her throat as she drank.

'Hm, yes. It is okay,' Akira said. 'I keep my best stock of wine at the New York apartment.'

New York apartment!

'How many, er, apartments do you have?' she asked. She couldn't help it, she had to know.

Akira laughed. 'Only three. The third is in Tokyo, of course.'

'Oh, of course.' Lisa gave a sober nod and wondered exactly what sort of man she was dealing with. Obviously he was very rich. And cultured. 'What do you do for a living, Akira?' she added.

He crossed his legs and his upper foot began to sway

nonchalantly as he answered. 'This and that.' Lisa's frown didn't go unnoticed. 'I am a businessman,' he said. 'Mostly, these days, I merely travel around, checking on the various companies in the Tanaka group.'

Lisa gulped. Of course, the Tanaka group. She was surprised she hadn't recognised the name. It was one of the world's largest industrial holdings companies.

'I'm impressed,' she said lightly. The last thing she wanted to do was show him how impressed she really was. She supposed men like Akira Tanaka were used to getting anything they wanted. Well, if he wanted her he could think again. As soon as she finished her champagne she was off.

'You are thinking of going so soon?' Akira asked. Ignoring her protests he leaned towards her and topped up her champagne.

'You needn't think you can get me tipsy,' Lisa asserted. 'I have drunk bigger men than you under the table.'

'Is that supposed to impress me?'

Flashing him an angry glance, Lisa wondered if anything ever dented his supercilious personality.

She shrugged. 'Not really. I just want you to know that I'm not some weak little woman who falls apart after a couple of glasses of champagne and allows herself to be seduced by strange men.'

A tiny smile touched Akira's lips and eyes. 'Really?' he said. 'So you think I plan to seduce you?'

'Don't you?' Lisa dared to glance at him again and this time she saw only amusement and friendliness in his gaze. It completely disarmed her.

Akira put down his glass and clasped his hands behind

17

his head. 'That depends,' he said. 'I would be lying if I said I wasn't attracted to you but—' he paused.

'But what?'

'But you are always trying to fight me and quite frankly I cannot be sure if you are worth the effort.'

Lisa gave a derisory snort. 'Please yourself. That's for me to know and you to find out.' Straight away she regretted her childish retort. She was positive she should be more sophisticated by now.

Akira reclined further, demonstrating how relaxed he felt despite her agitation. Or perhaps because of it.

'Make no mistake, Lisa,' he said, 'I shall please myself and – yes – I shall find out. In fact, I shall enjoy finding out.'

For the second time that evening Lisa heard him laugh aloud but this time it was far more than a mere chuckle. It was low and dark and treacly, a deliciously terrifying sound which thrilled her to the very core.

Chapter Two

It bugged Lisa that Akira seemed to have found the one
drink that went straight to her head and stayed there. To
be honest she hadn't drunk champagne that often before,
just the odd glass at weddings and so forth. Now, if he had
given her whisky, vodka, gin, or just about any other spirit
you'd care to name, she could have drunk glass after glass
and still remained sober and in control of herself. With
three older brothers she had learned the art of hard
drinking at an early age. But frothy little glasses of
champagne, five in all, were proving to be her undoing.

Akira seemed very relaxed, she noticed. He had reclined further on the sofa and in the last few minutes had
actually put his feet up and rested them on her lap.

'You don't mind, do you?' he asked, raising one silky
black eyebrow which reminded her of the caterpillars she
used to catch as a child.

Unable to think of a reason why she should object she
shook her head dumbly.

Akira sort of smiled. In the couple of hours she had
known him, she had come to realise that he rarely smiled a
proper full-on smile – the one that started at his mouth
and finished at his eyes, calling at all stops in between.

Most of the time his expression was either completely deadpan, or slightly less than deadpan. It was the slightly less than deadpan look which she called his other smile. At least the expression resulted in a barely discernible curve to the lips and a slight twinkle to the eyes.

'I really don't mind having your feet in my lap,' she said, wanting to best him, to spoil his amusement. It was an urge she had had most of the time since she met him.

Glancing down, she noticed how small his feet actually were. Narrow and perfectly shaped, they were probably no more than a size six or seven. Impulsively, she pulled off his black wool socks and noticed instantly that his toenails were nicely manicured and the skin on his heels and the soles of his feet was baby soft.

'I thought you might have tough feet,' she said, holding one foot and stroking it absently with her other hand, as though it were a cat.

He chuckled. 'Why?'

Lisa gave him a sideways glance. 'Because, being Japanese, I expected you to be a martial arts expert and have tough feet which you use to chop down small trees and large hoodlums.'

'Hoodlums!' He chuckled again.

'You know what I mean.' Lisa pursed her lips. 'Anyone involved in a business as large as yours must come across the odd crook.'

She watched covertly as Akira nodded. He was silent for a moment, staring off into space, apparently recalling something. Suddenly, he seemed to come back to reality.

'Give me a private demonstration of your karate skills,' he said unexpectedly, 'and I'll tape it on my new video camera.' He jumped up with all the enthusiasm and excitement of a small boy and just for a moment he reminded Lisa of Kazuo.

His sudden change in demeanor startled her. 'What? Here!' She glanced around, his living room was easily twice the size of the gym where she normally practised. Why not?

'Yes, here.' He began to move furniture away from the huge slab of black marble that doubled as a coffee table.

Gradually, it dawned on her that he meant her to use the table as a podium. 'Okay,' she said hesitantly, rising to her feet.

She waited uncertainly, feeling ever so slightly woozy as the champagne bubbles danced around inside her body. It seemed as though she too popped and fizzed with latent energy, the urge to perform for him suddenly overwhelming her.

He left the room for a moment and returned carrying the tiniest video camera she had ever seen. Japanese technology strikes again, she thought, wondering why she didn't feel even slightly daunted at the prospect of being filmed.

Akira walked towards her, eyeing her thoughtfully. 'That suit will not do,' he said. 'Please take it off.'

Lisa stared stupidly at him. 'Take it off?' She repeated. All she was wearing underneath were a tiny pair of bikini knickers.

'Yes, off. I want to watch your body move without the hindrance of clothing. I want to be able to see your muscles working.'

Now she did feel doubtful. Doubtful and a little scared of him. 'I don't think that's a very good idea,' she said slowly. 'Perhaps it is time I went home.'

Taking a step back, he sat on the edge of the table, his legs straight out in front of him and crossed at the ankles. 'Is that what you really want?'

To her own surprise she shook her head, spitting out a strand of hair that got caught in her mouth. She pushed it away with her hand, smoothing the rest of her hair back from her face. Already her uncertainty was changing to excitement. The special way he looked at her thrilled her all over again and, for a fleeting moment, she remembered the power of her earlier orgasm. Another one or two like that wouldn't do her any harm. If she left now she would probably miss out on one of the most promising sexual encounters she had ever had.

Slowly, she began to unfasten her belt and then unzipped the jacket. The edges fell apart exposing a long line of pale skin, from throat to navel. Dropping to bended knee she untied her shoelaces and removed the pair of white pumps that she habitually wore for karate practice. Her socks followed. Then she hesitated. Straightening up again she unfastened the cord that kept her baggy trousers in place. With a slight wriggle of her hips she let them fall to her ankles.

While she undressed she didn't dare to look at Akira. She knew he was watching her intently but felt unable to cope with the reality of her situation. It was easier to pretend that she was somewhere else, either at home or in the changing room of the leisure centre.

Her face fell. 'Oh, shit! I've just remembered something.' Stepping out of her trousers, she kicked them aside.

'And that is?' Akira's voice forced her to look at him

and immediately Lisa wished she hadn't. His eyes were penetrating, scanning every inch of her partially clad body and finally coming to rest on her pubic mound – the thick bush of dark curly hair clearly visible through the fragile white lace of her knickers.

Blushing wildly, she told him that she had left her holdall with all her clothes, money and car keys in a changing-room locker.

'You have the locker key though, don't you?' he asked, glancing back at her face. She nodded. It was pinned to the inside of her karate jacket. 'Then there is no problem. Your things will be quite safe where they are. You can collect them tomorrow.'

Knowing that she had no proper clothes, no car and no money made Lisa feel at a distinct disadvantage. Hell, even the keys to her flat were in that bag. The three other stewardesses she shared with were all on duty so there would be no one to let her in even if she did go home. *I'm trapped*, she thought, *trapped in the lair of a very scary man.*

As though he could read her thoughts Akira handed her a fresh glass of champagne. 'Here. Drink this,' he offered. 'You look as though you need to relax.'

She took the glass from him and gulped at it gratefully. Soon the delicate alcohol began to take effect. 'That is magical stuff,' she said, allowing the smile to return to her face.

Akira nodded. He didn't bother to sit down again but instead moved behind her and helped to remove her jacket, sliding it over her shoulders and down her arms. When he had disposed of the jacket he came to stand behind her again and placed his hands lightly on her upper arms. A moment later his fingers moved and began to knead her flesh, rotating thumbs loosening the taut muscles at the base of her skull, moving down her neck and across her shoulders with practised ease.

'Mm, that's heavenly,' Lisa sighed, allowing her head to drop back so that the feathery ends of her hair caressed her naked skin.

'If you want a proper massage you should ask Michiko to give you one,' Akira murmured. 'Her touch is so light and skilful you would swear her fingers can dance.'

Personal assistants who give massages, Lisa thought, *now there's an idea to conjure with.*

For the first time that evening she felt truly relaxed in his company. He obviously wasn't desperate for sexual release, he doubtless had Michiko there to see to that sort of thing. So the chances of him raping her were pretty remote.

Just as she felt her self-confidence return he dropped to his haunches behind her and whipped her knickers down her legs.

'Oh, God!' His unexpected action had a startling effect on her. Suddenly, her juices were flowing again, her sex throbbing. She could feel her buttocks clenching and unclenching under the heat of his gaze and his breath upon her skin.

'Turn around,' he said.

On unwilling feet she turned. Slowly. Inching her toes around until she faced him head on. Or rather, groin on. Despite her conflicting emotions she allowed herself a small, embarrassed giggle. His face was directly level with the tops of her thighs.

Keeping her legs tightly together, she forced herself to look down at him. His hands caressed her feet, his fingers working every tiny bone and sinew. They moved slowly, stroking her ankles, kneading her calves, her knees, her thighs. Finally, the backs of his fingers brushed lightly across her mound and then stroked lower, skimming the tight little purse of her outer labia.

The lightness of his touch sent a shudder through her, the torment almost as unbearable as the humiliation. To her relief, he rose to his feet and took her hand, guiding her as she stepped up onto the black marble table. It was about five feet square, leaving her in no doubt that she could execute most moves without falling off. Even if she did, it was only eighteen inches thick at the most. She was hardly going to break her neck.

Her fingers slipped from his as she moved to the centre of the table and he returned to the sofa. He moved it back, away from the table and then perched on the edge. Picking up the video camera, he brought the viewfinder to his eye and pointed the camera straight at her. For a moment he practised zooming in and out and then asked her to proceed.

Until this moment, Lisa stood ramrod straight, legs still together and her hands clasped tightly in front of her so that her arms obscured her full breasts. Now he wanted her to move and the ridiculousness of the situation suddenly struck her.

'I'm sorry. I can't do this,' she said, shaking her head. 'I feel like an idiot.'

'You look beautiful,' he assured her, 'and the camera doesn't lie.' He moved the grey box away from his face and actually winked at her. 'Please, Lisa,' he said, becoming serious again. 'Please, just do it for me.'

It was difficult to resist a man who begged. And she liked the way he spoke about her. When he said she looked beautiful she didn't feel coy about it. She believed him. He had a strange way of making her believe everything he said and it left her feeling desirable – a whole woman able to achieve anything she wanted.

With a deep breath she stared straight at him and gave a formal bow, conscious of the fact that her breasts swung invitingly. Straightening up, her cheeks slightly flushed, she took up the ready stance and then began to move.

At first she demonstrated only the various arm *kata*: lunge punches, reverse punches and a variety of blocking moves among them. And as she moved so Akira skirted around her, his concentration intense as the camera recorded her every action. His close presence meant she couldn't forget about the camera and felt herself blushing frequently as her breasts wobbled, or she was forced to move her legs apart.

'Show me some kicks,' Akira said after a while.

Lisa swallowed deeply. Kicks would be horribly shaming. Even more embarrassing than the *kata* she had so far demonstrated.

Ignoring her unwillingness, he repeated his request.

'Okay, but I need some more champagne first,' Lisa said, thinking she needed a lot more than champagne. It wasn't that she was ashamed about her body, or coy in any way, far from it. She had never been backwards in coming forwards – or simply in coming full stop. The main reason she didn't want to start doing kicks was because she knew full well that between her legs she was simply oozing moisture. She could feel her sex and her inner thighs coated with her own juices and dreaded him seeing the proof of her arousal for himself.

He waited until she had swallowed two flutes of champagne straight down, one after the other. Then he took up a kneeling position to the table.

'Give me a back kick,' he said, pointing the camera at her.

Lisa hesitated just for a moment. Suddenly, she slid her feet across the polished black marble, twisted her hips sharply and brought her right knee up close to her body. Then she kicked back, her leg arrow straight and carrying a lot of power. If Akira had been standing behind her she would have floored him for sure.

She could sense, rather than hear, the camera whirring, recording her movements.

'Hold that stance,' Akira instructed.

Gulping, Lisa forced herself to stand firm, bending forward from the waist to balance her right leg which was raised so far into the air that she was almost doing the splits. It was not a very ladylike position to be in, especially unclothed. To her shame, she felt her sex blossoming even more, her outer lips swelling and moving apart as her inner lips also swelled and peeped through the slit.

'Wonderful,' Akira murmured, moving across the table, almost slithering like a snake. He lay beneath her raised leg, filming her exposed vulva from below and then he rolled over onto his stomach and filmed her from another angle. 'This is great,' he said. 'You are really open and your vagina is virtually awash.'

A delicious warmth spread through Lisa as he spoke. He sounded so matter of fact in his appreciation of her body that she could hardly deny him the opportunity to look at it and to film her. And yet she felt terribly ashamed of herself and her blatant behaviour. Lowering her right leg slowly, she spun around and simulated a front kick and then one to the side. She finished with a round-house kick, just like the one that had injured Kazuo. The one that was responsible for her meeting Akira in the first place.

'God, I love these kicks,' she said aloud. Smiling down into the camera, she winked.

Akira sat back and pressed a red button on the side of the grey box. 'Okay. I think that will do.' He held out his hand and helped her down from the table.

The big question, *what now?* circulated Lisa's mind again. A quick glance at her watch told her it was only a quarter past one and yet she had no home to go to, or money for a hotel. She was so lost in thought that she didn't notice Akira stand up and walk over to her. Only when she felt his arms encircling her from behind did she realise.

His arms gripped her hard around the waist, pulling her back against him. 'You looked so beautiful,' he growled into her ear. 'Is it any wonder I want you so badly?'

Her buttocks felt something reassuringly hard nudge against them and yet she still asked, 'Do you?' as if she were a timid schoolgirl and not a woman of the world.

One hand broke free and roamed her torso, cupping and squeezing each breast in turn until she moaned aloud and felt her knees sag under the weight of her arousal.

Then the other hand moved down, the palm sliding over her belly, the fingertips becoming entangled in her pubic hair. They tugged gently at the silky curls, making her sex pout.

Still holding her, he walked her across the room until they stood in front of a full-length mirror. Her eyes were immediately drawn to the hand spanning her breasts and then lower, to the one that displayed her sex so shamelessly. Feeling a fresh surge of arousal, she watched their reflections as his fingers delved lower and spread her outer labia wide apart. Her clitoris looked huge, like a tiny cock – swollen and throbbing, desperate for release.

'Not yet,' he murmured, as though he could read her mind.

All of a sudden Lisa was seized with the urge to beg him. She wanted to throw him down onto the thick black carpet and straddle him. She wanted to take his cock, plunge it deep inside her and ride him until his inscrutable expression cracked. She wanted to make him come.

If she hadn't had the advantage of surprise, she would never have been able to floor him so easily. But as it was he was flat on his back with her astride him in seconds. He tried to throw her off but failed. Despite his overpowering presence he wasn't a big man, certainly no taller and only slightly larger in build than she. And she had the advantage of surprise and of being on top.

She sat astride his chest, the glistening flesh of her pouting sex only centimetres away from his face. Glancing at her sex, he then looked into her eyes and asked a silent question. Lisa wavered. She wanted desperately to fuck him but the promise of his soft, sulky mouth was too tempting to resist. Slowly, she inched forward until her pubic hair tickled his chin, then she rose majestically to her knees.

Akira looked up and saw her sex directly above his face. She seemed unsteady and wavered, sometimes hovering over his mouth, other times his nose and then his eyes. When she did this he fancied he should see right inside her, see past the reddened, swollen flesh and into the silky tunnel of her vagina.

Bringing his hands up he gripped her buttocks hard and forced her over his mouth, his lips fastening greedily on her, drinking in her nectar as his tongue drove her wild with desire.

She peaked again and again, helpless in the grip of Akira's hands and engrossed by her own lust. Finally, when she could take no more, she squirmed in his hands and he released her so that she could lower herself and sit lightly on his chest.

'I will fuck you in my bed,' he said, smiling up at her. 'It will be much more comfortable than the floor.'

He shifted slightly under her and she rolled limply off him, laying on her back on the carpet, arms and legs carelessly splayed as he got to his feet. Looking down at her he marvelled at the wonderful contrast of her pale body against the dark background. Her hair was a dark cloud, as black as the carpet and framing a heart-shaped face so beautiful and finely boned that he could have wept.

Everything about her was perfection in his eyes. Her almond-shaped eyes were huge and black, edged by thick lashes and topped by well-plucked brows. Set between two curving, apple cheeks her nose was faultless: smooth and straight and just slightly retroussé. And her mouth looked soft and inviting, the pale pink lips just slightly parted revealing a glimpse of even, pearly teeth.

Kneeling down beside her, he slid his arms under the backs of her knees and beneath her shoulders, then lifted her. As he stood up he staggered just a little and Lisa giggled, her head falling back to reveal a long, white throat. Entranced by the sight, Akira bent forward and planted a kiss just beneath her chin and then another at the base of her throat. Lisa turned her head and his gaze came to rest on her lips. In moments their mouths were locked, their tongues dancing around each other as they kissed and kissed. Finally, he broke away.

'My bedroom awaits,' he said for no particular reason other than to ease the undeniable tension between them.

Lisa was amused to find that he had a water bed. She expected a futon, or similar item of Japanese furniture. Instead he dropped her onto a surface that undulated beneath her.

'Oh, God, what is this!' She exclaimed. Putting out her hand, she tested the bed carefully, realising instantly what it was. With a giggle she said, 'I've never slept in a water bed before.'

Akira winked. 'You're not going to sleep in one now,' he said meaningfully. He was taking off his clothes as he spoke, draping each item carefully over the back of a chair.

At his words, Lisa felt a rush of desire. And when he flicked on a row of downlighters, dimming them instantly, she was able to see his body properly. The heat that had started up inside her grew to an inferno. God, he was fit! Although fairly small in stature, his musculature was good. Better than good. And his body seemed to gleam in the low, pinkish light. She didn't know how old he was but guessed that he was somewhere in his early thirties.

'Thirty-two,' he confirmed when she asked him.

He lay alongside her and stroked a thoughtful palm across her breasts. Her nipples hardenly instantly, the dark red buds swelling with her desire for him. She parted her legs slightly, just to ease the discomfort she felt – a slight tingling cum itching that was slowly growing in intensity.

'That's young to be in charge of such a huge conglomerate,' she murmured, sighing as he bent his head and took one of her nipples between his lips.

For a moment he sucked her, drawing the nipple deeper and deeper into his mouth until she felt the answering tug of arousal and groaned aloud. Then he raised his head slightly and said, 'My father is still in charge officially. But in reality he does very little. I make most of the decisions.'

He sounded so proud, almost like a young boy boasting of his exam results, that her heart went out to him. 'I think you deserve success,' she said quietly.

Her fingers played idly with his hair as he stroked and sucked her breasts. She felt so contented she didn't want to move. Nor did she feel compelled to take a more active part in the proceedings. There was such a sense of non-urgency about him. As though the world and everything in it would wait for them.

His voice came to her through a blissful haze. 'Tell me about you and about your ambitions.'

Lisa stared at the ceiling and told him about her job and her hobbies: reading, swimming and, of course, karate. She told him about her family: her father now dead, her mother and three brothers. She told him about her flatmates and some of the escapades they got up to. Escapades which invariably involved men.

Usually other men perked up at the prospect of being privy to the antics of four, sexually liberated women. Even though they were no longer called stewardesses, the old cliché, 'I'm Lisa, fly me,' still seemed to stick. Most of the time her job made it difficult for her to get men to take her seriously. Now here was a man who listened but did not interject with crass comments. Nor did he snigger, or raise his eyebrows suggestively.

Then, in a hesitant voice and just as he moved his head lower to slide his tongue across her belly and dip into her navel, she began to tell him about Flights of Fancy. He licked her – she spoke. He gave her burning flesh tiny wet sucks and she still continued to speak. Her dream consumed her to the exclusion of all else. Finally, in desperation, he plunged his cock deep inside her, taking her breath away and silencing her words.

The sensation of his hardness inside her was pure ecstasy, she thought dreamily, raising her pelvis to take him deeper and deeper. For a small man he felt huge, his girth filling her honeyed vagina so completely that she whimpered as she ground herself against him.

Akira groaned and plunged deeper still. 'I am going to fuck you hard,' he growled darkly, his jet eyes glittering as he commanded her gaze. 'So hard I'll make you scream.'

One hand slid over her shoulder to cup her breast and she arched her back, pressing herself into his palm. She felt so achingly hot, so full of desire that she could hardly bear it. As she wound her legs around him he thrust remorselessly, driving her deeper and deeper into a dark pit of carnality. Wild fantasies filled her head – men and women with roaming hands and flickering tongues. She had never had a woman but fantasised about it constantly.

Suddenly, his hand left her breast and he gripped her buttocks instead, forcing them apart and pulling her hard against him. His wiry pubic hair grazed her anxious clitoris and she came. Ardently. Forcefully. The pleasure peaking and peaking until she did, indeed, scream aloud. A moment later she watched his face change, his brow creasing in concentration, his lips drawn back in an agonised expression of desire. Then he came with a small, oriental cry of triumph, as though he had just smashed a house brick in half with his bare hand.

If she hadn't been pinned beneath his shuddering body, she would have felt tempted to get up and bow.

'Your Flights of Fancy concept is a good one,' he said when they had both got their breath back a little.

She nodded, feeling pleased. She had been mulling over the idea for almost a year now, working out the most minute details. Flights of Fancy would be the answer to every busy woman's dream. No more missed sex due to a hectic schedule. Women who made regular transatlantic flights for whatever reason could while away the hours being pleasured by the stud of her choice. Lisa's Boys she would call them. Desirable young men who enjoyed giving women pleasure. Men who wanted to make a career of it.

All she needed was the financial backing to lease a couple of planes and convert them to airborne pleasure palaces. Beauty treatments would be on offer as well as sex. Everything designed to make her clients feel as wonderful as possible and with no time wasted.

To her amazement she thought she heard Akira offer her the support she needed.

'What?' she said ungraciously, turning her head to look him squarely in the face. 'Are you serious?'

He nodded. 'When you get to know me you will find that I am always serious.'

The twinkle in his eyes gave him away. Lisa smiled.

'Don't play games with me, Akira.'

'I'm not.'

He pushed himself up and rested on one arm as his other hand stroked lightly across her stomach and up to her breasts.

She sighed. 'Flights of Fancy is my dream,' she said. 'I want to make it happen. I want to turn that dream into reality.'

Akira smiled a real smile and flicked her nipple. 'And so you shall. I have the necessary finance. You have the concept. Together we can make it work.'

A sigh of contentment drifted from Lisa's lips. She liked the way he said, *together*. For some strange reason it seemed more intimate to her than anything else he had said so far.

Chapter Three

The lobby of the nondescript Kensington hotel was hushed. To Lisa's far left sat an old gentleman, a retired military type, engrossed in a dog-eared copy of *Country Life*. While just a few seats away to her right, were a couple of well-dressed, immaculately coiffured women, both sipping from schooners of dark, ruby sherry and deep in conversation.

Lisa glanced at her watch. Her 'date' had precisely three more minutes before he was officially late, which didn't bode well. The previous evening she had endured a very difficult encounter with a bleached blond stud who had insisted she call him Raz – even though according to the print-out from the escort agency his real name was Christopher.

'Oh, that's a boring name,' he had said dismissively as he flopped into the chair opposite her in the hotel bar. He had then proceeded to allow her to buy him three pints of beer and tell her his life story which, she quickly discovered, she had no interest in whatsoever.

The decision to make her selection of 'boys' from various escort agencies' *crème de la crème* of manhood had been her own. It seemed the easiest and most sensible

37

route. Most of these men were already committed to carving out a career for themselves in the sex industry and therefore were not likely to be shocked by her proposal. If she ever got around to making one that was.

Christopher, or Raz, or whatever he wanted to call himself, was so disappointing that she hadn't bothered to demean herself by putting him through his sexual paces. Deciding to save herself for the real thing, she had paid him the amount they had agreed for the full evening and hastily bid him goodnight, explaining that she realised she had made a mistake. No doubt she had left him thinking that she was a frustrated shrinking violet who was content to remain frustrated for a little while longer. Why the hell should she care what he thought? There was no way she was going to let him fuck her for nothing.

'Excuse me, are you Lisa?'

A deep, honey voice floated somewhere above her head causing her to come out of her reverie and glance up. Immediately she found herself sinking into a pair of soft brown eyes, like those of a spaniel she'd had while she was growing up. The eyes were partially obscured by a heavy fringe of chestnut hair that looked silky and unmanageable, as though it had just been washed.

Lisa composed herself quickly and smiled up at him. 'Yes,' she said, extending a hand, 'and you must be Jake?'

Taking her hand and giving it a hearty shake, he nodded enthusiastically, again reminding her of a puppy. Then he asked her what she was drinking.

'Oh, no, allow me,' she countered, feeling flustered all of a sudden. She was the one who had hired him, therefore she was expected to pay for everything.

Her chair was soft and squashy, making it difficult for her to rise elegantly and she was grateful when Jake held out his hand to her again. Grasping it, she stood up and brushed the creases from her red linen skirt which she wore with a matching short-sleeved jacket. The choice of an all red outfit had been deliberate. Red suited her and gave her confidence. And boy did she need it. It wasn't every day she had sex with a complete stranger as part of her interviewing technique – especially when her un-suspecting partner wouldn't even find out he was on trial until afterwards.

Taking her lightly by the elbow, he guided her through the hotel lobby and into the equally colourless bar. Making sure she was seated comfortably at a table by the tall sash window, he insisted on taking her order and going to the bar himself. He returned a few minutes later with a long tumbler of gin and tonic for her and a campari and soda for himself.

As he sat down and picked up his drink he couldn't help noticing the way she raised an eyebrow inquiringly.

'I always drink this,' he explained, taking a sip as if to prove it. 'It was the first alcoholic drink I tried and I've loved it ever since.'

Lisa smiled and raised her glass to him as a mock toast. 'Same here,' she said, remembering how one day when she was about thirteen, her mother had inadvertently left the drinks' cabinet unlocked. Gin had been the first drink she'd tried and – at the end of a prolonged tasting session which had left her semiconscious on the living room carpet – had remained a firm favourite.

For a while they talked about 'safe' subjects, she wanting

to find out as much as possible about him without appearing to give him the third degree. Thankfully, he was quite happy to open up about himself. He told her his full name was Jake Rathbone, no relation to the actor, Basil, he pointed out hastily. He was twenty-eight, a professional escort, which meant he was not merely moonlighting as so many of them did, and had all his own hair and teeth.

Lisa laughed aloud. She didn't doubt that for a minute and liked him already, feeling certain that if his physical abilities matched his personality she would definitely offer him a job. Two drinks later she found herself ready to find out.

'About extras,' she said in a low voice as she leaned conspiratorially across the table.

Jake nodded. 'Yes, what about them?'

Very sensible, Lisa thought, to play it safe. She liked discretion in a man and she immediately added another plus point to her mental list of his credentials.

She sat back a little but still spoke *sotto voce*. 'How much?'

He answered candidly. 'A hundred for an hour, or two-fifty for the whole night.'

Lisa sat back completely. That much! The agency had been reluctant to go into many financial details, saying the escorts each had their own scale of charges and the agency just took a fee. It had been up to her to telephone Jake and make the arrangements. Even then he hadn't wanted to discuss the subject of extras on the telephone, other than to confirm that they would be available if she wanted them – and provided they hit it off on the night.

Draining her drink, she stood up and slung her bag over

her shoulder. 'Okay, let's go book us a room,' she said.

Jake stood at a discreet distance from her, pretending to be engrossed in a Degas print of a group of ballerinas, while she went over to the reception desk to make the booking. She had already checked that a room would be available if she wanted one and now she signed the register and handed the receptionist her credit card. Minutes later she and Jake were travelling up in the lift to the third floor.

The room was hardly palatial but comfortable all the same. Opening the mini bar, Lisa took out a bottle of champagne. What the hell, she deserved to celebrate. She was positive that she had just found the first of Flights of Fancy's key employees. Looking at the champagne bottle reminded her of Akira and she had to swallow deeply and bury her momentary disappointment when it was Jake's arms that came around her.

He took the bottle from her hands and opened it with professional ease. No fuss, no froth, just a slight pop and puff of expelled air.

'You're trembling,' he said, glancing at her hands, 'don't be nervous. I promise you some real good loving.'

His accent was strange. Cambridge English with American overtones. He had already explained to her that his parents were from Kansas and that his father was in the US airforce and had been stationed at an airbase in Suffolk since Jake was a small boy. With a wry grin, he said he felt more English than American, even to the extent that he preferred soccer to American football, or even baseball.

Lisa gazed at him as he poured the champagne and

41

handed her a glass. It was difficult to imagine that in a few minutes she would be putting him through his sexual paces and giving him marks out of ten.

The reality wasn't quite like that.

As soon as she put down her glass, the champagne only half drunk, Jake took complete control. Starting at the top button of her thin red jacket and working his way down, he stripped her naked in less time than it took for her to undress herself. It seemed entirely natural to watch him divest her of her clothing and for her to move her arms and legs obediently at his silent command.

He didn't undress himself but sank to his knees in front of her, his hands slowly stroking up and down the length of her legs as he stared intently at her face. Lisa felt herself weakening. A deep, soulful gaze such as his was hard to resist. Closing her eyes against it, she allowed herself to become consumed instead by the sensations that his gentle hands created as he stroked and kneaded her flesh.

She had opted only for one hour. Reasoning that if he couldn't put on a good performance in that amount of time there was no point in prolonging the agony. But he seemed in no hurry. Minutes were passing yet he still concentrated on her legs, his strong fingers deftly massaging each of her feet, then her calves and finally her thighs. Describing small circles upon her inner thighs with two fingertips of each hand, he worked his way inexorably up towards her sex which by this time was pouting with arousal. Moisture gathered on the lip of her vagina and she felt it spill over as he moved his mouth towards her and planted a gentle kiss on her lower belly, just above the triangle of pubic hair.

Lisa groaned. She felt his hands on her thighs, applying a

slight pressure. Shuffling her feet apart she whimpered softly as his warm breath caressed her blossoming sex and, a moment later, the tip of his tongue flicked lightly over her clitoris. Clutching his hair, she forced herself not to grind her mound against him but to let him continue at his own pace. This was after all a test, although she was firmly convinced by now that he would pass with flying colours.

Already her orgasm was building. The agonised bud of her clitoris pulsed and strained towards his teasing mouth and she felt his fingers skimming the slick folds of her labia. A moment later he delved inside her, the tips of his fingers finding her highly sensitive g-spot, just behind her pubic bone, and pushing her over the edge. Rocking gently on her heels, she rode the waves of her climax.

Someone was moaning loudly and she realised, with a pang of shame, that it was herself. Dear God! How could she look this man in the eye day in and day out and give him instructions like any normal employer without re-membering his special magic? One thing was certain, any future client who opted to be pleasured by Jake for the duration of her Flight of Fancy would certainly disembark with a smile on her face.

Coming out of her blissful reverie, she realised that Jake was guiding her gently towards the bed. The backs of her legs connected with the edge and she fell back, her legs inelegantly splayed. Jake looked down at her with a wolfish smile and unzipped his chinos.

'Well now, pretty lady,' he said in a deliberately accented drawl, 'we've still got half an hour to kill. Let's see how many more orgasms I can give you before my time is up.'

* * *

43

He managed four in all and by that time Lisa was practically cross-eyed with delirium, They had overshot his allotted hour but he didn't seem to mind. In fact, he seemed almost as contented as she.

When she had managed to get her breath back, Lisa offered him a job but to her surprise he didn't immediately jump at the opportunity.

'Ahm, not sure,' he mused, 'escort work suits me pretty well. I make a good living at it.'

'Whatever you earned last year, I'll double it,' she said rashly.

Propping himself up on one arm, he studied her through narrowed eyes. 'Are you serious?'

'Uh, huh.' Lisa nodded enthusiastically. Getting up reluctantly, she walked over to the dressing table where she had dumped her bag and took out one of the promotional brochures that she'd already had printed. Talk about optimism!

'Here, take a look,' she said, thrusting the brochure towards him. 'It's all perfectly kosher. Flights of Fancy is fully financed by a large industrial group and you are our first key employee – or at least you will be if you accept my offer.'

Barely able to contain her enthusiasm, she outlined all the details. If he accepted he would be in charge of five other 'pleasure givers', live in the lap of luxury and only be expected to make love to one woman per flight. Unless they had an orgy, that was. The orgies had been Akira's idea. One a week, he'd suggested, as a special incentive to their clients to fly on 'dead' days.

'You make it kinda hard to refuse,' he murmured,

glancing at the brochure and then at her. She knelt beside him on the bed, still naked, her face and skin glowing from the combination of their lovemaking and her excitement about Flights of Fancy. He didn't like to contemplate which enthused her more.

'One down, loads more to go,' she told Akira when she telephoned him the next day. At the beginning of the week he had flown to New York on business, having officially concluded his 'deal' with her, although he insisted before he went that she call him every couple of days with a progress report.

Lisa was more than happy to comply. Even though they had only spent one night together she missed him like crazy. It was as if she had known him forever and yet she hardly knew anything about him at all.

'I have a suggestion to make if you are interested,' he said. 'Something that will lighten your workload a little.' He said *workload* in an ironic tone which made Lisa giggle.

'What's that?' she asked.

Akira cleared his throat. 'You can borrow Michiko.'

For a long moment Lisa was silent. 'What do you mean, borrow her?'

'To help with your recruitment drive. I will send her back to England and she can vet some of your prospective employees. She's experienced. She's trustworthy and, let's face it, Lisa, darling, you can't be expected to sleep with every man in England.'

For a moment she was tempted to ask why not. Then relented. It was true that she could do with some help. Her 'boys' had to be right and it could take her all year to find them unless she had another pair of hands. She giggled to herself – hands didn't really come into the equation.

'Okay,' she said, nodding into the receiver, 'and thanks. But are you sure she won't mind?'

There was a pause, then Akira said, 'Michiko does whatever I ask her to do.'

'Oh.' His reply floored Lisa. There was no answer to that. For a moment she pondered on his arrogance before realising that Akira was the sort of man who had a way of persuading a person to do the unthinkable. For instance, she would never have dreamed of allowing herself to be filmed performing nude karate. Just the recollection made her laugh with embarrassment.

'What's so funny?' he asked.

'Nothing,' she said, 'I wish you were here now.'

'I know. So do I.' His voice was dark and promising. Above all, he sounded genuine.

'When are you coming home?' she said, annoyed with herself for asking the question but anxious to know all the same.

It sounded as though Akira yawned and she imagined him stretching like a sleek black panther. 'Oh, three more days, four at the most. By that time I should have wrapped up things here. Let's say Sunday to be on the safe side.'

'Okay, Sunday.' She hesitated, annoyed with herself again because she knew what she was going to ask. 'Can I see you then?'

She was reassured by the speed of his reply and the warmth in his voice. 'Of course. That would be lovely. Come to the apartment at nine and I'll make sure I have a couple of bottles of Dom Perignon on ice.'

Promising that she would be there, she remembered to ask about Michiko.

'I'll give her your telephone number so that she can call you and let you know she is ready to work,' he said. 'It will probably be tomorrow afternoon sometime.'

Lisa thanked him and said she would go ahead and set up a few 'dates' for the young Japanese woman. Now that her project was underway she really was anxious for Flights of Fancy to make its inaugural flight.

Michiko proved to be a godsend. To Lisa's surprise she appeared on her doorstep at three o'clock the following afternoon ready, able and more than willing. The excitement dancing around in her dark, slanted eyes told that much.

Not wishing to look a gift-horse in the mouth, Lisa went to her desk and picked up a couple of agency print-outs. 'Well, as you're so keen I've got a Shane – blond, brawny, six feet two – or a Tom – five nine, reddish-brown hair, beard. You can take your pick.' Lisa showed Michiko photos of both men and wasn't surprised when the young Japanese woman pointed to Tom.

'The shorter the better,' she said, laughing and glancing down at her five feet nothing frame. 'I can't imagine myself with a six footer.'

Lisa joined in the laughter. 'I met with a man this lunchtime who was hardly any taller than you,' she admitted. 'What a crazy situation that was. I had to go through with the sex part because he was ideal in every other way and I figured not all our clients will be giants.'

'Was it worth it?' Michiko asked.

Shaking her head, Lisa said, 'No way. Unfortunately,

his cock was to scale, if you know what I mean. I hardly felt it and in the end had to ask him if he was actually fucking me or not. He was pretty upset I can tell you.'

'Christ, no wonder!' Michiko exclaimed. 'You could have been a bit more subtle.'

There was no censure in her tone and Lisa smiled. 'Diplomacy is not one of my strong points,' she said. 'And I can't afford to waste time on no-hopers. After my remark he jumped up, threw on his clothes and ran. He didn't even wait for me to pay him.'

Michiko pursed her lips but Lisa could see she was trying not to laugh. 'I'm not surprised.' She rubbed her hands together and glanced at the print-out of 'Tom'. 'So what's the deal with this one? When do I get to put him through his paces?'

Lisa couldn't help noticing the other woman's enthusiasm. Perhaps she was becoming bored with catering to Akira's needs and was looking forward to a bit of variety.

'I should think tonight if you want to,' Lisa said.

Picking up her cordless phone, she punched out the number given on the print-out. Moments later she was speaking to the man himself and by the time she put the phone down Michiko had a date. After that she arranged a similar date for herself with Shane.

'Can you come over here tomorrow morning for elevenses so that we can compare notes?' she asked Michiko.

'Sure,' the young woman nodded.

Lisa promised that she would refund all expenses the following day and set about scanning various magazines for other possible candidates. She was already becoming quite anxious about the whole recruitment thing. Most of the details the agencies sent her told her whether someone was blatantly unsuitable and if not a telephone call was usually quite revealing. Now she was beginning to worry about running out of possible candidates before she had found the ones she wanted.

Picking up the latest copy of *For Women*, she considered the two and a half pages of personal advertisements placed by independent escorts. A couple sounded quite promising and she circled them. Then, on impulse decided to call them straight away. There was no answer on the first number but the second answered immediately.

He was called Curtis and described himself as broad, black and beautiful. His services, the ad said, included escorting and massage. Lisa took 'massage' to mean sex and so asked him outright. Being cautious Curtis spoke in riddles, offering to come to her flat the following day to give her one of his 'speciality massages' which would set her back one hundred pounds including oils. Lisa felt her stomach tighten at the prospect and at the delicious sound of his voice which was smooth and dark like melted chocolate, with overtly West Indian overtones. She realised her analogy was corny but could think of no more suitable description.

'Yes, okay,' she replied, slightly breathlessly, 'can you make it around two o'clock? I'll be on my own then.' She dreaded the possibility of any of her flatmates being around when he arrived.

Assuring her that, yes, the time would be alright, he confirmed the address of her flat and then rang off, leaving Lisa to wonder exactly what he would be like.

* * *

That evening she met with not one but two 'possibles', reasoning that if she allowed time for a couple of drinks and a maximum of two hours for sex with the first one, she could safely arrange to meet the second at a hotel around the corner at ten o'clock.

The second was Shane, the one she had telephoned that afternoon while Michiko had been there. His print-out told no lie, he was like a cross between Arnold Schwarzenegger and a young Robert Redford. Lisa took one look at him and fell instantly in lust.

Her earlier appointment had proved fruitless and after her afternoon escapade she was prepared to be disappointed yet again. The reality thrilled her to the very core. He was nice, he was solicitous, he was entertaining and best of all he was dynamite where it counted – between the sheets.

Looking back on the encounter she was unable to stop herself from laughing aloud. Between the sheets was really a euphemism as they had hardly got a look in. As soon as she and Shane stepped across the threshold into the hotel bedroom, he had grabbed her by the waist, lifted her up, ripped her knickers off and plunged into her there and then. All Lisa had been able to do was wrap her legs around his waist and cling on for dear life as, supporting her by the buttocks, he took her through three orgasms one after the other.

'Phew,' she said at long last, after he carried her to the bed, 'I think you must be superhuman.'

He grinned down at her in a blatantly lascivious way. He had pulled off his tee-shirt and his jeans were undone, revealing a generously proportioned cock that was still semi-erect.

'Depends on the woman I'm with,' he said. It sounded flattering but also believable and for all her bravado Lisa blushed to the roots of her hair.

When she finally got around to offering him a job with Flights of Fancy, he was more than happy to accept.

'Will I get to fuck you again?' he asked bluntly, his fingers still playing with her clitoris even as they discussed 'business'.

Lisa groaned slightly, her body undulating under his skilful touch. 'Maybe,' she said, 'I can't make any promises. I don't know how busy we'll both be.' For a moment she allowed her mind to drift along a familiar route where she received a bunch of tense and irritable looking clients on board a Flight of Fancy and then waved the same transformed group of women a cheery goodbye at the other end.

Shane skimmed the moist edge of her vagina with a single fingertip before plunging his finger deep inside her. 'Believe me,' he promised, 'we'll make time.'

With a shudder of delight Lisa tried not to think too much about the practicalities of her role. She hadn't really decided whether she would take an active part in the proceedings, although she supposed that she couldn't very well hold regular orgies and remain aloof. Enthusiastic participation would be called for to get the ball rolling and to put everyone else at their ease.

The next morning Michiko arrived looking so un-inscrutable that Lisa knew straight away her evening with the guy called Tom had been a success.

'Yes,' Michiko said in answer to Lisa's question and nodding enthusiastically. 'Yes. Yes. Yes. Yes!'

'He was good then,' Lisa commented drily.

Again, Michiko nodded. Flopping down onto the sofa she proceeded to tell Lisa every minute detail. How good-looking he was. How kind. How solicitous, etc., etc. And by all accounts he was absolute dynamite in bed.

'Better than Akira?' Lisa dared to ask, feeling wicked and deceitful, her stomach clenching as she waited for the answer she wanted Michiko to give – that she hadn't ever slept with Akira and therefore wouldn't know.

To Lisa's disappointment the young woman smiled guilelessly as she answered. 'Oh, no. Not better than Akira. But very, very good all the same. Definitely worth employing.'

'Did you make him an offer?' Lisa felt as though the bottom had just fallen out of her rose-tinted world but forced herself to put business first.

Michiko said she had and that his acceptance had been immediate and enthusiastic.

'That means we just need two more group leaders,' Lisa said, 'then the rest should be easy to accomplish.' Her plan was to put each of the five main employees in charge of a further five 'boys'. That way there would be a surplus of men for her clients to choose from. She didn't intend to cater for more than twenty women during any one flight. Her concept entailed keeping everything as exclusive and as personal as possible. She didn't want anyone feeling as though they were simply a number being processed on a conveyor belt. She wanted each and every one of her clients to feel special. To feel as though they were 'The One'.

She asked Michiko if she minded sticking around. Akira had already hinted that the young Japanese woman was an expert when it came to massage. And if her appointment that afternoon turned out to involve just a massage, she would appreciate Michiko's opinion of his performance – Flights of Fancy needed several masseurs as well as sexual studs.

'What if massage means what we think it means?' Michiko asked, tucking into the sandwich that Lisa had made for lunch.

Lisa laughed. 'In that case I'll fight you for him.' She was only joking. In all honesty, after bedding no less than three men the day before, she felt as though she could do with a break already.

Curtis turned out to be everything he had promised on the phone, from his dreadlock-style hair to his smooth, Belgian-chocolate skin. His eyes were a dark liquid brown and set well apart in a strong-boned, high-browed face. His nose and mouth were both generous but perfectly in proportion with the rest of his face and not completely West Indian in composure. Straight away Curtis admitted that only his father was Jamaican. His mother was Irish, he said, and he had been born and brought up in the London borough of Hendon. The broad, distinctive accent he adopted was as carefully contrived as his appearance.

Lisa noticed that he carried a bag with him and Michiko

piped up and asked him if it contained massage oils. When Curtis wasn't looking she winked at Lisa which made her giggle.

Curtis didn't miss either. 'Am I in for a threesome?' he asked cockily, shrugging his leather jacket off as though he was stripping for action.

Lisa felt her stomach contract painfully. A threesome wasn't part of her plan at all and yet the prospect of actually acting out a latent fantasy beguiled her. All at once she felt the telltale tingle in her sex and glanced at Michiko to witness her reaction to the suggestion. She was smiling broadly.

Curtis glanced from woman to woman. 'Where would you like your massage?' he asked.

Excitement surged through Lisa as she walked purposefully into her bedroom. She had prepared the double bed by covering it with towels. Curtis opened his bag and began taking out a number of bottles, arranging them on top of a chest of drawers by the bed. Michiko wandered over to him and examined them, picking each one up in turn and reading the labels. She nodded approvingly as she put down the last one.

'Michiko is something of a massage expert,' Lisa explained, realising that she hadn't introduced the young woman.

Curtis smiled winningly at Michiko. 'In that case I'd better make sure I do a good job.'

In a casual tone he invited Lisa to strip and exchanged a conspiratorial smile with Michiko when Lisa immediately blushed and scurried off into the adjoining bathroom to do his bidding. She returned wearing a white towel which she had wound tightly around herself. It seemed very odd to be unclothed in the presence of two people who were virtual strangers. Following Curtis's instructions, she loosened the towel and lay face down on the bed.

Kneeling beside her, Curtis pulled the towel down and folded it over until it only covered her buttocks. Then he reached out for the largest bottle of oil, poured a generous stream into a small stainless-steel bowl and added a few drops of another oil.

'I'm just mixing the base oil with Clary-sage,' he explained.

Lisa noticed that Michiko nodded approvingly. 'Clary-sage has special relaxation properties,' she said. 'Most people feel positively euphoric afterwards.'

'I could do with that,' Lisa murmured sleepily – just laying down had that effect on her. 'To feel anything more than dog-tired would be a novelty.'

To describe Curtis's massage technique as soothing would have been a gross understatement, Lisa thought. As his broad fingers worked the uplifting oil into every tiny knot of muscle, she couldn't help sighing with unrestrained pleasure. He had spent ages massaging her shoulders and back and was now working on her legs with long, firm strokes that eased all her muscles in one fell swoop.

Thanks to Curtis, she had forgotten her tiredness and her tensions. Her worries about the future, about Akira and Flights of Fancy all paled into insignificance as she floated on a cloud of total relaxation. There was nothing to worry about, nothing to fear.

Curtis finished massaging the backs of her legs and

delivered a playful smack to her towel-covered buttocks which unexpectedly sent Lisa's mind reeling, her body responding to his action as though he had just caressed her sexually. Glancing sideways, she noticed his face wore a knowing look that sent a *frisson* of excitement through her.

She knew what was coming next. She dreaded it and yet could hardly wait to hear his instruction. With an expectant look she watched as he rested his forearms beside her head and leaned right forward to whisper seductively in her ear.

'Turn over.'

Chapter Four

An insistent tingling sensation between Lisa's thighs made her blush as she slowly turned over and lay on her back. Glancing down she noticed with another surge of shame that her nipples were hugely swollen and standing to attention. For a moment she felt the heat of Curtis's gaze and then glanced to the other side of her where Michiko sat, perched like a little bird on the edge of the bed.

Having mixed a little more oil, Curtis knelt beside her again and began to massage her feet, shins and thighs. Pretty soon all thoughts of embarrassment left Lisa's head as she gave herself up to the sensation of his hands working her body. As he neared the tops of her legs she felt them part a little, almost of their own accord. Thankfully, Curtis ignored her change in position and reached out for the bowl of oils. Holding it above her, he allowed a thin trickle of oil to lay a trail down the length of her torso, from neck to navel.

Lisa sighed and arched her back. The sensation of the warm oil was so voluptuous that she suddenly found herself craving his special touch. To her relief, in the next instant, she felt his hands on her again, his broad palms and fingers spanning her waist, his thumbs pressing into her soft flesh and making small circulatory movements.

A movement to the other side of her made Lisa turn her head. Michiko had stopped perching and had moved properly onto the bed to recline next to Lisa, her head propped in one hand. Lisa's eyes widened as the young Japanese woman reached out her free hand and dipped one tiny fingertip into a puddle of oil that had formed between Lisa's breasts. Coating the fingertip well, she smoothed it along the length of Lisa's collarbone.

Lisa felt her stomach clench and tried not to respond as the fingertip slid back and forth. Her primary urge was to arch her back and implore either Curtis or Michiko to touch her breasts. The supple mounds felt huge and hot as though they were on fire and she longed for a soothing touch upon them.

Without meaning to, she groaned and allowed her eyelids to flicker open just in time to catch Michiko and Curtis as they exchanged a knowing look. Their expressions made her stomach clench even harder and she felt an answering tug in her womb. Before she knew what was happening both masseurs dipped their heads and began to lick and suck her throbbing nipples. Cupping her breasts in her hands, Lisa urged Curtis and Michiko to take more of them. Her lust was so strong and so unexpected that she felt almost demented by it.

As Curtis continued to tongue her breast, she felt his hand slide lower and lower over the flat plain of her stomach until his fingertips slid under the towel that concealed her pelvis. His fingers combed through her pubic hair, tugging gently at the soft curls to stimulate her sex. Ripples of pleasure ran through her as her clitoris started to respond, swelling and hardening, demanding attention.

'Please,' she gasped hoarsely, 'please.'

Curtis's wide mouth curved into a devilish smile. His fingers slid lower, driving a wedge between the swollen flesh of her outer labia and stroking the delicate petals beneath. Slipping a finger either side of her clitoris, he began to rub gently, sliding the fragile hood of skin that shielded her throbbing bud back and forth, deliberately driving her into the uncompromising arms of orgasm.

Through heavy-lidded eyes she watched Michiko quickly undress. She wore only a tight red skirt over a black T-shirt body and black opaque tights. Underneath the clothes she wore no underwear. Lisa didn't have time to think about the situation as it unfolded. Her arousal was already too great to put up much resistance as the young woman slid her body alongside hers and captured her mouth in a long, sweet kiss.

A groan reverberated at the back of Lisa's throat as Michiko's tongue explored her mouth and she felt Curtis's soft, woolly hair tantalise the sensitive flesh of her inner thighs. In moments his tongue was probing her vagina, matching Michiko's thrust for thrust.

It was almost too blissful to withstand. Lisa felt Michiko move gracefully across her so that their nipples jousted as their kiss continued. In desperation Lisa moved her hands and cupped the young woman's tiny breasts, pinching the hard red nipples between her fingertips until she elicited a whimper of pleasure. Encouraged by Lisa's wanton behaviour, Michiko slid her palms over Lisa's torso, smoothing the oil into her hot skin.

Relinquishing their kiss, the young oriental woman moved her lips over Lisa's cheek and jaw, just giving little licks and butterfly kisses as she worked her way down Lisa's throat to her right breast. With a loud moan, Lisa felt her swollen nipple spring to even more eager attention as Michiko closed her wet lips over it. Further down Lisa felt Curtis's fingers enter her as his tongue flicked across her clitoris, pushing her over the brink.

As she ground herself against his mouth and hands Lisa felt wave after wave of orgasm sweep over her, each one peaking higher than the one before until they finally began to abate. Watching almost in a dream, she saw Curtis move his hand up and stroke the backs of his fingertips down the length of Michiko's spine. Her eyes widened as the young woman groaned loudly and arched her back, her neat buttocks swaying tantalisingly.

Climbing across Lisa's temporarily sated body, Curtis gently pushed Michiko away from Lisa and arranged her limbs so that she was on all fours, her legs spread wide apart, her bottom jutting into the air. His fingers drifted across the blossoming flower of the young oriental woman's sex, gathering her moisture and slicking it up and down her blushing slit. He congratulated himself on his own good fortune. It wasn't the first time he had enjoyed more than one woman simultaneously but he had certainly never been partner to two such lovely and enthusiastic ladies before.

In a lot of ways Michiko and Lisa were very similar to look at. Both dark-haired, with neat features, huge dark eyes and plummy lips, there were, nevertheless, a few important differences between them. Skin tone was one. Michiko's colouring was typical of her race, yet Lisa was pale to the point of whiteness. Also, Lisa was considerably taller than Michiko and of a much bigger build, although certainly not overweight by any means. Whereas Michiko's limbs and torso looked slim and fragile, Lisa's were strong with well-toned muscles. She looked as though she worked out regularly and he instantly found himself wondering which gym she went to.

He glanced down at Michiko. His fingers were deep inside her by now and she had manoeuvred herself around so that she could delicately tongue Lisa's sex. The other young woman was shamelessly aroused, he noticed, her hands clutching her own breasts and squeezing them almost dementedly while she tried to spread her legs wider and wider. Thinking it was about time she was reminded what 'real' sex was all about, he withdrew his fingers from Michiko and quickly undressed.

Michiko hardly noticed that Curtis was no longer caressing her. She was so intent on the sweet, musky flesh beneath her mouth that she could think of nothing else. Her real disappointment came when Curtis made it obvious that he intended to fuck Lisa.

'No,' she mumbled, burying her face deeper between Lisa's legs, 'leave us alone.'

Curtis grinned. Okay, if that was the way she wanted it. He lay down on the other side of Lisa and raised her left hip until he could slide himself underneath her and push his cock into her waiting wetness. She welcomed him eagerly, her muscles gripping him and urging him deeper.

In that position Michiko was still able to lick and caress Lisa, although now her hands wandered to cup Curtis's balls from time to time and give them a tender squeeze.

Curtis groaned and willed himself not to come, but as Lisa began the climb to another orgasm he felt her tighten encouragingly around his cock. There was nothing he could do to stop his own climax. Lisa was bucking and grinding against him and he only had to glance down to witness the voluptuous sight of Michiko's tongue flickering over Lisa's straining clitoris. Throwing back his head he cried out an old African tribal war cry that his great-grandfather had taught him.

There was silence for a moment and then Lisa began to giggle. A moment later Michiko looked up and also started to laugh. Within no time they were all rolling around the bed, stark-naked and howling with mirth rather than lust.

'Oh God!' Lisa struggled to sit up and wiped the tears from her eyes with the back of her hand. 'I don't know which was more relaxing: the massage, the orgasms, or the laughter.'

Michiko grinned. 'It must have been the laughter because I feel relaxed and I haven't had the pleasure of the other two options yet.'

Lisa and Curtis exchanged guilty looks and Lisa decided to go and get everyone some refreshment. She had a bottle of white wine chilling in the fridge and a quick rummage through the kitchen cupboards revealed a couple of jars of green and black olives and a large bag of tortilla chips. Loading everything onto a tray, she carried it back into the bedroom.

It was difficult not to avert her eyes. All she could see at first as she walked through the door was the sight of Curtis's nut-brown buttocks heaving up and down. Then, as she surreptitiously placed the tray down on the dressing table, she couldn't help noticing the reflection in the mirror. Michiko was on her hands and knees again, her hips bucking against Curtis's hard belly as her tiny breasts shuddered to the vibration of his thrusts.

It was the first time she had looked at either of them properly since they undressed and now she found herself marvelling at the contrast of Michiko's waif-like form as she took the full force of Curtis's powerfully muscled body. For someone so fragile in appearance, the young oriental woman seemed to be matching him stroke for stroke and with as much vigour.

Pausing only to pour the wine, Lisa climbed back onto the bed and wriggled on her back until she was laying directly beneath Michiko. The young woman's breasts hovered tantalisingly above her, urging her to raise her head slightly and encircle one of them with her tongue. In ever decreasing circles, she licked the soft, slightly perfumed flesh until her lips enclosed a tiny nipple. The delicate bud hardened quickly in her mouth and she sucked on it, drawing it deeper between her lips and flicking her tongue back and forth across the tip.

Both Michiko and Curtis had begun to pant. Michiko's torso was covered with a thin sheen of perspiration and Lisa began to lap at every available inch of her salty flesh. The young woman undulated above her, giving tiny moans and whimpers and, as she arched her back, her upper body descended towards Lisa's face allowing her to lay flat and bring her hands into play as well as her eager mouth. There was no part of Michiko's torso that she couldn't reach and with a deep inhalation of breath to bolster her courage, Lisa slid her hand lower into the mass of wild, silky hair that covered Michiko's mound.

Lisa loved the sensation of the young woman's sex beneath her fingers. The hair was not at all curly but dead straight and as glossy as the hair that swung about Michiko's face in a smooth bob. Delving a little lower, Lisa's fingertips encountered the swollen flesh of her partner's sex, the clitoris hard and standing proud of her moist labia. With a small shudder at her own daring, Lisa ran her fingertips around the hard bud and then felt lower, grazing the base of Curtis's hard shaft with her nails.

The young man groaned at her unexpected touch which seemed to inspire him to thrust harder. Michiko was lost in her own private world, her lips emitting tiny gasps of pleasure, forming musical words that Lisa could not understand. The sounds she was making reminded Lisa of Akira and with a tingle of excitement she wondered what he would make of the situation she and Michiko were enjoying. No doubt he would love to join them, Lisa thought, and the very idea urged her to seek out her own clitoris with her free hand. Stroking both herself and Michiko simultaneously she allowed her body to float up and up, high on a cloud of voluptuous pleasure.

Hours later she found herself on the doorstep, waving goodbye to Curtis and Michiko and it was with a pang of regret that she watched Michiko ease her slender form into Curtis's low-slung sports car. He wouldn't hear of her taking a taxi home and had gallantly offered her a lift instead. The young woman's dark eyes had twinkled with something akin to expectation and Lisa felt envious of her as Curtis took her tiny hand in his huge one and led her outside.

Naturally, Lisa had offered him a job. In some ways she felt she would be doing Flights of Fancy a disservice if she didn't manage to persuade him to join the crew. His skilful massage technique was just the thing to put a nervous client at her ease and his dark good looks were an undeniable bonus. More so than the others she had already hired, the whole Curtis package would be excellent PR for the project.

After she had outlined her offer, Lisa realised, with an inward sigh of relief, that Curtis was not going to strike too hard a bargain. His enthusiasm for the proposal was immediate and enthusiastic, saying it was a brilliant idea and that he wished he'd thought of it himself. Proving that he had a good business head on his shoulders, he asked if the project was fully financed. He didn't want to give up everything and then discover that he had to start from square one again in six months' time, he said.

Without going into too many details, both Lisa and Michiko were able to reassure him about Akira's credit-worthiness. Curtis nodded approvingly, it turned out he knew the Tanaka group quite well as he'd been hired by their London head office on numerous occasions as an escort for visiting female clients.

By the end of the third month, Flights of Fancy was well on the way to lift off. Taking her courage in both hands,

Lisa had proposed a date another four weeks hence for the official launch. Again Akira had proved to be something akin to a fairy godfather. By offering the services of the global advertising and public relations agency that operated the Tanaka group account, he made sure that Flights of Fancy was properly publicised on both sides of the Atlantic. Furthermore, through business contacts in the airline industry, he had managed to lease two brand new jumbo jets which he had ordered to be gutted and equipped according to Lisa's precise instructions.

Between overseeing the refurbishment of the planes, organising suppliers of gourmet foods, fine wines and beauty preparations, as well as interviewing potential pleasure-givers, Lisa found herself with very little time to spare. Eschewing the need for sleep, she still managed to see Akira on a number of occasions. Sometimes she didn't meet up with him until after midnight but if he was tired he didn't show it – their encounters were every bit as enjoyable and erotic as the first.

The only thing that bothered her was that she was still searching for one elusive man. The fifth wheel so to speak. The one that would take on the responsibility of managing the final group of 'boys'. Team leaders had to be special people, with special abilities and character traits. Shane, Jake, Curtis and the one Michiko had interviewed, Tom, were all perfect for the job, but she had tapped the well of available young men almost to the point of exhaustion. There was just one person left to try who seemed remotely suitable but every time she tried to call the mobile telephone number given in his advertisement she encountered an answering service. Each time she had left a message but her calls had not been returned.

Feeling slightly frustrated before she even started, Lisa picked up her cordless phone determined to give it one last try. To her surprise it was answered on the second ring – by a woman.

She didn't sound in the least surprised when Lisa mentioned the advert she had seen and added that she was interested and would like to arrange a meeting.

'Oh, that Rio, he such a bad boy,' the woman said in a thickly accented voice, 'he sometime make me forget I am his loving sister. I just want to smack him so bad. You are the one who phoned four or five time, yes?'

Lisa agreed that yes, it was probably her but that she really didn't mind as long as she actually got to speak to Rio Fernandez eventually. At that a deep laugh rumbled down the phone and reverberated against her eardrums, making them itch.

All of a sudden, the woman's voice was replaced by that of a man. Although slightly deeper in pitch it was not dissimilar. 'I'm sorry about that,' he said. 'I *am* Rio. It's just that I sometimes pretend to be my own sister as a screening device. It works very well.'

'I'm sure it does,' Lisa said drily, wondering how reliable someone could possibly be if he pretended to be his own sister just to keep out of trouble.

'Well, what can I do for you – are you in need of an escort whose handsome looks and wonderful charm are only exceeded by his amazing sexual prowess?'

Lisa was stunned into silence for a moment. 'Modest, aren't we?' she finally said in an ironic tone.

His infectious laugh rumbled down the phone to her again. 'No. Modesty is not one of my many attributes,' he boasted, deliberately goading her, 'but then someone as dynamic as myself doesn't have to stick to convention. So, when do you want to meet?'

She heard the rustle of paper and realised he was probably flicking through the pages of a diary. It was bound to be black, Lisa thought. Or perhaps men as cocksure as Rio didn't use a little black book anymore. Perhaps they were so popular they needed to keep details of their conquests on a database. For one brief moment she imagined he would have them flagged in categories such as: 'big tits' and 'gives good head'.

Suddenly she found herself looking forward to meeting this man and maybe taking him down a peg or two. Either he was everything he claimed to be, or he was a total bullshitter. Hardly able to keep the laughter out of her voice, she made an appointment to meet him at her usual hotel the following evening at eight.

At first sight, Rio *was* everything he claimed to be, which Lisa found a little disconcerting. He was a bit on the short side perhaps for a lot of women. Certainly not taller than five six. But he was definitely an arresting sight. Resembling a younger version of Kid Creole, the Latin-American singer, his swarthy good looks were almost too good to be true.

Framed by a crop of thick, long, wavy black hair his face was finely boned, with high, well-defined cheekbones, a neat nose – ever so slightly Roman in appearance – and a wide, sulky mouth topped by a thin, pencil moustache.

Lisa couldn't help noticing that his body looked to be perfectly in proportion – slight but nicely toned. And he wore his clothes well, the loose designer suit in a subtle moss green draping his body in such a way that it enhanced rather than shielded it. On his feet he wore a pair of highly polished, black shoes, obviously expensive, possibly handmade. And the thin turtleneck jumper he wore under his suit looked as though it was cashmere.

When he leaned forward to shake her hand, his after-shave enveloped her in a beguiling cloud and a pair of deep sapphire eyes sparkled with all the warmth and promise of the Pacific Ocean.

'Hi! You must be Lisa.'

She didn't know how many times she had heard the same introduction and had looked into a pair of fresh eyes – *with* fresh eyes. But never before had she felt so instantly attracted to someone. Not even Akira who she had found frankly disturbing to begin with.

Let's go to bed – let's fuck now! her brain screamed as she allowed him to take her hand in his. Instead of shaking it he turned it over and placed a soft, sullen-lipped kiss in the palm.

'Yes, and you have to be Rio?' The words came out hoarsely, as though someone had come up behind her, put their hands around her neck and began to squeeze the very life out of her.

Dropping her hand, he took a step back, held out his arms and gave her a cheeky grin. 'The one and only,' he said.

Everything he did seemed deliberately theatrical and yet she could tell instinctively that there was nothing contrived about his actions. What Rio did and said was precisely who he was.

To her frustration he seemed in no hurry to get onto the main business of the evening. After a couple of drinks he insisted on taking her dancing. His choice was a dark cavern of a club in which a live band alternately played the rumba and the salsa interspersed with soulful ballads telling of unrequited love.

Lisa despaired of his choice. She wasn't one for dancing at the best of times and the complicated steps of the Latin-American dances, which he executed with perfect aplomb, left her feeling as ungainly as a baby hippo. When the band announced that the next dance would be the Lambada, Lisa groaned and tried her hardest to drag Rio off the dance floor. To her dismay he was totally uncompromising.

'This is an incredibly erotic dance,' he said, 'and you're wearing exactly the right outfit for it. It would be a shame to let it go to waste.' His sweeping glance took in her short scarlet dress with its flirty, swirly skirt under which she had dared to wear a matching lace g-string.

Shaking her head defiantly, Lisa tried even harder to demur. She had seen people performing the Lambada and knew that her skirt would end up swirling around her waist. Regardless of her being perfectly dressed for the dance, there was no way she was going to expose her buttocks to a crowd of strangers.

'You must. I won't take no for an answer,' he insisted. 'Don't worry, I'll lead, you follow.'

The music started up and Lisa felt herself being pulled unwillingly against him. One of his hands spanned the small of her back, pulling her even closer to his hard body and his free hand immediately sought her corresponding one. She felt his fingers entwining hers, as strong and as uncompromising as the man himself, and knew that she had lost the battle.

To her surprise, Lisa found her body responding naturally to the hypnotic rhythm. There was no doubt that Rio was a good teacher. Taking him at his word, she matched his movements exactly and soon found the pressure of his thigh against her groin unbelievably arousing. Her juices soaked the barely-there crotch of her knickers in no time and she began to panic that she would leave a telltale mark on his impeccable trousers.

As if he could read her thoughts he whispered into her ear not to worry and just let herself go. Needing no further encouragement, Lisa did just that, grinding her pelvis and swinging her hips provocatively as the captivating music took hold. Three quarters of the way through the dance she realised that quite a few of the others had stopped dancing and were simply watching herself and Rio. Playing up to the audience, Rio deliberately moved his hand lower over her buttocks, spanning them possessively as he deliberately urged the back of her skirt higher.

Loud whoops and catcalls greeted Lisa's ears, making her cheeks turn as scarlet as her dress. She could hear someone calling in a loud voice, 'What an arse – show me more, baby!' and cringed as she realised what a spectacle she was making of herself.

'Enough, Rio. Enough,' she gasped, trying to squirm away from him but he wouldn't let her.

'Finish the dance,' he growled threateningly, 'or I won't fuck you afterwards.'

Oh, God! Lisa felt her mind screaming again. She hated what he was doing to her, reducing her normally level-headed self to a quivering mass of shamefully aroused jelly. And yet in another way she wished the dance would never end, that she would not be forced to break away from him until his insistently rubbing thigh had brought her to orgasm.

It was a relief to be back at the hotel. To get there Lisa had practically had to plead with Rio but she was past caring. All she wanted to do was get him alone and find out if it had been worth the wait.

In the lift she got a taste of what she could expect. No sooner had the doors closed behind them than Rio pushed her back against the mirrored wall, his body slamming into her with a force that took her breath away. Fighting ineffectually against him, she heard herself groan aloud as his hand dived up under her skirt and pulled her flimsy knickers to one side. In the next instant his fingers were inside her, probing and stroking her hot vagina as she whimpered and squirmed against him. Seconds away from reaching orgasm he withdrew his fingers, smoothed down her skirt and moved away from her to recline nonchalantly against the lift wall. At that same moment the lift stopped and Lisa and Rio stepped out to be replaced by four other people.

'You seem to have that well timed,' she said with more than a hint of irony in her voice as she watched the lift doors slide smoothly to a close.

Grinning, Rio shrugged. 'I just do what comes naturally.' Taking the key from her, he began to walk down the dimly lit hallway until he reached the door of their room. 'After you,' he said, making a gallant sweeping gesture with his arm.

Despite herself, Lisa giggled and deliberately rubbed her buttocks against him as she squeezed past. Having just experienced his sudden, swift passion in the lift she expected him to throw himself upon her the minute he closed the door but yet again he surprised her by strolling nonchalantly into the bathroom instead. She stood stock-still, listening to the telltale sounds of him emptying his bladder and then cocked her head to hear what else he was doing. There followed the sound of his footsteps on the tiled floor and then a sudden *swoosh* told her that he'd turned on the shower.

First me, then the shower, she mused, feeling extraordinarily relaxed and expectant. Although they had not indulged in the most crucial part of their encounter, she already felt certain that she had found her elusive fifth man. Everything else from now on seemed like a mere formality.

Rio walked back into the room stark-naked.

'Oh, I – oh!' Lisa gasped as she tried not to stare quite so blatantly at him.

If he was bothered by her scrutiny he didn't show it. 'As soon as you are undressed,' he said, moving towards her, 'I'm going to start pampering you.'

It was a delicious prospect and Lisa found her fingers were trembling as she reached behind her back and fumbled for the zip. A huge, slithery eel of desire seemed to stir and uncoil itself slowly inside her and suddenly she felt hot. Hot and desperate to be rid of the thin little dress that now seemed to stick uncomfortably to her perspiring flesh.

'Hold on. Let me help you with that.' Rio was behind her in a flash, moving her hands out of the way and pulling down the zip in one fluid movement. As she took a deep breath of expectation, she felt his hands slide up her back and over her shoulders, pulling down the thin, shoestring straps that held it up. With a slight whisper the dress fell to the floor to pool around her ankles. 'Beautiful,' she heard Rio murmur. 'Fucking gorgeous.'

To her surprise he swung her around and captured her mouth in a deep kiss that took her breath away. Cupping the back of her head with one hand, he allowed the other to roam freely over her torso, skimming her stomach, pausing at her breasts to gently fondle each one. His caresses were soft yet insistent, inflaming Lisa to the point where she thrust herself shamelessly at him and gave a deep groan in the back of her throat.

He was still kissing her, his tongue plundering her mouth, but now his free hand moved lower, sliding under the waistband of her knickers and stroking the soft mound beneath. Lisa groaned and tried to spread her legs wider without actually overbalancing. She felt unsteady, as though she were drunk, and yet he held her so firmly that she dared to bend her knees a little to allow his hand proper access to her hungry sex.

She was still wet from when he'd caressed her before and now she felt his fingers slide into her easily. His thumb found her clitoris and began to rub it gently. Lisa moaned. Giving herself up to his caresses she allowed her mind to drift along a familiar erotic route. Like a passenger on a ghost train she felt herself being transported along a pitch black tunnel where lascivious ideas and fantasies lurked, all of them ready to jump out at her at any moment. One of them, Michiko, flickered into her mind and then disappeared just as quickly – the fleeting image of her naked body spread open and in the grip of lust strong enough to incite a fresh surge of arousal.

To Lisa's regret, Rio's mouth left hers and his fingers slid out of her body. 'This won't do,' he said softly, 'I'm forgetting my manners.'

Lisa laughed, realising that he probably had a 'routine'. One which was guaranteed to ensure complete satisfaction with his lady clients. If only he knew how much his unrehearsed actions excited her perhaps he would be tempted to drop his act. But she was intrigued to learn exactly what he believed constituted good sex. Damping down her eagerness to pull him back into her arms, she allowed him to pull her knickers down to her ankles then help her step away from the meagre pile of clothing.

'Go into the bathroom,' he ordered, 'I'll be with you in a minute.'

Lisa obeyed without question, wandering into the nondescript yet perfectly adequate bathroom with its functional white fittings. Unlike most hotel bathrooms of its ilk, this one, she noticed, had a separate bath and shower which she much preferred.

She didn't hear Rio come up behind her and her first inkling that he was there was a surprise hand on her right buttock.

'Oh!' She clenched involuntarily and glanced over her shoulder at him.

'You have a beautiful body,' he said, ignoring her startled look. His hands swept up and down her back, smoothing her shoulders, following the contours of her waist and hips. She groaned as he cupped both buttocks and squeezed them gently. 'I love a woman's shape,' he breathed into her ear, 'so sinuous. So sensuous. And your skin feels wonderful. So soft and silky I wish I could wear it next to my own.'

Lisa wanted to protest. His remarks were too much. Okay, she was quite pretty but she wasn't that remarkable looking. She certainly wasn't beautiful. Somehow, she kept her denial reined in. Flattery, even blatant flattery such as this, was good to hear. And she had met with and slept with so many men during the past few months who were not in Rio's league that she felt as though she deserved to have her ego massaged a little. The last massage she'd enjoyed had been at the hands of Curtis and what a delight he had turned out to be.

Chapter Five

Taking her hand, Rio led her over to the shower, pushed back the concertina door and guided her in. Then he joined her. There wasn't much space in the shower and Lisa felt acutely aware of the way certain parts of their bodies brushed together as they moved. Reaching past her, he unhooked a tube of shower gel then, turning her around to face him, he held the tube just above her left shoulder and squeezed.

The gel was cold, making Lisa gasp with surprise even though she knew it was coming. As the glistening blue stream slithered down her body, she felt goosepimples spring up on her skin and her left nipple harden. He squeezed a little more gel onto her right shoulder and then hung up the bottle again. With the flat of his palms he smoothed the gel across her upper chest and down the valley between her breasts. Working up a lather, he moved his hands in small circles over her stomach, one clockwise, the other anticlockwise, until her skin glowed pinkly.

Reaching for the bottle, Lisa squeezed some of the gel onto her palm, rubbed her hands together and then began to cover his shoulders with a cloak of bubbles. She looked into his face and laughed. Suddenly she felt completely alive, her whole body tingling with expectation and the sensation of his hands. Rio smiled in return and cupped her face in his soapy hands. Water cascaded between them, drowning Lisa's gasp of astonishment. Just for a moment his smile faltered and she noticed how his eyes darkened to navy as he gripped her face harder, his thumbs grazing her cheeks. Lisa sighed and felt his lips touch hers. This time his kiss was soft and lingering, lighting small fires inside her, setting her aglow.

'I want you,' she murmured hoarsely. 'I know you are keen to pamper me and everything but – oh God!' She broke off and reached down to clasp his cock which to her relief was rock hard. 'I need this,' she said. 'I need to feel it inside me. Right now.'

She was amazed that for someone with such a slight build he managed to scoop her up in his arms so easily. Stepping backwards out of the shower, he paused to stoop and grab a large towel before carrying her into the bedroom. She faltered slightly as he set her down on her feet and wrapped her with the towel, encircling her shivering body with the fluffy fabric and his arms. For a moment he simply held her, rubbing her back and shoulders with the towel as she trembled against him. Then he pressed against her gently, turning her around and pressing until she fell back onto the bed.

Suddenly, his composure seemed to desert him. Lisa could imagine how she must look – totally spread out and eager to take him inside her – and wasn't surprised when he fell on top of her.

What did surprise her was that he didn't thrust immediately inside her but rolled her over until she was on top of him. Straddling him, she felt between her thighs for his cock. Just for a moment she stroked it thoughtfully, her fingers sliding a droplet of his own juices over the bulbous head. Rio groaned and arched his back.

'Now. Now,' he growled urgently. 'I want you to fuck me now.'

What more encouragement did a girl need?

With a surge of renewed excitement, Lisa held his cock at the entrance to her body and plunged down hard. The reality snatched the breath away from both of them. Matching gasp for gasp, they fucked hard, Lisa riding Rio for all she was worth until he gripped her hips and began to lunge upwards instead. Still growling words of passion, he rolled her onto her side, hooked her leg over his hip and began to thrust harder still.

Feeling almost delirious with arousal, Lisa screamed out, her hoarse cries urging him on. 'Don't stop. Take me harder. Harder. Oh, God, don't ever stop.'

By the time they did stop they were too exhausted to do anything other than fall asleep. When Lisa awoke some six hours later, the first thing that struck her was how odd it was to have a man still in her bed in the morning. She rarely took men back to her flat after an evening out which usually meant an early morning goodbye and a taxi ride home at some ungodly hour. And during the past few months almost all her encounters had been of the, 'wham, bam, thank you very much, would you like a job?' variety.

Glancing across the bed to where Rio lay, half covered by the pale apricot duvet, arms thrown carelessly over his head, she wondered how he felt about last night. She was probably kidding herself, she thought ruefully, but, she had the distinct impression that her lover had been doing a lot more than merely satisfying her as part of his line of work. Were male escorts supposed to enjoy their duties quite that much? she wondered. Was his enthusiasm for her body all faked, or had she really felt something extra?

She didn't have to wait long to find out. Rio awoke with a lazy smile. 'Hi, you were fantastic last night,' was the first thing he said, the second being, 'come here, I want to fuck you again.'

Without a moment's hesitation, Lisa dived on him. Her arousal growing and peaking – growing and peaking.

They were interrupted by a sharp rap on the bedroom door. Wrapping the slightly damp towel around her that she'd discarded the night before, Lisa stumbled to the door, opened it a fraction and, with glazed eyes, met the baleful glare of a woman who, judging by her clothing, was the hotel's housekeeper.

'You should have vacated the room an hour ago, madam,' the middle-aged battleaxe said. 'If you just pay for one night that's all you get. All guests have to be out by ten o'clock. We're not a halfway house you know?'

'Yes, yes, okay,' Lisa grumbled, pulling the towel tighter around herself. 'I overslept that's all. We – I mean – I will be out of here in ten minutes.' She refused to add the words. 'I'm sorry.' If there was one thing she did regret about the interruption, overstaying her welcome certainly wasn't it.

The woman sanctioned Lisa's promise with a curt nod

and, lips still pursed crossly, turned to go off and harass someone else.

Closing the door with a sigh of relief, Lisa glanced over her shoulder at the bed. To her surprise it was empty, although the sound of running water coming from the bathroom told her exactly where Rio had disappeared to. When he came back into the room he was fully dressed, provoking a twinge of disappointment.

'Can you bear to put up with me for another hour or so?' Lisa asked him lightly. 'I need to put a proposition to you and the best place for it right at this moment seems to be over a plate of eggs and bacon.' Even as she voiced the suggestion she realised how dreadfully hungry she was all of a sudden.

'Sure.' Rio shrugged and nodded happily, apparently unconcerned about the details of her 'proposition'. 'I know just the place.'

Lisa dressed quickly in a pair of jeans and loose chambray shirt. Stuffing her dress and knickers from the night before into a small holdall, she picked up the room key and tossed it lightly into the air before catching it again. Then something occurred to her and she threw Rio a look of amazement.

'I've just realised. I haven't settled up with you yet,' she said. Dropping her bag down on top of the dressing table, she began to rummage through it until she found her purse. Inside was a wad of twenty pound notes. 'How much?' she asked candidly.

She noticed how Rio hesitated and put up a hand as if to ward off the money. 'Shit!' he said, shaking his head. 'I don't know if I can charge you for last night.'

Raising an eyebrow she asked why not.

'Because I enjoyed it too damn much, that's why,' he blurted out, looking unsure of himself all of a sudden.

Lisa smothered a smile. 'And aren't you supposed to enjoy it?'

'Well. Yeah. I guess. But I don't always.'

'But you still put on a good performance regardless?' she said.

Rio glanced at her warily. 'Yeah. I do. So what?'

She laughed. 'So nothing. Don't sound so defensive.' Peeling off a couple of hundred pounds, she fanned the notes out in her hand and thrust them towards him. 'I daresay this isn't as much as you would normally charge for a whole night,' she said. 'Tell me if it's enough.'

He took the notes hesitantly, stared at them for a moment, then his face lit up and he glanced back at her. 'This is nowhere near it,' he said, sounding as cocksure as the first time they met. 'But I don't want any more. And thanks. Thanks for everything.'

Picking up her bag again, Lisa walked toward the door. 'Don't start thanking me yet, Rio.' She threw the words casually over her shoulder. 'We haven't even got started on the good stuff.'

She had been referring to her planned offer for him to join Flights of Fancy, of course, and it was with a huge sigh of relief that she heard the magic words, 'It's a deal.'

Reaching across the small wooden table where they had breakfasted, she took his hand and shook it firmly. 'I can't tell you how pleased I am,' she murmured softly. 'There aren't that many men of your calibre out there.'

'Just five it would seem.' He threw back his head and laughed until some of the other diners began to throw him interested glances. Straightening up he became serious again. 'If you were not part of the package I don't think I would have accepted.'

Lisa looked uncomfortable for a moment. 'Don't say that,' she said, 'once Flights of Fancy gets off the ground – literally,' she paused and gave a soft chuckle, 'I doubt if we'll get to see that much of each other. I will be busy and you'll have your clients. Time will be in very short supply.'

His gaze was challenging. 'I'll make time,' he promised. 'Or perhaps I should have it written into my contract that I get to fuck my new lady boss at least once a fortnight.' Holding up his hands, palms facing towards her, he added, 'Just kidding.'

'So I should think.' Lisa tried to sound stern and failed miserably. There was too much laughter in her eyes, too much of a curve to her lips to expect him to take her seriously. In all honesty, if it hadn't been for her burgeoning involvement with Akira, she wouldn't have thought twice about agreeing to see Rio as often as he wanted.

Now she had her main recruitment problems sorted out, Lisa hastily turned her mind to the pressing matter of making sure that the planes would be ready to fly on time, as well as ensuring she had some passengers to go in them. In some ways she wished that she had set the launch date even further ahead. All of a sudden it was looming on the horizon and she didn't feel anywhere near ready enough.

Thankfully, Akira was a great support and a boost to her much-flagging motivation. After her experience with

Rio she didn't feel as though she could face another man. Or, to be precise, another fuck. But Akira wouldn't let her off that lightly. His solution to her jaded sexual appetites was to bombard her with huge bunches of fresh flowers: roses, carnations, orchids, some exotic blooms that she couldn't even recognise. All of them beautiful. All of them accompanied by erotic little messages.

After a couple of weeks of such overwhelming inter-floral seduction, she realised that she couldn't wait to see him again. Her whole body buzzed with her need for him. Even a simple act such as washing her hair reminded her of the sensuality of Akira's touch. He had washed her hair. Washed her all over in fact. And he had touched her all over. Even in secret little places that contained erogenous zones she didn't realise existed. Akira was imaginative. An ingenious lover and a fun one too.

Take ice cream. It wasn't for eating – at least not at first. In Akira's erotic, exotic world it was for smearing liberally all over the body and rolling about in on rubber sheets until they were both good and gooey. If not ice cream it was fresh berry compote, or rice pudding – a food which Akira claimed was the best thing the British had ever invented. And after all the smearing and rubbing in and rolling around came the best part. The licking it off. Lisa shuddered, cursing herself for thinking about it at all. How soon would it be until her inscrutable lover returned to London? Not soon enough for either of them it seemed. Unfortunately he was back in Tokyo so she couldn't even justify a flight to New York on the pretext of research.

Frustration was the key word in Lisa's vocabulary. Sexual frustration and the kind of frustration caused by sitting around, waiting for the man she really wanted. If it hadn't been for Flights of Fancy she might have gone mad in the meantime.

She had blithely left it up to Michiko to recruit the remaining personnel. And it seemed the young woman was enjoying the 'task' immensely – if her excited telephone reports were anything to go by. It made Lisa wonder how much freedom, sexual or otherwise, Michiko had enjoyed before she became involved in the project. Had her life been dictated by Akira up to that point? Was that how the oriental code of conduct operated?

Lisa was none the wiser. She had tried to broach the subject with Akira once or twice but he had been reliably enigmatic. Michiko was his assistant he said, then later admitted that she had been working for him since her father entrusted her into his care at the age of sixteen. No there hadn't been anything sexual between them then, he added when Lisa was forced by her own unquenchable curiosity to ask, implying that eventually there had been.

Strange as it seemed, even to herself, Lisa no longer felt envious of Michiko and her relationship with Akira. Curious, yes. Envious, no. In an odd way she felt as though, through the mind and body of the delightful young Japanese woman, her bond with Akira was strengthened. They had both been to bed with her. The very idea made her laugh but it was true nevertheless. She and Michiko had shared Akira. She and Akira had shared Michiko. It seemed right somehow. Very, very right. But not something she could confide to her friends.

Now there was another problem. When she agreed the deal with Akira she had given the airline her notice. The other stewardesses she shared her flat with had been shocked and envious in equal measure. That had been okay. Lisa could cope with shocking other people. What she didn't find very comforting was their complete scepticism about her plans. What sort of women would pay the money Lisa was planning to charge just so that they could join the mile-high club? Lots of them, Lisa had asserted with far more conviction than she actually felt.

She explained that the world was full of rich, busy, successful women who had all the money they could possibly need but no time to enjoy it. Some might just want to take a Flight of Fancy because they wanted to travel in luxury and be pampered by the multitude of beauty treatments that would be an onboard facility. Everything was included in the price. Including sex. Quite a few of her clients, she supposed, would thumb their cosmetically perfected noses up at the beauty treatments and go straight for the sex. Whatever the demand, she would make sure her clients were well catered for.

Akira telephoned her late that night. 'Everything is settled with the airport authorities at both ends,' he said. Typical Akira, Lisa thought, talking business when all she wanted to do was tell him how much she desired him.

'That's great,' she had enthused. 'When are you coming back?'

There was a long pause which turned her stomach to jelly.

'Not yet. I've got quite a few business matters to sort out before I can even think about coming back to England.

One of Japan's major car manufacturers is up for grabs and we, the Tanaka group, want a piece of the action. It will tie in well with our existing US activities. If everything goes to plan, after Japan I've got to go back to the States and sort out the export side. New advertising campaigns will have to be implemented and I don't trust the existing dealer network so I will probably have to organise a new one. All that sort of thing takes time.'

How much time? Lisa was desperate to ask. *When can I become part of your agenda again?*

Instead she gave him a progress report on Flights of Fancy. 'I'm going to see how the planes are coming on tomorrow,' she told him. 'Mark Jeffries said at the beginning of the week that they're on to the cosmetic touches now. I need to go through a whole heap of fabric swatches and decide on the decor.'

'How is Michiko doing – is she still bearing up under the strain?'

Lisa could hear the amusement in Akira's voice and it made her smile. 'Fine, as far as I know. All the main personnel are accounted for now. And she's been a godsend on the beautician side. As you know, she has a handle on that sort of thing. I wouldn't have a clue where to begin.'

'Simple,' Akira interrupted. 'You would have paid an expert to do the job for you. Stop thinking so small, Lisa. This is the time to think big and spend big. It's the only way to make a business work.'

She laughed. 'That's easy for you to say, you've got lots of money.'

The warmth in his voice was as encouraging as his words. 'So will you soon. I have every faith in you, Lisa.'

They spoke for a few more minutes, mainly about Flights of Fancy and then Akira said he had to go. As she put the phone down Lisa realised she had a smile on her face. God, it was good to speak to him again. Even if that was all they could do for the time being.

It excited her to see the inside of the planes Akira had leased. It made the project all the more real somehow. The two jumbo jets stood side by side in a huge hanger looking totally normal from the outside. As soon as she climbed inside, however, it was a different story. Her plan was to fly only one plane at a time across the Atlantic and back, from Heathrow to Kennedy, using them in strict rotation. That way she could keep absolute control throughout the flights and would always have a back-up plane if the unthinkable should happen.

A shiver ran through her as she surveyed her surroundings. There was no point in thinking that way. She *was* going to succeed. Flights of Fancy was going to be a huge success, if for no other reason than that Akira said so.

'As you can see, the lower floor has been partitioned off into twenty separate suites. They're a bit smaller than a room in some of the better hotels but I'm sure they will be perfectly adequate.' Rod Blackburn, manager of the refurbishing company, failed to hide a smile. What was the world coming to – flying brothels, whatever next?

Lisa could imagine his thoughts and was tempted to make a sarcastic response. Instead she asked about the fabric swatches and proceeded to spend the next few hours wandering about the plane, trying to visualise the final decor.

Each of the rooms had its own en-suite shower room, with basin, lavatory and bidet, and would be equipped with everything from a hairdryer to a fridge full of complementary champagne. On the upper floor there was a huge lounge bar, with a bank of TV monitors for screening all the latest films and music videos.

This would be where she would hold her first orgy. The first of many she hoped.

Glancing around she tried to visualise the impending scene. Everyone lounging around looking and behaving in a totally decadent manner. Happy, contented women served by a veritable army of gorgeous men. All the men she and Michiko had recruited were very different barring two important characteristics. One: they all loved women and loved to give women pleasure. Two: all were past masters in the erotic arts.

'Thinking about the profits, eh?' Rod Blackburn asked, coming up behind Lisa and jolting her from her depraved daydream.

Her eyes widened but she managed to compose herself before a blush started. 'Something like that,' she murmured.

'Your boss is a hard taskmaster, isn't he?' he added conversationally as they strolled back through the lounge towards the staircase. 'He's on the phone every other day checking up on our progress.'

Lisa was stunned by this piece of news. 'Really?' she said, then added frostily, 'Actually, *I* am the boss. And

Flights of Fancy is my baby. Mr Tanaka is merely my business partner.'

She didn't mean to be so abrupt but was still pleased to note that her sceptical companion looked suitably chastened. Clapping her hands together briskly, she gave him no time to think of a response. Instead, she asked him to show her how the kitchen was coming along.

Her next stop was the serviced suite of offices she had rented within the confines of Heathrow, near Hatton Cross. Here she had installed all the usual office paraphernalia, including several computers for databasing customer details. Eventually each client would have her personal predilections listed: type of man preferred, special dietary requirements or beauty preferences, everything, right down to her favourite drink.

Nothing would be too much trouble for Flights of Fancy. Luxury and pampering were the key elements and Lisa intended to make sure everything was absolutely perfect.

She had hired three women to handle the administration side of things, starting the following Monday. All of them, without exception, had been a little shocked when Lisa first outlined the concept to them but by the same token all were envious of the future clients and said if they could afford a Flight of Fancy they would take one like a shot.

That pleased Lisa because it confirmed that she was on the right track. When she opened the stack of mail that was waiting for her and found at least a dozen enquiries, she felt even more optimistic. Flights of Fancy was going to work, she thought happily as she logged all the details into the computer system. Not just because Akira had faith in her but because she had got it right.

Launch day was looming and Lisa was pleased to confirm to Akira that the flights each way were fully booked. Once again he had come up trumps, organising a similar office base for her at the New York end, and the number of enquiries that office had received was phenomenal. As Lisa had rightly surmised, the women who booked the flights were a pretty even mix of international business women, actresses and musicians and a large handful who were just plain rich.

Some of them were coy about their actual requirements, hesitantly mentioning being attracted by the idea of flying in luxury, while the majority were totally up-front and stated outright that they wanted sex and what kind of man they preferred. These were easy to deal with. With the help of the computer she was able to pair up one of her 'boys' with each client, knowing that in almost every case she had got it exactly right.

She had decided against going for a big launch. For one thing she didn't really have enough time at her disposal to organise the sort of event that such a project deserved. The press would have to be informed well in advance, catering organized and possibly a theme. Lisa mulled over the idea and promptly discarded it, opting instead to throw a huge orgy to mark the project's first three months of success.

Akira promised that, come what may, he would be there to kiss her feet and feed her grapes and Lisa had matched his enthusiasm for the whole idea. It took the pressure off a bit and gave her time to plan. It also reassured her that Akira quite freely envisaged their personal relationship extending that far into the future.

Chapter Six

Launch day dawned and with it the nest of worms which seemed to have been wriggling irritatingly around in her stomach for the past few weeks suddenly went berserk. Lisa opened her eyes and felt an enormous band of tension gripping her temples. When she got out of bed, her legs shaky and hardly able to hold her, she had to rush to the bathroom to throw up. Finally, feeling a little better, she brushed the hair out of her eyes and walked over to the window. There it was, a clear, cloudless, blue sky. The best possible flying weather. Everything augured well and Lisa was once again able to smile.

When she arrived at her office she found herself stepping into an atmosphere of controlled panic. Pretending to be composed, Lisa walked around reassuring everyone else. The plane was ready. The route, pilot and flight crew were all set to roll. In two hours the first Flights of Fancy passengers would check in at the special desk she had arranged in Terminal Three. Then they would all board the plane and soar off into infinity.

'It's all going to be alright. Nothing will go wrong,' she kept muttering to herself as she wandered around, checking and double checking everything.

Pam Jackson, one of the administrators she had hired, kept reassuring Lisa that everything was running like clockwork.

'Do you have your little introductory speech ready?' she asked Lisa who had sat down for a moment, leaned across the desk and rested her aching head on her arms.

Lisa glanced up in panic. 'Speech?' Then she remembered and her expression cleared. 'Oh, yes, my speech. It's in my briefcase.' She glanced down at the slim black case beside her chair. 'I don't know how I'm going to speak to all those women,' she added, looking panic-stricken again. 'I'll dry up, I know I will. I won't be able to say a thing.'

'Nonsense,' Pam said briskly, 'you've nothing at all to worry about. The passengers are just women the same as you. In fact you're doing something most of them would never be able to do in a million years.'

The older woman's reassurances went some way to relieving Lisa's anxiety, encouraging her to sit up straight and smile. 'Thanks. I needed that. There's nothing like a good talking to.' A soft chuckle escaped her, relieving the pressure inside her even more.

'Tell you what,' Pam offered, 'I'll make you a nice cup of strong coffee and we'll talk about the weather until it's time for you to leave.'

Lisa nodded gratefully and reclined in her chair, staring idly out of the window. Inside her head, she resumed her earlier mantra. Everything *was* going to be alright.

To Lisa's profound relief her clients were not the be-furred, bejewelled, talon-nailed ogresses that her feverish mind had conjured up. Her first reaction, as she watched the women board the plane and make their way upstairs to the lounge, was what an interesting mix they were. Some old, some young, some in jeans, some in designer dresses, some smiling and glancing around with interest, others looking frankly nervous.

She greeted each with a handshake and a friendly smile and couldn't help giggling inside as the women eyed up the five team leaders who were waiting in attendance: Shane looking blond and brawny; Jake the epitome of 'Alaska man'; Curtis bold, black and beautiful; Tom pleasant and totally unthreatening, his short reddish-brown beard freshly trimmed and Rio looking as mischievous as ever, his wicked eyes flashing.

'My, my,' one of the women remarked under her breath as she surveyed the line-up with blatant interest, 'a veritable smorgasbord of men, what a wonderful idea.'

Lisa couldn't help marvelling at the lift it gave her to hear such an off-the-cuff remark. All of a sudden her optimism soared. Flights of Fancy was a good concept – no – it was a brilliant concept and it was all hers, hers and Akira's.

In the lounge bar she opened the first bottle of champagne and waited until each of the twenty passengers and the five team leaders were seated ready for take off and had a full glass in their hands before launching into her speech.

She started out by welcoming everyone aboard the first ever Flight of Fancy and briefly outlined the concept and the choice of 'goodies' on offer. She mentioned the fact that the passengers who had booked men to accompany them on the flight had their requirements matched as fully as possible and that the said companions were already installed in the individual bedrooms, waiting. There was a collective gasp which Lisa took to mean approval, or perhaps awe at the women who were daring enough to state exactly what they wanted in advance. Then one woman, a slight blonde wearing jeans and a leather jacket with matching cowboy boots, tentatively raised a hand.

Lisa glanced in her direction and said, 'Yes, can I help you,' in what she hoped was a soft, friendly voice.

The woman was hesitant. 'If we er – I mean if one of us – that is me,' she began and paused to take a deep breath before continuing in a rush. 'If I want a man but haven't booked one, can I still have him?'

Smothered laughter rippled around the room. 'Of course,' Lisa said. 'There are twenty five men altogether, at least one for each of you if you want them. You can either see their details and a photograph first, or you can pick one out in person, it's up to you.'

The woman blushed and managed a nervous smile. 'I think I'd like to look at the details first,' she murmured.

Another ripple ran round the room, this time from other women who hadn't booked a companion for the flight but who now decided it wasn't such a bad idea after all.

By the time the toasts were made and the champagne drunk, the plane had already taxied to the runway and was ready to take off. The soft leather armchairs were fitted with safety belts and Lisa instructed everyone to buckle up. Again the lounge rippled with excitement, take-off was always a special moment for Lisa and it seemed everyone there was just as keen to get airborne.

Through the porthole windows she could see the familiar landscape of the airport sliding past, gradually slipping away faster and faster until the ground suddenly seemed to drop away and they were rising and banking over the outskirts of London.

As soon as it was safe to do so she invited the women to follow the stewards to their rooms, encouraging anyone who was interested to stay behind and go through the details of the men on offer. Half went, half stayed and of that half all of them picked out a man who, they claimed, was their idea of physical perfection.

It was such a relief to see everyone going off with expectant smiles on their faces. Three of the women who went straight to their rooms opted for beauty treatments rather than sex, another one claimed she just craved eight hours of uninterrupted solitude, while the rest welcomed the man of their dreams into their temporary boudoirs.

Lisa was surprised that Rio wasn't one of the men chosen. 'Hi,' she said softly, when he wandered into the lounge, 'do you want a drink.' She waved a careless hand at the countless bottles of champagne still on ice and the well-stocked bar.

He shook his head and then amended his decision to a glass of champagne. Picking up a bottle he eased out the cork and topped up her glass before pouring himself a fresh one and sitting down beside her on a soft, cream leather sofa.

'I can't believe no one chose me,' he said, looking more downcast than she had ever seen him.

Lisa tried to lighten his mood. 'Different strokes for different folks,' she murmured, placing a comforting hand on his knee and squeezing it.

Rio glanced at her. 'I suppose.' He looked down at her hand and then back at her face. 'Are you busy right now?'

Shaking her head happily, Lisa smiled right into his eyes. 'No. Are you propositioning me?'

He nodded.

'Well, then,' Lisa said, rising decisively to her feet and picking up the bottle of champagne, 'it's just as well I've got an identical bedroom all to myself. Ourselves,' she amended.

As she walked down the staircase ahead of Rio, it struck her that this would be her own initiation into the mile-high club, the idea thrilling her almost as much as the prospect of fucking Rio again. It was odd really, he was absolutely nothing like Akira. Apart from the fact that they were both small and dark, the two men were like chalk and cheese and yet she felt just as much desire for this cheeky, lascivious young man as she did when she was with her oriental lover.

Was there something wrong with her, she wondered, to fancy two men like crazy at the same time? Or was there something very right about it? When all was said and done, she was still a free agent and she did have a lot of sexual energy at her disposal. Plus she was on a high from the morning's activities so far. No wonder the thought of a few hours uncomplicated fucking seemed desirable.

Pausing only to tell the head steward that she was going

to her room to do some 'work' and did not want to be disturbed unless it involved one of the passengers, or was a dire emergency, she opened the door to her room.

Rio dived on her the moment the door was closed behind them. Almost ripping the buttons from her pristine white blouse, he forced her bra over her breasts and began fondling and sucking them avidly. With an agonised groan Lisa allowed her head to drop back, arching her back and offering even more of herself for his delectation. Further down, between her legs, she felt the crotch of her new, fifty pounds a pair, silk knickers become soaked with her juices.

She began to gasp. Her whole body was on fire yet Rio seemed intent only on her breasts. Squeezing them together, he flicked the pointed end of his tongue over her nipples, inciting further whimpers of arousal.

'Rio, please,' she gasped, fumbling for his belt, 'for God's sake fuck me.'

Taking her hands away from his body, he tutted. 'Impatience will get you nowhere.'

Lisa tried to glare at him through heavy-lidded eyes. 'I'm not impatient, just randy as hell.'

Stifling a grin, he shook his head decisively and muttered, 'Same thing in my book,' before lowering his mouth to her breasts again.

She gave in gracefully, or as gracefully as she could. Clutching his head between her hands she urged him to bite her nipples.

'Not hard,' she said, 'just lightly. Just little nips.'

To her delight he obliged her, sucking the taut buds deep into his mouth before clamping his teeth down gently around their base. Moving from breast to breast he sucked and nibbled her. Finally, he raised his head and smiled wolfishly.

'On your knees, young lady.'

Lisa was taken aback. Her first thought was: how dare he? – and the next, oh God, this is wonderful!'

Dropping to her knees in front of him, she reached out and began to caress his cock through his gabardine trousers – part of a 'uniform' of clothing that she had chosen for her 'boys' to wear. Navy trousers and short sleeved, white silk shirts worn with a loose silk-mix jacket. Rio had discarded his jacket somewhere along the line and, glancing up, Lisa couldn't help noticing how wonderful his tan looked against the pure, ice white of his shirt, his arms strong-looking and covered with a light mat of dusky hair.

It delighted her to feel the outline of his erection through the material of his trousers and this time when she reached for his belt buckle he didn't try to stop her. Instead, he allowed his fingers to delve into her hair and encouraged her to take his cock in her mouth. Lisa complied eagerly. She loved his cock, it was quite large and broad with a smooth bulbous head but, best of all, at some stage he had been circumcised so she could see all of it – every vein, every sinew straining and yearning as his desire mounted.

She mouthed him expertly and with great relish. Giving head was something she loved to do with the right man. Some, quite frankly, were not all that appealing, but Rio deserved everything she was going to give him.

As she came up for air and just began to flick the tip of her tongue delicately around his glans, she glanced up and noticed that he had his eyes shut. A beatific smile suffused his face and she marvelled at her own capability to give another person such obvious pleasure. Gripping the base of his stem hard, she ran her tongue all the way down the length of his cock, sliding it up and around and down again, until she felt a telltale surging sensation beneath her fingertips.

'Do you want me to come in your mouth?' he asked hoarsely.

Lisa took her mouth away from him almost regretfully. 'Yes,' she said, 'if that's what you want.' She didn't doubt that he would taste absolutely divine.

Enclosing him with her mouth again she began to suck steadily, her fingers massaging the sensitive spot on the underside of his shaft. Within moments he came, flooding her mouth with a salty jet. Swallowing hard, she sucked him gently for just a moment or two longer and then released him. Glancing up, she saw that he was looking down at her with a dark, promising expression in his eyes.

'I think you deserve some of the same,' he said thickly.

There was a chair just behind her and so Lisa sat down. Rio knelt before her, sliding his hands up the length of her legs, delighted to encounter the portion of bare flesh above her stockings. 'You are one hell of a sexy woman,' he growled, massaging his skin, his thumbs delving between her thighs to prise them apart.

Lisa felt a surge of excitement at his words and actions. She felt sexy. He made her feel sexy. Straight away she opened her legs for him and raised her bottom obligingly as he pushed her short navy skirt up over her hips until it was bunched around her waist.

'It'll get creased,' she protested feebly.

'So what,' Rio countered, 'put on a fresh one. Knowing you, I'll bet you have a complete change of clothes hanging in that wardrobe.' He nodded in the direction of a bank of built-in cupboards painted light blue to blend in with the decor.

She was so busy blushing and nodding sheepishly, that she hardly noticed when he ripped her knickers clean away from her. Fifty quid down the drain, she wanted to cry out but her words were drowned by a strangled groan of pleasure as he spread her labia wide and plunged his tongue inside the hot, waiting wetness of her vagina. Instantly, desire ran up from the tips of her toes to the top of her skull, spiralling her into a vortex of pleasure.

In room eleven Katya Sandusky was still anticipating the pleasures to come. From where she lay, reclining against a huge mound of satin pillows, she could see her reflection in the mirror opposite: slim apart from a few lumps and bumps that she intended to consult her plastic surgeon about as soon as she got home, long, well-toned legs, a pretty face with huge wide-spaced eyes and her crowning glory, a silken sheet of waist-length chestnut hair.

Glass of champagne in hand, she awaited her companion with a mixture of excitement and nervousness. She had never paid for sex before and, in a roundabout way, this was what she was doing. Although when she made the booking she hadn't stated outright that she wanted a man to share the flight with, she had known it was her real reason for taking a Flight of Fancy.

Her husband, the darling, assumed the new service was aimed at women purely for pampering purposes. As one of Wall Street's rising stars, the work ethic meant far more to him at this stage than relaxation, including sex which usually had to be 'slotted in' rather than spontaneous. Katya accepted the situation for what it was. She knew it didn't mean he wasn't in love with her and she felt as strongly about him as the day they had married four years ago. No other man could take his place in her affections but she loved sex. She needed it. She craved it. Sex without complications was the ideal solution. *And, let's face it*, she thought, blowing a kiss to her reflection, *what better way to fill the tedious hours of a transatlantic flight*.

A light knock on the door roused her from her contemplation.

'Come in,' she called, trying to quell the surprising knotting sensation in her stomach. Her voice sounded weak, she realised and, when the door didn't open immediately, she cleared her throat and called out again.

Sam Sturgess was looking forward to his day's work. He had woken with a smile on his face and had positively leaped out of bed, fuelled by his eagerness to get on with the day. If he stopped to think about the events that led up to this moment, he found himself wondering if it was all an elaborate hoax.

Having been a male escort for two years, the idea of indulging in paid-for sex with a woman he had never met before didn't phase him. It was a job and one he enjoyed very much. What man wouldn't? But this was a little different. Michiko, the little Japanese girl who had booked him two months earlier, had blown his mind with her offer. Part of him loved the idea of earning a regular salary while still doing what he loved best, while another part baulked at the notion of being employed.

All doubts were wiped out the moment he boarded the plane. A quick glance around told him that here was a concept that was so outstandingly brilliant and yet simple that it couldn't fail. And the facilities were excellent: comfortable, welcoming rooms, all kinds of luxuries on tap and best of all the knowledge that he wasn't working to a timescale. With up to seven hours at his disposal each time he couldn't fail to put on a good performance.

Katya's first impression of the young man who entered her room was: Wow! She had pounced on his details when she saw the photograph of him but the tall, athletic-looking man who walked through the door was far better in the flesh. The photograph had only been a head and shoulders shot but the cropped blond hair atop a strongly masculine face had attracted her instantly. If she had seen the body that came as part of the package she would have probably creamed her knickers there and then.

'Hi, you must be Sam?' she said, not bothering to move as he nodded and closed the door behind him.

'And you are Katya?'

She felt a *frisson* of anticipation as she nodded in reply and watched wordlessly as he walked across the room like a man on stilts, his navy-clad legs covering the small expanse of rose-coloured carpet in a few strides. Instead of coming straight over to the bed, he went to peer out of one of the portholes.

'Looks as though we're well and truly on our way,' he said as he turned away from the window.

Feeling rooted to the spot, his stare was as unavoidable as it was unintentional. His eyes took in the vision of her reclining against the pillows, champagne flute in hand, and all at once he realised he had stepped not into a hoax, but into a dream.

Although she had discarded her shoes she was still fully dressed. He had already noticed the black court shoes which lay on their sides, sole to sole, like a pair of lovers, reminding him of his reason for being there, but now all his attention was arrested by the woman herself.

She looked fairly young, only in her late twenties at the most, but her demeanour was as understated and self-assured as the dress she wore – a black-and-white-striped shift dress which was plain but beautifully cut, the hemline just skimming the midpoint of her shapely thighs. Her legs were bare, displaying a beautiful tan, and she wore no jewellery save a thin gold band on her wedding finger.

Pointing to the open champagne bottle and clean glass on the bedside table, Katya offered him a drink. He accepted with a smile that lit up his face and she eagerly shifted across the bed to make room for him to recline next to her. It felt so strange, she thought, to be laying fully dressed on a bed, next to a man whom she knew nothing about, knowing that they were going to spend the rest of the flight having sex.

A moment of silence passed between them as they each sipped their champagne, then they both spoke up at once. Laughing, Katya insisted he go first.

'I was just going to say, I think Flights of Fancy is the best thing that could have happened for women,' he said.

Katya shivered inside, loving the deep, gravelly sound

of his voice. It held so much promise, spoke of his masculinity and ultimately turned her insides to water. It was a good job she was already laying down.

She nodded. 'I agree, although I must admit I did feel a bit nervous about making the booking.'

'Well, we're in this together. It's a first time for both of us.'

He slipped his free arm casually underneath her shoulders and held her lightly. Smiling down at her, he held the glass to his lips and then to hers in a gesture that seemed so intimate she almost whimpered.

'Have you done this sort of thing before?' she asked. 'Been a—er—companion to strange women.'

'There's nothing strange about you.' His pale blue eyes twinkled. 'But yes I have and you've no need to worry. We'll take everything nice and slow. Just as it comes.'

A second shiver ran through Katya. The way he spoke was so beguiling, almost like a lullaby, enfolding her with a sense of rightness about the whole situation. And the mere mention of 'coming' made her stomach feel as though it had turned itself inside out.

Feeling suddenly nervous, she reached out to the other beside table to pick up a packet of Marlborough and a thin gold lighter.

'Do you mind?' she asked, glancing up at him.

He shook his head. 'No. I don't smoke myself but you go ahead.'

She shook a cigarette out of the pack, placed it between her lips and was gratified when he took the lighter from her and flicked it into life. Inhaling deeply, she allowed herself to smile at him. So many thoughts were running through her head. He had a nice face which bore a gentle, relaxed expression, his arm around her felt good – strong and protective, not at all threatening – and her desire was mounting by huge degrees. *This is not going to hurt either me or Peter*, she decided, the realisation filling her with profound relief, *this is not an affair, just sex.*

After a few more puffs, she put her cigarette out decisively and took a long swallow of champagne to kill the taste in her mouth. 'Would you kiss me?' she said.

From that moment on it all seemed to happen naturally. Sam tightened the grip around her shoulders, pulling her to him. His head dipped, the expression in his eyes softening as his lips lightly brushed hers. Katya sighed with pleasure, giving herself up to the deep, searching kiss that followed.

As his hand came up to caress her breasts she felt a tingle of sensation run through her, from the nipple which hardened under his palm, to the very pit of her womb. All at once she yearned for him, wanting him to spread her legs wide and fill her up. Behind her back she felt him reach for her zip. It came down in a single, fluid movement, the strap of her dress dropping to reveal the upper swell of the breast he now caressed.

She moaned, aching to press herself into his hand but lacking the nerve.

'Shall we take this off?' he murmured softly, taking her breath-stopping silence for acquiescence.

Disengaging slightly, he leaned away from her and pushed both straps down her arms and over her hands. Her dress pooled around her waist and she delighted in the muted groan of approval that her sudden display elicited. Under the dress she was completely naked, a fact which he soon discovered.

'And there you were when I arrived, looking like butter wouldn't melt in your mouth,' he said. He gazed up into her eyes before taking a hard, pink nipple between his lips.

'I know. I'm totally shameless really.' Katya tried to giggle but found herself moaning instead and murmuring: 'Yes, yes,' as he began to suck gently.

She had no qualms about urging him on now. Her breasts felt aflame and so sensitive to the touch that she couldn't help crying out when his fingers sought her other nipple and began to toy with it. He changed sides and she arched her back again, trying to push her nipple as deep into his mouth as she possibly could. His caresses were so sensual that she felt lost in sensation, trembling excitedly as her clitoris began to tingle and nudge its way between her blossoming sex lips as it swelled and hardened.

As his knee insinuated itself between her legs, she felt herself opening out to him. She could feel the wetness trickling out of her but she paid it no heed as she bore down on his thigh and ground herself against the hard muscle. Only his clothes stood between them and the glorious sensation of flesh upon flesh.

To her relief, that was only a temporary imperfection in an otherwise blissful state of affairs. To Sam, removing his clothes while pleasuring a woman was second nature. His shirt came off as he continued to suckle her breasts. His trousers came down and off while he rolled her onto her back and slipped his fingers between her legs. Like Katya, underneath he wore nothing at all.

Kicking off his socks, he caressed her outer labia, easing

them apart to reveal the prize beneath. She was wonderfully receptive, opening out under his fingertips with an eagerness that belied her apparent passivity. He much preferred women like her to the voracious kind: the ones who demanded things of him and took their pleasure without any apparent regard to aesthetics.

He liked sex but he preferred the erotic. The slow build-up. The gentle touching and caressing. The feeling that he was leading his partner into a vale of delights that would always be special to her.

'Mm, that's so good,' Katya whispered, spreading her legs wider.

He has a magic touch, she thought deliriously, like a musician playing an instrument with all the learned skill and dedication that it entailed. She felt as though she wanted to urge him on still further. Her vagina was so wet and open that she longed for it to be filled and yet he held her delicately on the brink.

He moved across her slightly and she felt his cock brush tantalisingly on the taut flesh of her thigh. Reaching down, her questing fingers encountered it immediately, a long, fairly slim wand of muscle that felt as hard as a rock. With the proof in her hand, she felt at that instant as though she were the most desirable woman on earth. Some men took a little work to get to this stage, he was hard for her already.

'Does madam approve?' he murmured, his lips stroking her cheek and continuing down the length of her throat.

Arching her neck, Katya smiled dreamily. 'Oh, yes. Madam approves,' she said. 'In fact, madam is over the moon.'

* * *

Lisa was just subsiding from yet another bout of ecstasy. The past couple of hours had been wonderful but Rio had still not fucked her yet. He was teasing her deliberately, he said, making her wait until he was ready. She pouted but to no avail. Trying to remind him who was boss didn't work either.

'Right here and now, I'm the one calling the shots,' he'd said, in a tone that brooked no argument.

She smiled dreamily to herself as she watched him raise his head from between her widespread thighs and grin at her lasciviously. There was no way she was going to argue. She was loving every minute of it.

'Come here,' she said, reaching out her arms to him.

Slithering up between her legs, he positioned himself over her. His upper body supported by his hands, he allowed the tip of his glans to skim the moist entrance to her body.

'How much do you want this?' he teased as he ground his pelvis slowly to circle her sex with his cock.

'You know how much I want it,' Lisa gasped. 'I've been wanting it for the past two hours.'

'I might let you have it in a minute.'

'You'd better.'

He tutted. 'There now, you've just earned yourself an extra wait.'

'Rio!' Her tone was somewhere between laughter and a warning.

In return he was uncompromising. 'I warned you I would be in control.'

'Yes, but—' Lisa tried to squirm towards him but he pulled back and shook his head reprovingly.

'Patience, Lisa. Patience.'

She hated him, she thought, knowing that she didn't really. Being in control was her domain. This jumbo jet and everything that surrounded her was her empire. And yet here she was, allowing herself to be dictated to by someone her own age and enjoying every minute of it.

'Don't tease me, Rio,' she sighed. 'Doesn't it make you feel good to know how much I want you?'

He nodded, a confident smile on his face. 'Of course.'

'Bastard!'

A soft chuckle greeted her outburst and in the next instant he lunged deep inside her, driving all other protestations away from her lips on a hoarse scream of pleasure.

Chapter Seven

New York was New York – noisy, grimy, busy as hell and the most exciting place on earth as far as Lisa was concerned. Unfortunately, she had precious little time to see any of it. Even taking the time difference into account, which meant that they landed at Kennedy some three hours after they took off from Heathrow, by the time she and the crew had disembarked and gone through customs it was late afternoon and she had promised to meet Akira for dinner that evening.

It had been a wonderful bonus, Akira phoning her to tell her that he had managed to juggle his schedule so that he could be in New York at the same time as her. Even just one night together was better than nothing.

Thinking back to the end of the flight, Lisa recalled with countless tingles of pleasure how many compliments Flights of Fancy had received from the passengers on the inaugural journey. Comments varying from: 'Absolutely wonderful', 'I didn't realise it was possible to feel this relaxed', 'My chosen man certainly seemed to know what he was doing' and 'I'm certainly going to book my return flight with you', all served to elevate her to cloud nine without recourse to a plane.

After the last satisfied customer had disembarked, she and her 'boys' had enjoyed a very boozy debriefing in the lounge bar. All of those who had been pressed into service looked and sounded very pleased with their lot – and rightly so, she thought with an inner glow of fulfilment. The past few months had been hard work but now, in the aftermath, worth every single minute.

Her only difficult moment, if it could be called that, was when she turned down Rio's offer to take her out to dinner and then on to a club.

'I know this great place,' he had said enthusiastically, 'where all the patrons wear fancy dress. The last time I went one woman was dressed as Cleopatra and led an ocelot around on a diamond studded lead.'

Lisa frowned. 'It sounds wonderful but I really can't, Rio. I – I've already promised to meet someone for dinner tonight.'

He was quick to pounce on her refusal. 'But you told me you don't know anyone in New York. You said you'd only been here once before.'

She felt frustrated. Why was he being so pushy and why the hell did he seem to assume that they now had a relationship?

'Look,' she said, as gently as she could, 'I made this arrangement before we left. It came as a total surprise. I didn't think he'd be able to make it.'

'He?'

'My business partner, Akira Tanaka.'

She wondered why she was trying to play down the situation. Why hadn't she just told him outright that Akira was her lover? Deep inside she knew she was deliberately hedging her bets. She liked Rio, really liked him. He was fun to be with and an excellent fuck. In a lot of ways he turned her on far more than Akira ever had and yet she knew that with Rio, what you saw was what you got. Whereas Akira was still almost a total mystery. His inscrutability got to her, teasing and beguiling her, maintaining her interest. If the truth be known she was still dying to find out more about him and what made him tick.

'It's no go I'm afraid, Rio,' she said more firmly now. 'I promised Akira and that's an end to it.' She pretended to jolly him along and punched him lightly on the shoulder. 'Come on. I'm sure there are plenty of pretty women out there in the huge metropolis who would be over the moon to receive your special brand of attention. And we'll see each other again tomorrow evening on the return flight,' she added encouragingly.

It was a relief when the old mischievous light returned to his eyes and he smiled. 'A good fuck makes the time fly as fast as the plane itself.'

Lisa stood up and began to collect up some of the empty glasses which she placed on a tray. 'That's right. You never know, you might get to do some real work tomorrow.'

To her surprise his expression clouded over. He seemed troubled and all at once warning bells went off in her head. Her heart sank. She didn't want to do it but she had to put him straight about a few things and apparently the sooner the better.

'Don't come to rely on me, Rio,' she warned. 'I'm a busy lady. I've just started all this up.' Pausing, she indicated the practically empty lounge with a wide sweeping gesture. Taking a seat opposite him, she leaned forward, her palms pressed together on her lap as if in prayer. 'I have to be able to devote myself to Flights of Fancy. That means *always* being available – what we did today should really have been a no no – and I particularly need to keep my business partner informed every step of the way. Without his financing, Flights of Fancy would be sunk without trace.' She noticed a worried frown cross Rio's face and added hastily, 'I don't doubt that by the end of the year the service will be breaking even. Possibly turning a profit. But the point is, just because it's up and running – or rather flying – I can't afford to slacken off. I must be free to do what I have to do, when I need to do it.' She didn't think she could be any clearer than that and thankfully, judging by the way his anxious expression had disappeared to be replaced by a relaxed smile, he seemed to have got the message.

'Point taken, boss,' he said, stressing her title in an amused tone.

'Well, just you remember it,' she retorted, wagging a finger at him and pretending to be stern. 'If you don't buck your ideas up I'll make you call me "Mistress" instead.'

With her head thrown back to let out a prolonged, throaty laugh, Lisa missed the way Rio's expression changed and darkened. Had she seen it, she would have known she had inadvertently touched a nerve.

Akira was waiting for Lisa in the rooftop restaurant of his hotel. Despite her best intentions she was late, only ten minutes or so but she knew that to punctual, do-a-million-things-at-once Akira, her tardiness would be seen as a gross aberration.

As she sat down, nodding gratefully to the black-and-white-clad waiter who assisted her, she noticed the way her inscrutable Japanese companion tapped the face of his platinum Rolex.

'Late,' he said sternly.

'Sorry.' Lisa pulled her chair further towards the table and picked up her napkin. Stalling for time, she shook it out and smoothed it across her lap. When she glanced up she noticed, with a start of surprise, that Akira was actually smiling.

'I was just teasing you,' he murmured, reaching across the table for her hand which lay limply between the two of his as he spoke. 'I have got a sense of humour you know, Lisa.' He paused, his expression darkening a little as he added in a low voice, 'It's little things like that which make me eager for us to get to know each other better.'

A small trembling sensation started up at the soles of Lisa's feet and ascended quickly to the top of her head. 'I – I'd like that,' she stammered. 'The trouble is, it seems you and I are destined to be on the opposite sides of the world most of the time.'

He brushed her doubts away with a light laugh and signalled to the waiter. 'Chateau Lafite-Rothschild, nineteen eighty five if you have it,' he ordered before turning to Lisa, his face still bearing a smile. 'You better than anyone should know how quick and easy it is to get from place to place these days.'

Lisa glanced down at her lap. 'I know but—'

'No buts,' Akira insisted, squeezing her hand until she

winced slightly. For a small man he possessed amazing strength.

'Okay.' For the first time that evening, Lisa relaxed back in her chair and picked up the glass of wine that the waiter had just poured for her. 'Now do you want to hear all about the first Flight of Fancy, or would you rather talk about the weather or something?'

Teasingly, he pretended to consider her suggestion. For a brief moment he held his glass up and she touched the rim of hers to his.

'To the first of many,' he said softly, holding her gaze with his own until she was forced to look away and gulp at her wine in confusion.

She couldn't help wondering what his toast really meant. Realising it was probably intended to refer to Flights of Fancy, her woman's intuition, or perhaps wishful thinking, gave her cause to think his words meant far more than that. It wasn't love, she told herself firmly. Not only didn't she have the time for such an emotion, neither did she need the complications that a love affair entailed. What she had with Akira, and to a certain extent with Rio, was fine. Absolutely fine. No strings. No complications. Just great sex.

'I want you to use my apartment whenever you are in New York,' Akira said as they began to eat the first course: oysters for both of them.

Lisa wasn't that fond of oysters at the best of times and nearly choked on the slippery thing when he made his offer. She swallowed deeply, took a gulp of her wine and dabbed at her lips with the edge of her napkin. Finally, she glanced across the table at him.

'Are you serious?'

He nodded. 'Perfectly.' Pausing to swallow another oyster first, he added, 'It makes sense. The place is empty most of the time and hotels are so impersonal and an unnecessary expense for you. Please, I'd like you to stay at my apartment. It would give me a lot of pleasure to think of you lying in my bed while I am thousands of miles away.'

His suggestion and the reasons behind it sounded so intimate it made her shiver visibly.

'Are you cold? He looked at her – a deep, penetrating look that hammered on the door to her very soul.

'No, not cold,' she whispered, shaking her head, 'stunned maybe. And very grateful for your offer.'

Akira waved his hand dismissively. 'I don't want you to be grateful to me,' he said, sounding as though he meant it. 'You are an independent woman, Lisa. You're strong, emotionally and physically.' He paused to smile and she realised that their thoughts had simultaneously shifted to the karate class where they had first met. 'And you know what you want. Best of all, you have the determination to succeed.'

'Gosh,' Lisa murmured breathlessly, sitting back in her chair and rocking childishly on the back legs. 'I am wonderful, aren't I?' She was joking but Akira surprised her by nodding emphatically.

'Yes, you are,' he said. 'To be truthful, I've never met a woman quite like you before.'

His words made her feel funny. There was a hollow place in her stomach that no amount of good food and wine could fill. She realised she felt anxious. Mixing business with pleasure was complicated – perhaps too complicated. She had told herself that enough times in the past and yet here she was doing exactly that, breaking her own rules and probably her heart into the bargain.

'I don't want things to become too serious too quickly,' she warned.

They were interrupted by the waiter arriving with their entrée and she noticed Akira remained silent and avoided her eyes until he picked up his knife and fork. Even then he paused until the waiter was well out of earshot.

'I don't love you, Lisa,' he stated bluntly, his words shocking her. 'But I do find you extremely attractive, mentally and sexually. You have already demonstrated to me how adventurous you can be and we have had fun so far, yes?'

'*Hai.*' Lisa spoke softly, using one of the handful of Japanese words that she had managed to learn. It meant yes.

His expression became dark and compelling as he reached across the table again and this time took both her hands in his. Under the table she felt his foot insinuate itself between her relaxed thighs. Glancing around to make sure no one was watching them, she opened her legs a little and sighed as his toes tickled her satin-covered mound.

'Will you come back to my place with me tonight?' Akira's voice was as soft and compelling as the movement of his foot between her legs.

Lisa squirmed slightly in her seat, surreptitiously giving him better access to her moistening vulva. Glancing around she realised, with an inner sigh of relief, that no one was paying them any attention. Her eyelids began to droop under the weight of her burgeoning lust and, consequently, the look she gave Akira was all the answer he needed.

'Excellent,' he said, withdrawing his foot and signalling to the waiter once more. 'Then shall we go?'

She was shocked that he wanted to leave straight away. 'Don't you want dessert, or coffee, or something?' she asked hesitantly.

A heavy hank of black hair flopped over his brow as he shook his head emphatically. 'I took the liberty of arranging for dessert to be awaiting us in my limousine,' he said.

Threads of anticipation zigzagged through Lisa's body. What could he have in mind? Stumbling to her feet, she scraped the legs of her chair across the dark green tiled floor, the harsh noise causing the other diners to glance around. Wishing the ground would open up and swallow her, Lisa clung gratefully to Akira's arm.

'I forgot to tell you how beautiful you look this evening,' he murmured, seemingly oblivious to her excitable condition.

The blush that had been threatening Lisa for the past minute or so suddenly suffused her cheeks and throat. Still ignoring her reaction, his eyes swept the length of her body from top to toe, taking in the piled-up hairstyle – a haphazard confection from which long, black, corkscrew curls dangled and danced around her head, with longer tendrils caressing her cheeks and the nape of her neck – and the fluid red silk dress she wore, with its deep plunging neckline front and back. He smiled, pleased with his own good fortune, the sweep of her spine was almost as enticing as the delicious curves visible at the front.

'Shall we?' he said, guiding her through the restaurant and out into the lobby.

They stood silently side by side, waiting for the elevator to arrive and when it did, he showed no apparent eagerness to step inside. As soon as the elevator doors closed, however, he became a changed man. Aside went the inscrutability and calm demeanor to be replaced by a raging passion that took Lisa's breath away.

For eight floors they devoured each other in a kiss that left Lisa breathless and panting. Between the wide vee neckline of her dress, her creamy breasts rose and fell in frantic harmony.

'Akira, what are you doing?' She stared wide-eyed at him as he calmly reached out and pressed a red button which stopped the elevator instantly.

His smile was devilish. 'Buying time.'

Lisa had no time to think up a response, already Akira was pushing her down to the floor, rucking her dress up to her waist as he did so. As she lay back gasping, wondering what on earth she was doing and if it was all a terrifyingly erotic dream, Akira unzipped the fly of his dress suit and, snatching the crotch of her knickers aside, plunged straight into her.

Immediately, Lisa's legs wrapped themselves tightly around him, gripping him tightly as she bucked her pelvis, trying to match his rhythm. She couldn't keep it up, he was driving his hard cock inside her so hard and so fast that she could barely think straight. In a rush, she felt her clitoris swell and explode seconds before he cried out and came inside her, his hips jerking spasmodically, his breathing ragged.

They lay in blissful aftermath for about two seconds before Akira seemed to come to his senses and revert to his usual sanguine self. Jumping to his feet, he quickly cleaned himself with a handkerchief and zipped up his trousers. Lisa was less energetic. She wobbled, Bambi-like, to her feet and immediately sought one of the elevator walls for support. Leaning one shoulder against it, she weakly accepted Akira's offer of a clean handkerchief and dabbed half-heartedly between her thighs before pulling her knickers back into place and her dress down.

Smoothing the pure silk over her hips and thighs, she nodded to Akira that it was safe to restart the elevator. On the ground floor they were greeted by stony faces. No one would dare say anything to Akira, she realised with startling perception. He was obviously well known and respected – that much was obvious, if for no other reason than the acute deference the head waiter and staff of the restaurant had shown him earlier.

Holding her elbow lightly, Akira guided her through the vast lobby and out of the hotel.

'Do you visit this place a lot when you come to New York?' she asked, watching with only partial interest as a sleek, white, six-wheeled limousine turned the street corner and began to drive down their way.

'Oh, off and on,' he declared in such a falsely airy manner that Lisa wondered what he was trying to cover up.

Was this where he brought all his women? So what? Surprisingly, she didn't even feel a twinge of envy at the thought. Right there and then he was with her and that was all that mattered.

Lisa's questions were drowned by the throaty gurgle of the limousine drawing to a smooth halt beside them. Now she couldn't help but take notice of the fantastic automobile. She tried to peer inside, wondering if a top celebrity was about to make an appearance, but the glass was so darkly smoked that she couldn't see a thing.

Akira seemed in no hurry to move off to hail a cab so Lisa watched as the driver's door opened and a chisel-jawed chauffeur emerged. Way over six feet tall and dressed in a grey flannel suit piped with red, a peaked cap disguising his appearance, the Greek-god of a man reminded Lisa of every chauffeur she had ever seen in films.

'Arnold Schwarzenegger, turned ace driver, at your service,' she giggled to herself.

'Lisa!' Akira's voice started her out of her reverie. She had been watching in a daze as the chauffeur stepped around the front of the car, walked to the rear passenger door – just a matter of feet from where she and Akira stood – and opened it with a flourish. 'Get in. We don't want to spend all night on the sidewalk, do we?' He nudged her gently in the small of her back, his palm pressing her forward until she found herself about to step into the car. Glancing down she noticed that an aluminium plate on the sill pronounced the name Lincoln Continental.

'Oh, so this is what one of those looks like,' she murmured to herself. All at once she realised what Akira was doing, where she was going.

'Do you want me to get in this?' she gasped, whirling her head around to meet Akira's inscrutable gaze.

He nodded patiently. 'Get in the car, Lisa.'

On wobbly legs she stepped inside. It was a revelation. Instead of the rows of seats that she imagined the limousine contained, the front part of the passenger area comprised a few soft leather seats, while towards the back a jacuzzi bubbled invitingly.

'That—that is amazing,' she stammered, pointing in disbelief at the foaming pool.

Akira couldn't help a smile. 'I thought you might like it. He reached out and opened a fridge. 'And see, in here I have fresh berry compote and champagne.'

Lisa trembled. She knew what that combination meant. One glance into Akira's eyes revealed the deep, dark sensuality that lurked in his soul. He looked at her with the intensity of a man who has the prize he most desires within his grasp.

Her own juices flooded her and, weak limbed, she groped around for something firm to support her. With grateful fingers she encountered the butter-soft leather of a small club chair and sank her trembling body into it gratefully.

Akira watched impassively before turning his attention back to the fridge. 'Do you want both?' he asked.

Dumbly, Lisa nodded.

Using a silver ladle, he divided the berries between two cut glass bowls and then uncorked a bottle of champagne and poured some into a couple of tall flutes blown from green-tinted glass. Accepting the glass he handed to her, Lisa sipped gratefully, her eyes still scanning the interior of the car. The chauffeur was back behind the steering wheel and Akira uttered a few curt instructions in Japanese before pressing a button which activated a dark screen of glass. The screen rose smoothly, cutting them off from the front of the car. Moments later she heard the engine gurgle into life and was only vaguely aware that they had begun to move.

Akira turned his attention back to her. 'Take off your dress, Lisa,' he said softly. 'Don't worry. No one can see you and the car won't stop until I give the instruction. It's just you and me gliding gently through night-time New York.'

His description beguiled her almost as much as the thought of being naked in front of him. With trembling fingers she unfastened the gold clips on her shoulders which kept the dress in place. It pooled around her waist, revealing her bare breasts, and she wriggled out of the rest of it as seductively as possible. Her knickers, a damp scrap of matching silk, followed quickly.

He nodded approvingly as she sat before him as nature intended. 'Do you know one of the things I really like about you, Lisa,' he murmured, kneeling before her, 'is the way you appear totally at ease with your body. Being naked is no big deal to you is it?'

She shook her head. 'Not really,' she said, gasping as he reached out and pinched her nipples between thumb and forefinger. 'But you help a lot, Akira, I mean—' She paused to glance down and watch Akira's fingers at work, twisting and pulling at the distended buds of her nipples. 'You make me feel so desirable, it's easy not to feel embarrassed.' She finished her sentence on a sigh as countless darts of pleasure zinged through her, igniting all her erogenous zones simultaneously.

Taking note of her obvious arousal, Akira released her nipples and sat back on his heels. 'Time for dessert I think.'

Reaching out for one of the bowls filled with berries, he motioned to her to kneel on the thickly carpeted floor beside him. Lisa scrambled to do as he instructed and waited patiently in the curiously submissive position that she knew Akira liked – back straight, shoulders relaxed, knees just wide apart enough to display her sex and her palms resting on her thighs. With a shiver of anticipation she watched him dip a perfectly manicured finger into the bowl and scoop up some of the sweet and sour confection.

The colour, as he smeared a trail of berries across the upper swell of her breasts, was a deep crimson. Like blood but much thinner. It trickled down her breasts, teasing her, rougeing her nipples to an even deeper red. Lisa sighed again and allowed her head to drop back. They had played this game before but never in the back of a moving limousine, never gliding along the mysterious grid of streets that constituted one of the world's most vibrant and exciting cities and never in such an atmosphere of dark sensuality.

Akira was coating her stomach with the berries now, smearing them haphazardly over her taut flesh, his hand sliding lower over her belly and down between her parted thighs.

Whimpering with barely contained lust, Lisa spread her thighs wider apart and arched her back until she was almost bent double. She could feel his fingers, slick with berry juice, sliding over her moist vulva and into the groove between her outer labia. Her clitoris seemed to jump and twitch as his fingertips skimmed it, teasingly, lightly. All at once a harsh groan tore from her throat as he stroked her swollen sex lips and spread them wider, one finger circling the hard stem of her clitoris with maddening dexterity.

The juice had dried on her breasts and torso. Her skin felt tight and blushed of its own accord under the roseate film of juice.

'I'm such a dirty girl,' she whispered, as Akira had taught her. 'I need to be cleaned.'

A gruff laugh touched her ears and she raised her head slightly to see his dark, silky head moving lower, his lips just hovering over her stomach.

'Yes. Oh, yes please,' she urged, arching her back still further.

'Naughty,' he murmured darkly, delivering a light slap to her exposed vulva. 'You are such an impatient girl, Lisa.'

A million responses to his humiliating words and action jostled in her mind but none of them seemed to count for anything. All she wanted right at that moment was the feel of his mouth on her anxious flesh, his tongue lapping at her juice-streaked breasts and torso. It didn't matter that he wanted to treat her as his plaything when they were alone together. She knew he respected her and handing over her pleasure to someone as talented and inventive as Akira was liberating in itself. Oh, the relief not to have to think, or feel guilt. To be able to give herself up to the beauty of the moment was an acquired skill which she had learned from the master himself.

'You must know when to relax and let go,' he had told

her the second time they got together. 'Stress is okay in small doses. It can even be constructive. But you have to be able to release it when *you* want to.'

He had gone on to teach her a few Thai-Chi-based relaxation exercises and had then taken her liberated mind and body to new heights of ecstasy. It was no accident, she knew, that her orgasms were much more powerful now. Thanks to Akira she had learned to submerge herself in the moment and forget everything else.

The touch of his tongue, delving inquisitively into her navel, brought her back to the present. Like a sleek-coated dog, he lapped at her straining body, cleaning her completely. To her delight he lingered on her nipples before creating a wet trail down the centre of her torso to her sex.

As soon as his mouth touched her vulva she cried out and when his tongue began to lap at her swollen clitoris she could hardly contain herself. She wanted to hang on to her climax, to prolong the delicious moment but her arousal was too strong. Within minutes she was forced to concede defeat as a wave of heat and lust swept over her and exploded at the very point where his tongue wriggled like a sidewinder.

She lay in a crumpled heap on the floor of the limousine. Carelessly foetal, she rested on her side, her knees slightly drawn up, her hands clasped in front of her face. Akira stroked her back softly and rhythmically, his palm sweeping from the nape of her neck to curve over her buttocks. After a few minutes he squeezed her bottom gently and asked her if she would care to join him in the jacuzzi.

Lisa nodded wordlessly and rose unsteadily to her hands and knees to crawl towards the inviting bath. Sinking into the effervescent warmth with a contented sigh, she allowed the water to enfold her, cleansing the last traces of berry juice. Akira immersed himself opposite her and immediately, his toes began an exploratory journey starting at her feet and ending up at the apex of her thighs. One foot ruffled her pubic hair and she smiled, truly and completely relaxed for the first time that evening.

'Did I tell you you look beautiful?' he asked, handing her the champagne flute that she had discarded some time ago.

She nodded. 'Yes, but don't let that hold you back.'

'I won't. You are beautiful, Lisa. One of the most beautiful and sensuous women I have ever met.'

'Flatterer!' She laughed lightly but secretly felt thrilled. He wasn't disposed to flattery, she knew that. When he said something he meant it.

He glanced down at his lap and then back to her face. 'There is something hiding under these bubbles that urgently requires the delicious gift of your body,' he said.

'Really?' she teased lightly, edging towards him.

Straddling him, she waited until he slid a little lower and she could feel the tip of his cock brushing her vulva. Already aroused, her vagina seemed to open even wider and she enveloped him with ease, sliding her hot channel down his shaft until he was buried inside her up to the hilt. Then she began to grind her pelvis, slowly at first, then faster and faster. Gripping his hair, she pulled his head back and kissed him hard, sucking his tongue deep into her mouth and caressing it with her own.

His hands had been holding her lightly by the waist but now they slid slowly up between their bodies to cup her breasts. The bubbles of the jacuzzi popped and fermented all around them as they rocked and ground together. She could feel his desire growing, his cock expanding inside her to tantalise the velveteen walls of her vagina.

'You feel so good, Lisa,' he growled into her ear, 'I could go on fucking you for ever and it wouldn't be enough.'

'Oh God, Akira!' His words drove her to fever pitch, urging her to grind her hips even faster. The swollen bud of her clitoris grazed his belly and she felt the first waves of orgasm wash over her. Now she was frantic, squirming mindlessly on top of him until they both climaxed in unison.

An hour later, Lisa and Akira were both dry, fully dressed and seated in the club chairs sipping champagne as though they had enjoyed nothing more than pleasant conversation. The limousine drew to a smooth halt and in the next moment the door opened. As she stepped out onto the sidewalk, Lisa noticed they had arrived back at the same place they had started.

Gazing up at the familiar façade of the hotel, she turned to Akira with a questioning look.

Even for someone who had turned inscrutability into an art form, it was impossible to disguise the merriment in his eyes. 'This is where I live,' he said. Pausing only to thank the chauffeur and tell him that his services were no longer required that evening, he took Lisa's hand and led her back inside the hotel. 'The twenty-fourth floor is all mine.

Although that's not strictly true. The whole hotel is mine. Tanaka group owns the lot and three others like it in Chicago, Boston and Los Angeles.'

'Wow, I'm impressed.' Lisa forced herself to adopt an ironic tone when in truth she *was* impressed. Very.

He smiled and took her over to the elevator. 'So you should be.'

This time, throughout their ascent to the twenty-fourth floor, they remained upright and fully dressed both knowing that they had all night and possibly the following morning to be together. Despite Lisa's fears about becoming involved, the realisation that she was with a man who meant more to her than great sex filled her with a warm glow. The future had never looked rosier.

Chapter Eight

Katherine Dwight was in a state. Her usual calm, neatly ordered self was all of a fluster and she knew precisely why. It almost made her swear when she thought of the trick that had been played on her by so-called well-meaning friends.

'A birthday present for you, Katherine,' one of them had said amid a chorus of giggles.

'Yeah, one you'll never forget,' said another, coarser member of their little group.

This was accompanied by a round of out and out sniggers which made Katherine instantly wonder if all her moralistic WASP friends had been replaced by aliens overnight.

Katherine was a statistician. A lady who let her head rule her heart and everything else besides. At twenty nine she believed she had everything any self-respecting woman could wish for: a white-collar husband, two well-behaved children – boy first, then girl – a flexible job, a reliable house-maid and a select group of very good friends. Now her thirtieth year was dawning and everything seemed set to change.

First of all came the offer to deliver a lecture at one of

England's top universities, all expenses generously covered in advance. Then the discovery that her friends had clubbed together and paid for a luxury flight over for her. Her birthday present? – the chance to totally abandon herself to pleasure.

It wasn't a concept that she was overly familiar with.

During the course of the next few weeks she surprised herself by gradually becoming accustomed to the notion of having her hair done en-route and perhaps a manicure and pedicure. Her friends laughed at her tentative suggestions and pointed out that everything listed in the brochure was included. *Everything*. It was then her eyes alighted on the paragraph about sex.

She was speechless. Ruddy-cheeked with indignation and gripped by an overwhelming sense of anxiety, she refused to acknowledge – even to herself – that, deep down, sex with someone other than her husband was something she would consider. Shaking her head in denial, she remonstrated with herself. Educated, well-brought up girls like her wore white organza dresses to their prom and wore a similarly virginal outfit on their wedding day.

Ross had still been a virgin too, bless him. Their wedding night had been tender but covert, with the duvet pulled up to their chins and all activities of the marital-duties variety carried out strictly under a concealing layer of duckdown. As time went on nothing really changed. She wasn't overly embarrassed to undress in front of Ross but he always made sure he averted his eyes at particularly revealing moments, and in return she treated the whole act of changing clothes with dispassionate haste.

There was nothing erotic in their relationship. Nothing of the kind she had read about in *Cosmopolitan*. Even the birth of their two children had been a women-only affair. Ross said he would rather not if she didn't mind – referring to his being present at the actual event – and Katherine was quick to breath a sigh of relief and assure him that no, she didn't mind, not at all.

Now here she was, waiting in the departure lounge of Kennedy airport to board a plane that was filled to the gills with sexual studs. The prospect filled her with terror of magnified proportions. All the assurances in the world that she wouldn't be compelled to do anything more than relax – alone – for the duration of the flight did nothing to assuage her blind panic.

What was she letting herself in for? How did she know that hordes of men wouldn't fall on her like ravening beasts the moment the plane took off? She would be helpless – unable to escape and hopelessly overpowered by all that masculinity.

A wicked trickle of something nasty soaked into her pants and she had to fight down the urge to rush to the ladies' room to try and repair the damage. The first call for boarding came and she found herself caught up in a small wave of other women, most wearing designer clothes and secretive smiles, all obviously bound for a Flight of Fancy.

As she boarded the plane, she had the odd sensation of stepping into a small, very exclusive hotel. Following behind a tall young man in a smart navy suit, she and several other women climbed a flight of stairs to the upper deck. A smiling, dark-haired girl introduced herself as Lisa and another young man handed her a glass of champagne and led her over to a comfortable leather armchair.

Hastily refusing his offer of assistance with her seat belt, she crossed her legs primly at the ankle and surveyed the scene as the rest of the passengers appeared and took their seats. There followed a short introduction and refills for those who wanted more champagne. Then a short interlude followed as the plane actually took off. As soon as people were allowed to unbuckle they were straight on their feet and heading for the staircase.

Katherine remained rooted to the spot.

A minute or so later Lisa spotted the tightly wound-up woman in the ill-fitting Prince of Wales check skirt suit and went over to her.

'Hi, do you need some help? I can get a steward to show you to your room.'

Katherine shook her head wordlessly. 'I – I don't know why I'm here,' she whispered in a voice that definitely wasn't hers.

Lisa took stock of the situation immediately. *This must be the birthday-gift client*, she realised.

'You know your friends booked a man for you, don't you?' she said candidly. 'Do you want him now, or would you rather wait a while first?'

Katherine felt as though someone had just hacked her into a million pieces and then put the bits back together all wrong. Her limbs wouldn't work. Her body felt wooden, her face stiff. Even the hairs on her head felt as though they were at odds with each other.

'Look,' Lisa added kindly, dropping to her haunches beside the frightened woman. 'You don't have to have him. Or you can have a look and send him away again. It doesn't matter. He won't mind. We can always find you someone else more suitable. Or no one at all. It's entirely up to you.'

Turning her head slowly, Katherine looked into Lisa's face and saw kindness and sympathy. To her surprise she began to cry. Fat, wet tears rolled down her face as she heaved with sobs that tore at her chest. As though a dam had been breached, she felt the frustrations of the past eight years well up inside her and flow out. Ross had never given her an orgasm. That was the crux of the matter. Never. Not one.

'I don't know that much about s-sex,' she admitted in a broken voice.

Lisa handed her a clean, white handkerchief, edged in lace. 'It doesn't matter,' she said softly. 'All Flights of Fancy lovers are experienced men. They do all the work, not you. You just lay back and enjoy as much, or as little, as you want.'

'It sounds wonderful,' Katherine gasped, managing a tentative smile.

Lisa smiled gently. 'It is, believe me.'

Gulping, Katherine dabbed at her eyes before turning to look at Lisa again. 'I – I know this is an awful imposition but – but would you mind taking me down to my room and just sort of be there with – with the man for a little while?' She said the word 'man' in the same way that a potential victim might say werewolf, forcing Lisa to bury a grin.

Instead she helped Katherine to her feet and said, 'Of course, no problem. I'll stay as long as you want me to.'

* * *

Realising that her 'special treat' client would probably be more nervous than most, Lisa had deliberately matched her with Jake. She knew from her own experience that he would be tender and thoughtful and because he was American he would therefore be that little bit more familiar.

He was already waiting inside the room when they arrived. Seated in a maroon-velvet club chair with an open bottle of champagne nestling in a black ice bucket on the dressing table beside him, he looked totally at ease. As Lisa entered, followed by a trembling Katherine, he stood up, greeted Lisa with a smile and turned his attention immediately to the woman behind her.

His first thought when he saw Katherine was, *Hell, this one's going to be a challenge!* Followed by, *Why in heaven's name does she wear her hair like that?*

As if she could read his mind, Katherine's right hand immediately fluttered to the tightly coiled, wheat-blonde bun that stuck rigidly to the back of her head.

Apparently oblivious to the tension in the room, Lisa made the necessary introductions before walking over to the ice bucket and pouring some champagne for herself and Katherine. The other woman accepted the glass gratefully and perched nervously on the edge of the bed.

Katherine didn't want to think about what she was actually sitting on. Just the word *bed* held too many dreadful connotations. Instead she tried to clear her mind and concentrate on what Lisa was saying.

'Jake is American. Although I expect you've already worked that out for yourself.' Lisa laughed lightly and threw a smile at both Jake and Katherine. Jake grinned and said, 'Sure am,' while Katherine tried hard to stretch her lips into an alternative expression to naked fear.

Taking centre stage, Jake leaned forward in his chair and began to animatedly describe the place where he had been born and raised. Pretty soon his light-hearted comments and wickedly incisive descriptions of the small population of Wynnville began to take effect.

Almost against her will, Katherine felt herself begin to unwind a little. Accepting a second glass of champagne from Lisa, she hardly took her eyes off Jake's face as he spoke. She was trying to work out how old he was. Probably around the same age as herself, she realised, although no one would know it to look at them. He looked youthful, relaxed and tanned, while she felt like a pale shadow of her spinster aunt in Oklahoma.

All at once she was filled with anger. Anger at herself and at Ross for not encouraging her to make more of herself. Most of her friends wore their hair long and flowing, or stylishly cropped. Even the suit she was wearing now was tantamount to fashion fever as far as she was concerned. Nearly all her clothes were in drab, sensible colours and fabrics that didn't show up creases or sticky fingermarks, but just the other day she had been gripped by the sudden urge to splash out on something completely different. Something that was, in her eyes at any rate, totally outrageous. Thus, the plaid suit with it's hip-hugging skirt that just skimmed her knees. Most of her other clothes were loose cut with hemlines that reached her ankles. This suit was by far the most revealing thing she had worn in a long time.

Just then they were startled out of one of Jake's tales –

rampaging cattle in the Arizona desert – by the sound of Lisa's bleeper.

'Oops!' she said, jumping to her feet. 'Sounds as though someone somewhere wants me.'

She glanced apologetically at Katherine who was beginning to look terror-stricken again. But thankfully the woman raised her hand and said that of course Lisa must go, that she had taken up too much of her valuable time already.

Assuring her that it wasn't the case, Lisa bade both her and Jake a cheery farewell and quietly hoped that things would eventually work out between them.

Long minutes of painful silence followed. Katherine quaked as Jake stood up and was immediately relieved when he asked if she minded if he use the bathroom.

'No. Please. Go ahead,' she said.

Left by herself she gave in to the temptation of a third glass of champagne.

When Jake returned he was quite surprised to see that the bed was no longer occupied and that his client, Katherine, was seated on the chair chanting under her breath. Presently her eyelids fluttered open and she stared at him.

'A friend of mine dragged me off to a consciousness-raising seminar last February,' she explained, surprised to find that her voice had returned to its normal, controlled pitch. 'At the time I thought it was a load of old phooey but I didn't think it would do any harm to give it a try now.'

Jake smiled and sat down on the corner of the bed so that their knees just brushed. 'I don't think I need to ask if it did any good.'

Catherine nodded emphaticlly, the movement dislodging a couple of hairpins. Unusually for her she ignored
them and let them lay where they feell onnthe thick cream
carpet.

'Oh, yes. You should try it – really,' she urged.

Jake realiised he liked the animated look in her eyes, it lit
up her whole face, transforming her instantly. 'You look
beautiful when you smile,' he said.

It was only a half-lie. The glow that had appeared along
with her words lit up her eyes, forcing him to notice them
properly for the first time. They were a deep amber colour,
with little flecks of green, reminding him of a favouriite
marble he had owned as a child and had lost to his best
friend. No amo nt of cajoling or just plain bribery would
make him swap it for another one and Jake had found
himself missing that marble aas if it had been a dear friend.

'I love your eyes,' he murmured, almost to himself.

Katherine thought she heard him say he loved her eyes
but couldn't be certain. *Silly woman*, she scolded herself,
*what would a good-looking man like him possibly find
attractive in you?*

Reaching out for a second bottle of champagne, he
offered her a refill. Immediately, Katherine began to shake
her head.

'Oh, no. I've already had three.' She wished she hadn't
shaken her head quite so hard. Now she felt as though she
were swimming underwater. Glancing down she noticed
that he was ignoring her protests and was in the process of
topping up her glass.

he bubbles popped and fizzed, tickling her nose as she
held the glass to her lips.

'Tell me about yourself,' he said, relaxing back on the bed a little.

Trying to ignore the image he presented, Katherine demurred. 'There's nothing really to tell.'

He wouldn't give up that easily. 'How old are you?'

For a moment she gave in to the temptation to laugh. It was a low, throaty laugh. A laugh that reminded Jake of the smoke-filled atmosphere of intimate nightclubs.

'Would you believe today is my thirtieth birthday?' she replied.

Of course, he already knew but he nodded encouragingly as though it was the first he'd heard of it. 'And what are your plans when you get to London?' he asked. 'Sightseeing, or just hitting all the hotspots?'

This time Katherine couldn't help the laugh that bubbled up inside her, vying with the champagne. 'Silly!'

His expression became intense. 'Why shouldn't you. You're not under age are you?'

This time she blushed and shook her head.

He tried a different tack. 'Tell me about your job,' he said.

Taking another gulp of champagne for courage, Katherine began to steadily outline the vagaries and responsibilities of her part-time position with New York analysts, Simpson, Hale and Brand. Describing her work was easy, she loved it and the facts and figures loved her. They didn't make any demands on her, or cause her problems – they just *were*.

'I – I'd like to see my name added to that list one day,' she admitted hesitantly.

Great heavens! She surprised herself there. It was an

ambition that she hadn't even fully acknowledged. What hope was there of a wife and mother attaining a partnership? She felt privileged to have a career at all. Briefly, she explained to him about the seminar and the fact that she'd been invited to speak.

Jake's face lit up. 'Wow! A celeb.'

Katherine actually giggled, he noticed.

'It's no big deal.'

'Yes, it is. It's a very big deal. Hell, I can't even add three-figure numbers together in my head.'

She didn't doubt the truth in that. Lots of people were number blind. 'May I have another glass of champagne?' she asked, feeling uncommonly bold all of a sudden.

'Sure.' He picked up the bottle and poured. As he placed it back in the ice bucket, his fingers drifted to hers where she held the stem of the champagne flute. 'You have nice hands,' he said, stroking the soft portion of flesh between her thumb and index finger.

Katherine felt a shiver start up inside her and had to force herself not to snatch her hand away. 'Thank you,' she said softly. 'I'm always moisturising them.'

Now she felt stupid. What on earth made her think that he would be interested in any part of her beauty routine? In fact, when she came to think about it, putting on a few dollops of handcream *was* her beauty routine. Suddenly she started to realise just how meaningless her life really was and resolved to do something about it as soon as possible.

Glancing into Jake's open, trustworthy face, she realised that right here and now was where she could make a start. Why not jump in at the deep end for once, surely then the shallow waters that followed would be a piece of cake in comparison?

'I – I really like you, Jake,' she said softly but with only a hint of her earlier nervousness.

He took her cue. 'Good. I really like you too.' He paused and gazed deep into her eyes wondering if it was too soon to kiss her. 'Did I mention that you have wonderful eyes?'

She nodded, dislodging another couple of hairpins in the process. Jake glanced at her shoulder, where they dangled precariously, picked them up and placed them on the dressing table. To Katherine it seemed like a very intimate thing to do and all of a sudden she experienced another rush of wetness between her legs.

'I think I need the bathroom,' she muttered hastily.

Jake moved obligingly out of the way and she got to her feet unsteadily. All at once her head swam and a wave of nausea swept over her. Feeling distraught, she clapped a hand over her mouth and mumbled, 'Excuse me,' before fleeing to the safety of the pink-tiled bathroom.

She knelt in front of the toilet pan, retching and wondering why nothing was happening when she remembered that she had been too nervous to eat all day.

Gradually, she became aware of a presence behind her and moments later a large hand began to gently stroke her brow.

'Are you okay?'

She didn't dare turn around. Instead she mumbled that she would be in a minute or two. The hand continued to stroke her and another began to describe small circles on the back of her neck. Trembling but with an emotion she didn't recognise, but which definitely wasn't nervousness, she allowed herself to bask in the moment.

After a short while she began to feel better and felt a rush of shame to be sitting on a strange bathroom floor, clutching the lavatory bowl as if it were her best friend. As if she were moving in slow motion, she released her grip and sat back on her heels. To her delight Jake's hands didn't leave her but, instead of stroking her brow, he ran a single crooked finger over her cheekbone, following the contours of her face.

Turning to look at him, she found herself drowning in his compassionate gaze. After that it seemed the most natural thing in the world to accept his kiss. Closing her eyes, she felt his lips move against hers, pressing gently, the tip of his tongue flickering over her bottom lip. Katherine sighed. Kissing was okay. No. Correction. Kissing was wonderful. She and Ross didn't kiss nearly enough. They had in the old days, all the time but, since the wedding, the act had been replaced by other, more intimate things.

She shuddered suddenly, trying and failing to imagine how it might be if she allowed Jake to touch her like that. There was no way she could visualise his naked body, especially not his penis. In fact, the very idea of trying to imagine it shocked her to the core.

Jake was taking her hand and helping her up, she realised.

'I think we'd be more comfortable in the other room,' he suggested.

She couldn't help noticing he didn't use the word bedroom and felt grateful to him for the fact.

This time he led her gently to the bed and she sat down. He offered her more champagne but she refused.

'I think I've had enough,' she said, 'at least, for the time being.'

'Okay, whatever.' Jake smiled and reclined on the bed, his right hand idly stroking her arm.

After a few minutes Katherine began to feel distinctly warm. A light film of perspiration broke out on her forehead and she began to undo the buttons of her jacket. She shrugged it off her shoulders, relieved that she had opted to wear a silky black camisole underneath. Catching sight of herself in the mirror, she realised that, worn by itself, the camisole made her look unusually sexy.

What helped was the fact that her carefully contrived hairstyle had now started to droop in earnest and long tendrils of blonde hair fell around her face and neck. Models spent ages trying to get the same effect, she realised – the just-got-out-of-bed look. With a small tremor of anticipation she glanced behind her where the rest of the vast bed loomed.

To her surprise, she found the sight more enticing than terrifying and longed to stretch out full length upon the cream satin quilt.

As if he could read her mind, Jake suggested that they recline a little instead of sitting bolt-upright.

As she shuffled backwards to the head of the bed, Katherine felt the beguiling sensation of her hands and nylon-clad feet slithering over the quilt. It felt so soft and warm. She just wanted to lay there for a little while. Close her eyes. Think of nothing.

* * *

When she awoke, she was surprised to find that Jake was still lying beside her. With a jolt she remembered where she was and what she was supposed to be doing.

'What – what time is it?' she gasped, sitting up hurriedly.

Using the flat of his palm against her shoulder, Jake pressed her gently down again. 'Only nine twenty New York time,' he said. 'We've still got another four hours' flying time.'

'Oh.' She lay back and stared up at the ceiling. She was aware that he was hovering over her as though he were unsure what to do or say next.

Glancing sideways at him, she caught his gaze again and, like the time before, he leaned forward and kissed her. This time the kiss went on – a long, uninterrupted exploration of each other's lips and tongue. His left hand was resting lightly on her stomach, not moving, although she could feel the heat of his palm through the thin silk camisole.

As they kissed his fingers began to move, surreptitiously massaging her stomach and stroking her left side. She didn't do anything to encourage him but neither did she feel inclined to stop him. It was all perfectly innocent and it was nice. It gave her a warm feeling.

Presently, she noticed how his fingertips just skimmed the undersides of her breasts. Still she didn't feel like stopping him. They circled her breasts with slow, rhythmic strokes and still she didn't feel like stopping him. They brushed lightly over her nipples and she felt a strong urge for something indefinable in the pit of her belly.

Panicked at first, she forced herself to remain calm. It wasn't as though Ross hadn't ever made her nipples go hard before, she reasoned. Although she couldn't quite remember feeling such an odd sensation between her legs. It was as though something or someone was teasing her down there, like blades of grass, or the spray from the shower.

Just to ease the sensation a little, she uncrossed her legs and wriggled slightly.

'Is that skirt stopping you from feeling comfortable?' Jake asked softly.

She glanced quickly at him, expecting to find that the quiet American had turned into a raving sex maniac. With relief she noticed that his expression was still soft and open and his eyes betrayed no hint of rampant desire. Strangely though, she did feel as though he fancied her a bit. Just a little tiny bit. It was just the way he treated her, the odd few comments he'd made, like the one about her eyes.

'Yes, a bit,' she admitted, 'and my tights. My body always swells up when I fly.' Sudden images of Peter Pan and Wendy flashed through her mind and she laughed.

'Care to share the joke?'

Struggling to sit up and undo her zip, she told him and was gratified when he laughed too.

'You don't look too badly swollen to me,' he said when she had wriggled out of her skirt and tights. Underneath she wore a pair of French knickers which matched her camisole. They had come as a set and it seemed a criminal waste of money to wear one without the other.

In all honesty, it surprised Jake that such a good body should be lurking under those shapeless clothes. In the check suit she had looked quite plump but now, clad only in black silk, her figure looked encouragingly slim.

'You don't mean it,' she murmured shyly, looking at him from under pale lashes.

He was quick to put her straight. 'I do.' Taking a chance, he ran an assessing hand over her stomach and belly and down over one hip. 'You feel amazing.'

Heat flooded her as he spoke – a shaming blush, which started at her throat and suffused her face, and an even more shaming heat in her womb. *Dear lord*, she thought, almost delirious with surprise, *I think I'm becoming turned on.* The euphemism made her laugh again, only this time she wasn't willing to share the joke.

When Jake moved to stroke her breasts again over the camisole, she found she didn't feel any where near as reticent as before. And when he slipped the straps over her shoulders and began to cover her throat and upper breasts with soft, butterfly kisses, she found herself sighing with undisguised pleasure.

This was as far as she would let him go, of course, nothing more, she decided. As he slipped the straps lower, uncovering her breasts completely, she thrashed about in confusion. Desire conflicted with common sense, arousal with decency.

'Please,' she whispered, 'please don't.' But his tongue was already circling a nipple, driving her mad with impatience for him to suck the tender bud.

Softly caressing her other breast, he glanced at up her. 'Do you mean that – do you really want me to stop?'

The word *yes* sprang to her lips but all at once she felt defeated. 'No,' she gasped. 'No, I don't want you to stop. I – I like that.'

Smiling his approval, Jake returned to licking and

caressing her breasts. Then he did it, he sucked one nipple and then the other.

'Oh, ah!' Passion inflamed her. Really strange things were happening between her legs now and she felt a strong urge to touch herself there. Squirming on the satin quilt, she tried to ease the throbbing sensation.

Lost in her own haze of arousal, Katherine missed the moment when one hand left her breasts and began a slow but determined journey down her torso. She felt his fingertips trace the outline of her hipbone and then the sensation of her pants rubbing her mound. It took another long moment before she realised that it was Jake's hand doing the rubbing.

'Oh, heavens. Oh, no.'

She tried to sit up but couldn't. His other hand and his mouth were still caressing her breasts. She was pinned to the bed, trapped and helpless. All of a sudden she felt the barrier inside her explode into smithereens. This was her fantasy coming true, she realised with a surge of lust, this was her being forced into submission. Anything that might happen from now on would not be her responsibility. She was powerless to resist.

Taking her silence as acquiescence, Jake slid his hand between her thighs. To his surprise he found that she was soaking wet. Christ, the discovery excited him. Miss Prim harbouring a wet crotch, what a revelation! He had expected her to be as dry as a bone. Encouraged, he allowed his fingers to slip inside the loose leg of her knickers. They toyed with her pubic hair for a while, stroking and fondling while Katherine whimpered and squirmed.

His manipulations grew bolder. Deftly, he slipped his middle finger between her labia, stroking the soft petals of flesh beneath while his other fingers squeezed and massaged her puffy lips.

Suddenly, she stopped squirming and became completely rigid, her legs went stiff and she seemed to grip his finger with her sex. A hoarse scream shattered the moment and in a second she became as limp as a rag doll.

Katherine lay in a haze of euphoria wondering what had just happened to her. It was unbelievable. Heat. Lust. Passion. A desire to be touched anywhere and everywhere. Was it really her?

'That orgasm was just for starters, honey,' Jake said, stunning her when she already felt as though someone had drained her lifeblood.

Orgasm! Was that what it was? Was that what orgasms were all about? *Christ! Yes, goddamn it, Christ! I don't care if it's blasphemy. Christ. Christ. Christ!*

'Are you okay?' Jake sounded concerned and he stopped touching her. Instead his hands stroked her face.

She couldn't speak. Staring at him wordlessly, she just couldn't make her lips form words. Using all her strength, she nodded weakly.

'That's good, real good,' he murmured in a lower, much relieved tone.

His hands left her face and resumed stroking the rest of her body. Not just her breasts and sex this time, but her arms and shoulders, shins and thighs, hair and neck. Surreptitiously, he removed the last few pins from her hair and fanned the wavy strands out around her face.

Now she looked nothing like the woman who had walked into the room behind Lisa.

The sight of the blonde, demi-goddess lying beside him suddenly galvanised his own arousal. Hell, if there was one thing he wanted above all else right now it was to see her naked.

Ignoring her feeble protests, he pulled the camisole off over her head and her French knickers down her legs. She tried to curl up instantly, protective hands fluttering over her mound but he refused to let her.

'No,' he said gently, 'you're beautiful. I want to look at you.'

'You can't, you can't. You are not my husband,' she wailed uselessly. To her relief Jake didn't laugh.

Instead, he gently moved her hands out of the way and stroked her mound. Almost against her will, Katherine found herself relaxing again.

'That *is* nice,' she murmured, opening her legs a little despite the insistent little worms of trepidation wriggling around inside her.

Still stroking her, he bent his head and began to drop light, teasing kisses on her stomach, kisses which drifted a little lower and a little lower with each passing moment. As his nose brushed the soft down covering her pubis she suddenly came to her senses again.

'What are you doing? Don't – you mustn't!' It horrified her to realise that his face was so close to her private parts. It didn't matter quite so much that his hand was there but faces were something else entirely.

Ignoring her, he continued to kiss and lick her flesh, then work his way across her lower belly and across the tops of her thighs. His breath whispered over her sex, driving her mad with the same sensation she had experienced earlier. Arousal.

Before she had time to protest, his tongue delved lower, burrowing into her soft bush, tantalising the very top of her slit. She felt herself becoming wet again and despaired of the mess she was probably making on the quilt. *This is no good*, she thought, *I can't let him do this*. But it was already too late. She knew she was powerless to resist.

As his tongue touched her clitoris he felt her twitch. Praying she wouldn't try to stop him, he deftly circled the hardening bud, occasionally flicking the tip of his tongue across it. Still she didn't protest, so he allowed his fingers to come into play, toying with her outer lips under he felt confident enough to spread them wide so that he could caress her soft, inner flesh.

Katherine moaned and flexed her hips, opening her thighs wider in automatic response to the way he stimulated her. Christ, it felt good, she thought, ignoring her mother's stern warning about taking the Lord's name in vain. Christ, it felt damn good!

During the more lucid moments of her encounter with Jake she couldn't believe the way she responded to him. Could she really allow a man total and utter access to her body? To her own amazement it seemed the answer was a resounding YES. Once he had made her come a second time, simply by whatever it was he was doing between her legs, she let all her inhibitions fly right alongside the plane. When he was certain she was ready, he slipped his penis into her and she almost swooned.

This was it! This was sex in all its unfettered glory. Katherine wasn't Katherine any longer. Not homely wife and mother Katherine, concerned with facts and figures, dietary requirements and pristine laundry. This was wanton, outrageous Katherine. Katherine the lover. Katherine the great.

Tightening her vaginal muscles around his hardness instinctively, she brought him to a shuddering climax.

He looked at her in astonishment and she, Katherine the great, returned his gaze unflinchingly. 'That was really amazing,' she said, a satisfied note to her voice, 'but this time around, do you mind if I go on top?'

Chapter Nine

Two magpies landed on Lisa's windowsill the day the first Flights of Fancy orgy dawned, their appearance only adding to her existing optimism. Her time spent with Akira in New York had been wonderful and everything business-wise seemed to be operating far better than she could have hoped. Her 'boys' were happy, the rest of the crew were happy and above all she had not received a single complaint from the clientele. Flights of Fancy was well and truly up and running.

She made sure she got to the office early that morning and, during the course of several cups of coffee, carried out last minute checks on everything. She knew that this flight would be vastly different from all the others. For one thing an orgy took a lot more organisation than a simple transatlantic flight. She needed mood music, she needed good food and wine – grapes by the crateload, of course, for those with true Bacchanalian tendencies – and she took the precaution of double checking that the crew were all fully aware of the nature of the flight.

In effect, it was to be a closed set. Only those actually taking an active part in the orgy would be allowed any access to the lounge bar. She didn't want to run the risk of voyeurism, or people taking part who shouldn't. From comments that had been made, she knew there were several stewards who had expressed a keen interest in joining in the fun but Lisa had answered their requests with a flat, 'No.'

Although it would mean one extra woman, she had also taken the precaution of inviting Michiko to join them. If the worst came to the worst she and Michiko could get the ball rolling, although she had no particular desire to take a very active part. In truth, this aspect bothered her a little. Even though the orgy had been her idea it was not something she had actually experienced before.

Akira had given her a lot of constructive advice which prompted a certain number of questions to form in Lisa's head about the extent of his past erotic activities. But she knew better than to ask. He never queried her past, or her present for that matter and she felt loath to do the same. They were free agents, both of them, living for the moment and enjoying their snatched time together in the best way they knew how.

A quick glance at her watch told her it was time to go. She needed to get over to Terminal Three and make sure that everything was okay at that end. Gathering up her briefcase and overnight bag, she wished everyone in the office a cheery goodbye.

The first thing that struck Lisa as the passengers boarded the plane was how vastly different they were to the usual crowd. Naturally, she had expected a looser, more up-front type of woman to book the orgy flights. Women who were unsure of themselves or their sexuality would hardly be likely to take part but still she was shocked by the blatant sexuality of the clientele.

From their details she knew that most were in showbusiness: starlets, minor actresses and musicians of varying descriptions. Lisa wasn't prone to making snap judgements about people but she supposed that their attitude to casual sex was part and parcel of their unique world. She knew the casting-couch phenomenon was still very much in vogue, despite claims to the contrary, and the music business was renowned for its free and easy attitude. Anything went with these women and today that would certainly be the case – she hoped. Her secret fear was that the orgy would turn out to be a complete flop.

First to come over and talk to her was a starlet called Candy. Thinking instantly how much of a cliché she looked, Lisa fought to smother a grin. Candy was a bouncy little blonde with narrow hips clad in blue designer jeans that looked as though they had been sprayed on and pneumatic breasts which strained under the scant covering of a white cropped tee-shirt. All the time she was speaking to Lisa her wide blue eyes were darting around, eying up the available talent and, to some extent, the competition.

'Aren't your men hunky!' she enthused in a deliberately breathless voice. 'And so many to choose from.' Her inflection was so acute that Lisa half thought the young woman might orgasm there and then.

Smiling pleasantly, Lisa agreed that, yes, they were hunky and added that all were extremely skilled lovers.

'I can't wait,' Candy said, turning to accept a glass of champagne from a passing steward. 'Should I get my kit off now, or do we have to be airborne first?'

Lisa couldn't help chuckling. 'That's entirely up to you but I planned to wait until the plane had taken off before officially starting the proceedings.' To her own ears she thought she sounded stuffy and regretted it immediately, although Candy didn't appear to notice.

Thankfully, the next person to come up and greet her was Michiko. Lisa greeted her warmly with a kiss on both cheeks and then a quick hug. It felt strange to be holding Michiko in her arms again. They had hardly met since their interlude with Curtis – most of their conversations since then had been by telephone – but now that the young woman was there again in the flesh, so to speak, Lisa found herself anticipating the forthcoming event with a lot more enthusiasm than she had before.

'I'm really glad you could make it, Michiko,' she said. 'This all feels so weird.'

Michiko laughed. 'Of course it does. At the last orgy I went to, everyone stood around for ages, fully dressed, looking as though they were on their way to a funeral and had ended up in the wrong place by mistake.'

'God, I hope that doesn't happen today.' Lisa couldn't hide her feelings but Michiko reassured her.

'I shouldn't think so.' She glanced around and then added confidently. 'No, I know so. Look at these women. They are all positively wetting themselves to get started.'

Lisa had to admit she had a point.

Unlike the clientele on the other flights, these women were more than happy to mingle and chat to each other. It was as though they were all members of the same exclusive club, which, at the end of the day, was exactly what Flights of Fancy was all about. There were none of the usual coy or assessing glances of the, 'is she here just for the sex?' variety. They were all there for sex, every one of them, and with as many partners, male or female, as they wished.

Lisa deliberately kept her usual introductory speech short. For one thing it was difficult to interrupt the chattering women and get them to their seats in time for take off and for another she didn't want to bore them. The whole point of the exercise was to make things seem as free and easy as possible. This time Lisa would not be the boss, as such, she would be one of them.

At first she had been wary about the extent of her own involvement but Akira had very sensibly pointed out that she couldn't very well sit on the sidelines and watch. She would have to throw herself into it body and soul. Lisa had giggled and said she didn't know if her body would be up to it after the night they had spent together but he had merely smiled sardonically and assured her that, yes, it would.

'You have the sex drive of a roomful of ordinary women,' he said, which Lisa took to be a compliment.

Deep down she wondered if she had wanted him to mind about her activities, or at least show some indication of sexual jealousy, but she knew that just wasn't his way. And she had to admit, his open attitude was one of the reasons she liked him so much.

A tannoy message from the Captain interrupted her thoughts and the babble of excited chatter that surrounded her. Acting on instructions, all the women hastily found a seat and got ready for take off. Talking was fun but the delights to come in a short while were far more appealing.

As soon as the 'fasten your seatbelts' light went out, an excited babble started up again. Lisa got the ball rolling by inviting everyone to swap their chairs for the more comfortable sofas and large squashy cushions that were piled up in enticing mounds.

Her 'boys' were the first to move, divesting themselves of their jackets, shirts, socks and shoes before reclining artistically around the room and looking every bit as tempting as the furnishings. Generous ice buckets, each containing a couple of bottles of champagne, and bowls of fruit and delicate little savouries were strategically placed within easy reach of anyone who wanted them.

She noticed Candy, and another young woman who looked as though she modelled herself on the cartoon character Betty Boop, make a beeline for the squashy cream leather sofa where Shane sprawled confidently. At an unspoken instruction from Lisa another of her 'boys' got up and wandered over to join them. He was the right choice. Both Candy and 'Betty' gave him an assessing look which ended with a smile of approval.

Candy wriggled up the sofa to make room for him and managed to lose her tee-shirt in the process, encouraging the new arrival to immediately bury his head in her generous breasts.

In another part of the room Curtis was entertaining a tall, angular woman who, according to Lisa's notes, wrote lyrics for a couple of the most enduring female soul singers.

And on a pile of sateen pillows at their feet a Chicano actress called Ramona was getting to grips with a couple of men.

'Greedy,' Michiko murmured in Lisa's ear, nodding in the direction of Ramona who was giggling as one of the boys struggled to remove her tight leather trousers.

'I can't believe it's all happening like this,' Lisa said, her glance alighting on similar scenes all round the plush lounge. 'I honestly thought they would need more encouragement.' As she spoke she wandered over to an unoccupied mound of cushions and settled down comfortably.

Michiko reclined next to her and accepted a glass of champagne from Lisa with a light kiss on her lips. The next thing they knew, both were anxious to put their glasses down quickly and turn the kiss into something more promising.

Just as Michiko's lips left hers and began a slow, tantalising journey down the side of her throat, Lisa glanced across the room and noticed that Rio was standing alone, watching them. 'Come and join us,' her smile invited, to which he responded like a shot.

As he knelt at their feet, both Lisa and Michiko looked down at him, watching with idle interest as his hands began to stroke their ankles and calves simultaneously. Lisa shifted, kicking off her high-heeled shoes. Her legs were bare and under her 'uniform' she wore no underwear.

Michiko wore tight black leggings, with a loose red tunic, but she offered no resistance when Rio reached up and began to pull the leggings down. Underneath she wore a tiny red g-string which soon followed the leggings, and Lisa's skirt and jacket, to build a small heap on the carpet beside them.

Glancing at Michiko's dark bush, Rio paused, appearing to need Lisa's confirmation that it was alright to touch. She nodded, almost imperceptibly, and his hands began to travel further up their legs, pausing to stroke the backs of their knees before continuing their journey.

Resuming their kiss, Lisa felt Michiko's sigh of pleasure dust the inside of her mouth. She couldn't see anything but assumed that Rio had reached his ultimate destination. His hands had left her body for now but the young Japanese woman's delicate caresses made up for it. Groaning with unrestrained pleasure, Lisa felt Michiko's fingertips dance lightly over her hip and across the twin moons of her buttocks.

Lisa allowed her own hands to drift over Michiko's hair, revelling for a moment in its silken feel, before travelling lower, over her finely-sculpted shoulders, pushing the loose-necked tunic down until one perfect breast was revealed. The nipple was already hard and Lisa caught the rosy bud between her thumb and forefinger, pulling gently and twirling it between her fingertips.

She felt Michiko squirm and wondered how the young woman was feeling right at that minute. By angling her own head, she could see Rio's nestled between Michiko's thighs. With a hoarse groan Michiko arched her back, prompting a surge of envy in Lisa. Rio's mouth was magic and at that moment she longed to feel his clever tongue burrowing between her own swelling sex lips.

As if he could read her mind, Rio moved, the fingers of his right hand replacing his mouth between Michiko's legs. In the next instant she felt the soft caress of his long, curly locks brushing her thighs. Trying in vain to restrain her whimpers of pleasure, Lisa twisted her body at the waist so that she could offer more of herself to him and instantly felt his tongue moving over her anxious sex, soothing and exciting as it travelled up and down the length of her slit.

Her orgasm was instantaneous – a powerful torrent of heat and desire that transcended everything else. Screaming hoarsely, she threw back her head and ground her clitoris against the flat of his tongue. Michiko's orgasm followed, her own pleasure a growing series of waves that eclipsed Lisa's ebbing flow of elation. Moments later the two women relaxed back against the mound of pillows and shared a knowing smile of contentment.

Rio glanced from one to the other wondering what he had done so right in his life to deserve the pleasure of two such lovely women at the same time. It was a first for him. In all his years' experience with women, sex had always been one-to-one. This was his greatest fantasy and now it was coming true. Careful not to break the thread of eroticism that joined the three of them, he divested himself of his clothes surreptitiously and then reached for the buttons on Lisa's blouse.

As she carelessly shrugged it away from her body and Michiko scrabbled to pull her tunic over her head, he couldn't help marvelling at the differences and similarities between the two women. First the breasts, which came into view simultaneously, Lisa's full and firm, tipped by tiny pink buds and areolae that were hardly any darker in pigment than her nipples. Then Michiko's, tiny but perfectly formed, almost all their surface taken up by circles of dark brown tipped with luscious, cherry-like nipples that seemed to strain towards something unseen.

Although Lisa was quite a bit taller and of a larger build than the doll-like Michiko, their figures were equally entrancing. Michiko's was neat and compact. A place for everything and everything in its place, whereas Lisa's body was more rounded, more generous, her well-toned flesh filling his hands wherever he touched her.

Ignoring Rio for a moment, Lisa and Michiko simultaneously rolled onto their stomachs to watch a writhing mass of bodies across the room. It was difficult to count the number of people involved, although it seemed that there were less flashes of breasts and female buttocks than there were of hairy male chests and thighs, or swaying cocks and balls.

There were a lot of raucous laughs and salacious comments coming from the tangled bodies and for a moment Lisa felt tempted to join them. Then, just as she was about to turn her attention back to her own partners, she noticed a tall woman rise majestically from the centre of the group. Like a contemporary reproduction of Botticelli's 'Birth of Venus' she posed, naked yet adorned by a rippling mass of flame-red hair. It covered her shoulders and breasts, cascading down her spine in silky waves to stroke the curves of her generous hips and bottom.

One of the men in the group raised his head and called to her – something about feeding him – but Lisa couldn't quite make out what he said. To her surprise the woman raised one leg and gracefully straddled him, then she lowered herself over his face. In absolute amazement, Lisa watched as the man opened his mouth to accept a controlled sprinkling of grapes, which the woman dispensed from her vagina. As the grapes rained down between the woman's sturdy thighs, Lisa, Michiko and Rio abandoned their own pleasure to watch the spectacle.

'Do you think you could do that?' Rio directed his question to neither woman in particular but both looked keen to take up the challenge.

'Here, let me.' Lisa reached out and grabbed a nearby bowl of grapes. Putting the bowl down between herself and Michiko, she drew up her knees and allowed her thighs to drop open inelegantly.

She reclined back against the cushions. 'As it was your idea, Rio, would you mind doing the honours?' she said, flashing a pointed glance between the bowl of grapes and her exposed sex.

Rio was quick to comply. Taking a handful of the grapes, he moved between Lisa's legs and gently pressed one into the slick channel of her vagina.

Lisa moaned. The grape felt cold and slippery, an unusual intruder into her body but not an unwelcome one. Gripping the grape, she accepted another and another until she felt stuffed full. She had to keep her vaginal muscles tightly in check as she watched Rio do the same to Michiko. The grapes filled her, the slippery ovals pressing against each other, the lower ones threatening to slip out at any moment.

'Hurry up, I can't hold on,' Lisa complained, laughing.

A wicked light flashed in Michiko's eyes. 'If you drop

one you have to feed *me*,' she said.

Lisa felt a *frisson* of arousal. The idea of straddling the young Japanese woman and filling her mouth with grapes straight from her vagina – the act witnessed in close quarters by Rio and at a distance by a roomful of people – thrilled her. Laughing nervously, she felt something give between her legs. Unsure whether she felt disappointed or elated, she watched as a single grape popped cheekily from her bulging sex.

'Yes, yes!' Michiko exclaimed with undisguised glee. 'Now you are mine.'

Careful not to dislodge another grape, Lisa laughed cautiously. 'Yes, but the same goes for you. If you lose a single grape while I'm feeding you then you have to feed me.'

They glanced at Rio who gave a discreet cough and, when he knew he had their attention, made a slight *moue*. 'So where do I fit into all this?' he said.

Lisa shrugged, the sudden movements disturbing her breasts which jiggled invitingly. Michiko glanced at them and caught one in the palm of her hand.

'I do believe the poor boy is jealous,' she said mischievously, toying with Lisa's nipple as she spoke.

Pretending to be outraged, Rio lunged for the giggling young woman and pushed her back against the cushions. As she fell she cried out and the three of them watched as a lone grape rolled across the silken cushion between her thighs.

'That's it. You've had it, Rio,' Lisa chuckled, but he was already one step ahead of the conniving young women.

'I propose another forfeit,' he said, glancing from one to the other.

Lisa smirked back at him. 'Go on.'

'Well—' he paused, pretending to dust imaginary stray hairs from his shoulders '—if either of you shows a lack of self-control and lets more than one grape go at a time, that person has to switch to feeding me.'

Michiko glanced at Lisa and shrugged. 'I'm game,' she said with a devilish glint in her eye.

Lisa felt a strong surge of warmth overtake her. 'So am I,' she said. 'Get ready for feeding time.'

Michiko lay back again and waited patiently as Lisa positioned herself over her mouth. She stared up between Lisa's thighs, momentarily marvelling at the shape and tone of them before her keen eyes alighted on the bulging pouch of the other woman's sex. She could see the grapes nestling together like ova just inside Lisa's vagina, the lips of her sex spread wide.

'Okay, Lisa. I'm ready.' Michiko opened her mouth, her lips forming a wide but perfect 'O'.

Concentrating hard, Lisa flexed her muscles slightly to release a single grape into the waiting mouth. All she could see as she glanced down was the deep, wet cavern of Michiko's mouth and the young woman's eyes – hard, black nuggets fixed pointedly at Lisa's gaping sex, waiting for the next grape to fall.

Michiko tasted the second grape and licked her lips lasciviously. 'Honey-coated, my favourite,' she purred in a way that almost made Lisa come there and then. Willing herself not to capitulate, Lisa flexed her muscles again and allowed another grape to drop. This time

Michiko wasn't ready and the grape bounced against her lips and rolled across the cushions towards Rio.

He pounced dramatically on the grape, placed it in his mouth and appeared to be savouring its flavour, like a wine buff. 'An excellent vintage,' he said, his blue eyes twinkling wickedly. 'Please, Michiko, allow me to eat of the vine.'

Both women laughed simultaneously, each wondering if an orgy was the right place for fun and games. Everyone else seemed to be so intent on the whole thing. Now the lounge was strewn with naked bodies, all apparently moving from one to the next, to the next on an endless conveyor belt of sex.

Rio left Lisa with no more time to think. Grabbing her by the thighs, he pulled her back towards Michiko's feet where, just a fraction away, his face was turned up expectantly. Glancing behind her to where Rio lay, Lisa took aim, arched her back and let another grape go. After a moment or two she couldn't manage to squeeze out another grape and began to laugh again as Rio insisted on rolling her on her back and 'checking', his fingers opening her out and probing her vagina until her laughter turned to groans of arousal.

Pouting, Michiko tapped Lisa on the shoulder. 'What about me?'

Mouthing, 'Sorry,' Lisa motioned to her to straddle her face. Rio had just nestled his head between her legs and a surge of eroticism encouraged her to feed from Michiko while Rio fed from her.

In a triangle of lust, the three ate from each other and when each was sated, for whatever reason, they swapped around. Rio buried his head between Michiko's thighs while Lisa chased his swinging cock with her hands, caught it and immediately fed it between her eager lips. Like the first day of spring, pleasurable memories filled her mind as she reacquainted herself with the feel of him and the slightly salty taste of the droplet of pre-come that oozed from the tip of his glans. Grasping the base of his cock with one hand, she cupped his balls with the other, enjoying the rough, weighty sensation in her palm. Not knowing if it was her imagination or not, she fancied she could feel them throbbing, feel the desire surging through his veins as she licked and sucked him with all the relish of a child with a lolli-pop.

Michiko's anxious groans touched her ears. She sounded as though she were seconds away from sky-rocketing into oblivion. Sucking harder on Rio's cock, Lisa silently urged him and Michiko on and felt a curious flash of delight as they both orgasmed simultaneously, Rio spurting a torrent of warm, salty come into her mouth as Michiko let out a prolonged, 'Aaaah!' followed by a string of unintelligible Japanese.

With the careless abandon of a house of cards touched by the breeze, they fell apart. Dropping away from each other and back, to recline against the mound of cushions. Lisa licked a stray drop of Rio's come from the corner of her mouth and smiled, first at him and then Michiko.

'My turn again,' she said.

The day was waning and along with it, the orgy. Most people had all but given up by the time the plane reached mid-Atlantic and the next couple of hours saw the others fall like ninepins. Now the whole room heaved with a different kind of activity – sleep. Every one of the guests and Lisa's 'boys' were out for the count.

Only Michiko still fought the threads of drowsiness that tried to draw her into their black web. Glancing down to her left and right, she saw the gently snoring forms of Rio and Lisa. She gazed at them fondly for a moment, curiously reminded of her brother and sister and the way, back in the half-forgotten recesses of her Japanese childhood, they had all been forced to sleep together in a single, bare room.

The opulence of the jumbo jet was hardly a fair comparison and, hugging her knees to her chest, she thanked her own good fortune. If it hadn't been for Akira she would have been destined to become one of the thousands of prostitutes that worked the bars and nightclubs of downtown Tokyo. He had rescued her just in time – sold to the highest bidder. And no matter how much he assured her she was not only a valued employee but also her own woman, she had remained morally and financially indebted to him ever since.

Reclining back against the cushions, Michiko allowed her mind to wander to New York where her boyfriend awaited her arrival. At least, she hoped he was still waiting. They had only spent a short time together before she had to leave for England and she had been away for several months. Two brief telephone calls had confirmed his continuing interest but Michiko was still wary of men. She didn't always trust what they said, no matter how sincere they seemed. Only Akira had been able to restore her faith in the male sex and he had encouraged her new relationship with almost fatherly zeal.

'Just don't leave me too quickly,' he had joked when she plucked up the courage to confide in him, when she felt more or less certain that there was something worth disclosing. 'I'll have a hard job replacing you but I want you to be happy.'

Akira knew Michiko demanded nothing more of life than to be with one man who she loved, her arms filled with almond-eyed, mop-haired babies. Chun, her boyfriend, was Chinese and approaching the end of his training as an attorney. He would soon be making good money and able to support Michiko and a family, which is what he claimed he wanted more than anything else in the world.

The young woman hugged her future around her, covering her indolent nakedness with a warm layer of love and responsibility. Decadence was okay but she had never really been cut out for it. That was Akira's style. Now he had Lisa – his perfect match – and for the first time she felt confident about leaving him.

A few of the passengers began to wake up, stretching and groaning as they massaged over-used muscles. Like anemones they stirred and vacillated amid the sea of bodies that surrounded them.

The sounds touched Lisa's sleeping ears and woke her. She came to gently, with a smile on her face which brightened even more as her eyes alighted on Michiko's gentle gaze.

'Hi,' she said. 'Did I fall asleep?' All at once she felt guilty about abandoning her responsibilities but Michiko was quick to reassure her.

'They all did,' she whispered, her slow glance leading Lisa's around the room.

Lisa giggled softly. 'Thank Christ for that. They must have had a good time if they all wore each other out.' Struggling to sit up a little, she looked down to where Rio lay at their feet, his arms and legs splayed carelessly.

'I can't help thinking he likes you more than a little bit,' Michiko observed, nodding in Rio's direction.

With a sigh, Lisa nodded. 'I know. I'm worried that it's going to become a problem. Akira and I—' She paused and raised her hands in a defeated gesture.

'Don't worry about Akira,' Michiko said confidently. 'When he's ready to make his move, you'll know it.'

It seemed an odd thing to say and Lisa shivered with anticipation. Was Akira the one she really wanted? Or was it Rio? Or neither? Was it time for her to stop being footloose and fancy-free?

As if she could read Lisa's mind, Michiko said, 'Akira isn't the sort of man to place restrictions on anyone, not even the people he loves.'

The L-word caught Lisa unawares. 'Do you think Akira is in love with me?'

Michiko shrugged. 'It's early days but yes, I'd certainly say he likes you far more than any of the others I've met.'

Lisa was tempted to ask about the others but by this

time most of the passengers were beginning to stir. She glanced at the digital clock above the bar. In just over an hour they would be landing at Kennedy.

Chapter Ten

It was four o'clock New York time when Lisa finally exited JFK and climbed into a waiting taxi. Giving her instructions to the driver, she sat back and idly watched the passing scenery as they drove through Queens and across the East River to Manhattan's Upper East Side where Akira's apartment awaited her.

Unforunately, she mused, he wouldn't be there. He was back in Tokyo for the foreseeable future, putting together yet more lucrative deals and masterminding takeovers, no doubt. But for once she didn't mind. She was looking forward to a little solitude. A whole weekend to herself closeted in the luxury of his apartment, with the vibrant city pulsating around her seemed the perfect antidote to two months' hard slog.

It surprised her how tired she really felt. If she thought about it honestly, the flights themselves were not that demanding. Once the initial introductions were made and all the passengers were safely ensconced in their individual cabins, it was easy for her to chill out and relax. There were rarely any complaints or queries, so she was hardly ever disturbed. And usually, when she had finished her paperwork, she would either settle back on her own bed for a good long read, or invite one of her unoccupied 'boys' to join her.

That was how she had come to know Mark as more than just an employee.

Mark, like Rio, was young and mischievous, with a wicked sense of humour, but that was where their similarities ended. He was as fair as Rio was dark. And tall, very tall, with well-defined muscles which proved his claim that he worked out every day come what may.

She sometimes thought what she liked best about Mark was his total dissimilarity to either Rio or Akira. He made no pretence at finesse and did not bother to spend time pondering the aesthetics of any given situation. He made it clear he simply enjoyed fucking for the sake of fucking. And at times, she felt, that was just what she needed. Mindless fucking could be deemed erotic in itself – if that was what suited her mood. Twice so far it had suited her and twice Mark had provided the outlet she craved.

She had arranged to meet him, along with a couple of other 'boys' and their chosen companions, at a bar the following evening. It was intended to be her only foray into the outside world that weekend and she felt sure that after twenty-four hours in her own company, she would welcome the change of pace. That still left her with the whole of Sunday to relax and recover from the night before.

Akira's apartment was bright and welcoming. Michiko was there but insisted she was leaving straight away.

'I'm spending the weekend with my boyfriend's parents,' she said, brushing her silky black hair away from her face with a trembling hand and tucking a strand behind her left ear.

It was a gesture of nervousness that Lisa had come to recognise. She knew all about Michiko's boyfriend but didn't realise it was that serious.

Michiko glanced at the bulging suitcase by her feet, then back at Lisa. 'I have a confession to make,' she said cautiously. 'Chun asked me to marry him last night.'

'Go on!' Lisa sounded as incredulous as she felt. 'What did you say?'

Clearing her throat, Michiko wavered before finally admitting that she had said she would think about it.

'I meant seriously,' she added. 'In that respect I suppose this weekend will be the ultimate test.'

'How come?' Lisa asked, sitting down on the arm of a nearby sofa.

'If his parents don't like me then I won't be able to marry him,' Michiko explained. 'Although we are both from a similar part of the world, our cultures are totally different. The Japanese are essentially a spiritual race, whereas the Chinese are – are—'

'Practical?' Lisa offered diplomatically before adding, 'But does it really matter what his parents think? You don't have to live with them. You and Chun could be happy regardless.' A small vestige of romanticism still led her to believe that love could conquer all.

Michiko shook her head sadly. 'It doesn't work like that for me I'm afraid,' she said. 'When I have children I want them to be part of a loving extended family. In a way it would sort of make up for my own childhood.'

Lisa understood and said so. One day recently, over a boozy lunch in a Chelsea bistro, Michiko had told her the whole story – about her life growing up in poverty in

Japan, her fortuitous meeting with Akira and, finally, her move to New York.

At that moment they were interrupted by the buzzer on the intercom. Flicking a switch on the wall, Michiko studied the closed-circuit television by the door to the lobby.

'It looks as though my cab's here,' she said, glancing over her shoulder at Lisa.

The other woman nodded. 'Okay,' she murmured as she stood up to hug Michiko's tiny body to her own, 'just – have a good time, okay? Just chill.'

They both laughed and then Michiko picked up her suitcase and hobbled out to the elevator with it. 'See you Monday,' she called, as the doors began to slide together. 'Oh, and by the way, there's a message from Akira on the pad in his office.'

The doors closed and Lisa remained rooted to the spot for a heart-stopping moment before dashing back inside the apartment and making straight for Akira's desk. There were only a handful of words on the bright yellow pad: 'I want you but I will have to wait. Next Saturday. My apartment in London. Eight thirty. Be there.'

A *frisson* of anticipation ran through Lisa as she absorbed the words. 'I want you' seemed to smack of something more than mere sex. She had sensed the last time she spoke to him that he wanted to say more but as she tried to encourage him to open up, so he became more brusque and finally finished the conversation with a curt, 'I'll be in touch.' At that moment she had thought perhaps that was it. The end – at least on a personal level. But now, it seemed, that wasn't it at all.

All of a sudden the prospect of the weekend seemed less inviting and more like interminable. Worse still, the coming week would be unendurable. She laughed at her dramatic use of words, yet nevertheless it was true. Ninety-eight percent of the time she was a level-headed, successful business woman, with a private life that held no complications, only tons of fun. Then Akira would call her or, better still, see her in the flesh and she would be lost – an idle piece of jetsam floating on a sea of pleasure and anticipation.

Damn the man! she thought, suddenly cross with herself for behaving so illogically. *I'm going to relax this weekend if it kills me.*

On Saturday she awoke to the muted sounds of traffic twenty-four floors below and the *coo* of a lone pigeon which had landed on the windowsill outside. Lisa lay in bed and studied the bird thoughtfully. Was it a symbol of what she had become, she wondered idly – a lone creature who flutters about here and there without ever really coming home to roost? If she was a bird, she was not a homing pigeon but a magpie. She had no real place and no one she could really call her own.

For a moment or two she envied Michiko's relationship with Chun. Despite the young Japanese woman's fears about cultural differences, their relationship was simple and straightforward. Love. Marriage. Babies. If it was possible for someone like Michiko, who had such a terrible start in life, it should be possible for her too. The question was, had she had enough of playing the field?

She thought back over the past six months. To all the

men she had fucked and whose performance she had assessed. And to all the men she had fucked for fun. Was there another dimension to life other than sex and business? Could she reasonably hope for more?

Hating the way she was allowing herself to sink into introspection again, she decided to go out after all. Getting up quickly, she showered and then pondered what to wear. Inside the apartment the air-conditioning was blasting away but outside she knew the streets would be scorching. New York in the height of summer had a way of turning ordinarily sane people mad.

Deciding to risk it, she opted for a loose pair of drawstring trousers in white cotton, and a matching blouse. On her head she wore a straw boater and on her feet a pair of flat sandals. The best way she knew to get around the thriving metropolis was on foot.

Lunchtime found her seated in Riverside Park, her view of the Hudson River unobscured as she sat on a bench and munched a bagel. The filling was smoked fish with cream cheese, an old favourite which she could never pass up. She had covered nearly all the Upper East Side, occasionally catching a bus ride to save her feet, then jumping off a few stops later when she spotted something that looked interesting.

Now she was fed up with walking and was getting all hot and dusty. As soon a she had finished her bagel, she decided, she would catch a cab and get the driver to take her to Fifth Avenue where she could shop till she dropped. She wasn't planning to meet the others until nine that evening, so she would have plenty of time to get back to the apartment and take a quick nap before she had to get ready to go out.

She only had time for four stores – Macy's, Bergdorf Goodman, Bloomingdale's and Saks – but they were each worth a whole day in themselves. Staggering out onto the sidewalk, her arms weighed down with carrier bags, she hailed another cab. Hang the expense, she thought, she couldn't face the subway and her feet had long ago given up the ghost. Akira was always telling her to 'think rich' and now she was. And she had the credit-card slips to prove it!

Back at the hotel sleep came easily to her. Under the light Porthault cotton top sheet, her naked body ached with weariness. She was glad she'd had the forethought to book an alarm call. When the telephone rang beside her, she would have sworn that she had only been asleep for ten minutes and yet the clock told a different story – three hours.

'Right, thank you,' she said briskly into the receiver before slamming it down hurriedly and jumping out of bed.

The shower revived her and soon she was stepping into her outfit for the evening: a new dress, black and cream silk, the monochrome colours blending as though someone had just stirred an Irish coffee. Her tan was developed enough for her to keep her legs bare and on her feet she wore a pair of strappy, cream sandals.

Feeling good enough to eat – or at least drink – she stepped into the elevator, moved on into a waiting cab and gave the driver the instruction to take her to the Monkey Bar on Fifty-Fourth Street.

She had never been there before and her eyes were out on stalks the minute she stepped into the jungle that surrounded her. True to its name, the Monkey Bar was a riot of verdant leaves and cheeky-faced apes, their grins coming at her from all sides.

Mark was by her side like a flash and when she asked he explained that the bar was actually quite old and that all the murals were originals which had been recently touched up.

Having already consumed the best part of a bottle of champagne while she was getting ready, Lisa giggled at the phrase.

Mark grinned. 'Honestly, Lisa, I can't take you anywhere.'

'Oh, yes you can,' she quipped, feeling extraordinarily happy and carefree. 'I'm yours for the whole night.' Her eyes twinkled with promise as she spoke and in the next instant she felt the telltale wetness of her own arousal seep into the crotch of her designer knickers – a mad impulse buy at Macys.

'Okay, you're on.' His look said it all. The assurance of sex. Free and unencumbered. Of mindless fucking and heaps of laughs.

It quite made Lisa's day.

Barney, Luke, Neil and Gary were the other 'boys' who had elected to join their boss for a social evening. With them were four girls: Natalie, Charlene, Mary and Bobo. Lisa had to struggle not to raise her eyebrows when she was introduced to the latter. But despite her strange name, Bobo seemed a very pleasant, level-headed young woman.

While Neil and Gary went to the bar to get some drinks, nudging their way past the high bar stools with padded seats fashioned to look like giant stuffed olives, Lisa surreptitiously weighed up the four women.

Natalie was the quietest, she decided straight away, and the most serious. Her long brown hair was woven into a tight plait, the end of which tickled the base of her spine, and on the bridge of her freckled nose she wore John Lennon-style glasses with purple lenses. It meant Lisa couldn't see Natalie's eyes, which she found quite disconcerting. Although she was sure the young woman's mind was on far more highbrow things than what she thought of her boyfriend's boss.

Charlene was totally different to Natalie. Bright and bubbly, she kept up a stream of continuous chatter with Bobo, who was just as animated. The two young women were both blondes, although Charlene's hair was styled in a sleek bob while Bobo's was a wild mass of curls.

Which left Mary, a dark, softly spoken girl of Irish descent who was barely out of her teens. For some reason Lisa felt motherly towards her and tried to draw her out a little, encouraging her to laugh along at Bobo's wicked jokes. Only Natalie seemed either unwilling, or unable, to join in.

Mark sat next to Lisa and kept his hand on her knee. She didn't mind his proprietorial air, it was quite clear that the others had paired off and so Mark was naturally 'hers' for the evening. Just then Neil and Gary returned, each bearing a tray laden with wicked-looking cocktails.

Lisa fought her way past the sliced fruit and sipped her concoction. 'It tastes lethal,' she said, smacking her lips and bending her head to take another sip through the straw.

'That's the general idea,' Neil butted in, 'we get you girls drunk and then we can have our wicked way with you.'

Lisa laughed. 'Don't you ever get bored with sex? I would have thought fucking for a living would encourage you to take up more cerebral pursuits in your spare time.'

A deathly hush fell over the table.

Lisa glanced around with surprise. 'What – what did I say?'

Mark leaned sideways and whispered in her ear that the other women didn't know what their men did to earn an honest crust.

'Oh, shit!' Lisa gasped. 'I'm sorry, I didn't realise.'

Natalie was the first to laugh. The sound shocked everyone, not least Lisa who suspected that the quiet girl had actually fallen asleep behind her purple specs. It was a deep, throaty laugh which was so infectious that soon everyone was giggling helplessly.

'My God, Luke?' Bobo exclaimed, wiping a stray tear from her cheek. 'Do I understand right that you boys are hookers?'

Neil, Barney and Gary looked uncomfortable and glanced down at their feet which shuffled nervously beneath the table but Mark chipped in brightly.

'Not hookers. Professional lovers. There is a difference,' he added, trying to look serious.

Taking up the thread, Lisa briefly explained the Flights of Fancy concept. If it hadn't been for the background music you could have heard a pin drop.

'So how do Bobo and I get on one of these flights?' Natalie asked.

'Easy,' Barney quipped, 'come into a fortune.'

Lisa couldn't let that remark pass. 'Oh, come on,' she said, 'it's not that expensive.'

All four men turned their eyes to heaven.

'Okay,' she conceded. 'A Flight of Fancy is a bit special – hence the price. You've got to take in the overheads. It's not a cheap service to run.'

Mark held up his hands in defence. 'Alright, Lisa, keep your hair on,' he said. 'We're not casting aspersions on your business acumen.'

'I should think not,' Lisa asserted briskly before allowing her stern expression to soften into a smile. 'Now, who wants some food? I'm starving.'

After a brief word with one of the waiters, they all trooped down into the circular, sunken restaurant. The menu was not cheap and, feeling extraordinarily magnanimous, as well as a bit guilty about her unintentional faux-pas, Lisa elected to pick up the tab.

'Are you sure?' Mark said, eying the bill. 'You pay us well enough. I think we can afford to go Dutch.'

But Lisa waved away his concerns with the tip of her new platinum Mont Blanc pen – another impulse buy, this time from Bergdorf Goodman.

'Quite sure,' she said firmly. 'Call it a bonus for two months' hard grind.' Pausing to laugh at her own little joke, she tucked the bill in her handbag. 'Anyway, all I'll do is claim it back as a business expense.'

Suitably mollified, Mark stood up and gallantly offered

her a waiting arm. 'Shall we dance, boss?' he said, his cheeky grin returning in full measure.

They went on to a second place, this time a club where the smoky atmosphere and incessant beat soon had Lisa's head throbbing.

'Can we go?' she asked apologetically, after they had only been there an hour. 'My head is splitting and I can't stand this smoke.'

Mark shrugged affably. 'Sure, where can I take you?'

Lisa hesitated. The most comfortable place she could think of was Akira's apartment but she wouldn't dream of taking him there. Instead she asked him where he was staying. He named a modest hotel in Greenwich Village.

'It's not up to much and I've only got a single bed,' he said, looking unsure of himself all of a sudden.

Lisa, however, was all smiles. 'That doesn't matter. It just means we'll have to get closer than before.' Her memory flickered back to the couple of occasions when they had romped around on her wide double bed in her inboard cabin.

Mark shrugged again. 'Okay, boss, your wish is my command.' He put up his hand to flag down a passing chequered cab.

'Don't keep calling me boss,' Lisa said, laughing.

'Okay, boss – I mean, Lisa.'

The laughter lingered in her voice. 'I'm warning you, Mark.'

He pretended to duck as she feigned a punch.

* * *

Mark's hotel might have been modest but it was clean and comfortable, with a well-stocked mini bar.

'What'll you have?' he asked, squatting down in front of the teak-veneered door and opening it.

Lisa peered inside. 'To be honest, I think I've had enough alcohol,' she said. 'I'll just have one of those.' She pointed to a bottle of mineral water and added, 'Do you have any paracetamol to go with it?'

Mark handed her the bottle, took out a beer for himself and then loped off into the bathroom to return with a couple of white pills nestling in his broad palm.

Lisa took them and popped them in her mouth. Swigging the water straight from the bottle, she swallowed and smiled. 'Thanks.'

Taking a seat on the end of the bed – the only place to sit apart from a padded chair tucked under the kneehole of the dressing table – Mark gazed up at her.

'Shit, you're beautiful, Lisa,' he said. 'I don't think I've ever mentioned it before.'

She shook her head. 'No, you haven't but I appreciate it all the same.' Reaching out to ruffle his short blond hair, she smiled wistfully. 'Mark, do you ever get the feeling that you're on the wrong track?'

His eyes widened. 'What do you mean? Surely you're not having second thoughts about Flights of Fancy?'

'No. It's not that.' Lisa squatted down in front of him and rested her chin in the gap between his knees. 'I mean personally. Don't you sometimes think that there's more to life than just fucking and having fun?'

Letting out a long, slow breath, Mark reclined back on

his elbows and studied her face. She seemed troubled, he realised. It wasn't just what she said but the way she looked. Older somehow, less vibrant.

'Is that a proposal?' He meant it as a joke, a feeble attempt to lighten her mood but it backfired on him.

'Would you marry me, Mark?' she said. 'Would you be content to give up your lifestyle, work a nine-to-five job and help me bring up loads of babies?'

'How many?' He stalled for time. Fortunately, Lisa sat back on her heels and let out a peal of laughter.

'Oh, God!' she howled. 'You should see your face. *How many?* I don't believe you said that. Shit, you crack me up, Mark.'

He leaped on her then. To demonstrate his relief and to shut her up. All too soon their mock-fight, which involved a lot of tickling and rolling around on the floor, turned into something far more erotic.

'Watch your dress, Lisa,' Mark warned, eying the threadbare carpet warily.

She lay underneath him, panting, tendrils of damp hair clinging to her face and neck. Earlier that evening she had started out with a neat chignon but now her dark curls tumbled down unchecked.

'Thanks for your concern,' she said. 'I guess I'd better take it off.' Nudging him out of the way, she sat up and pulled the dress over her head.

With long, muscular arms, he reached out and draped it neatly over the back of the chair. Then he glanced back down at her and his breath caught in his chest. He had meant what he said. She did look beautiful. As she reclined back on her elbows he could see the proud swell of her breasts heaving over the fragile cobweb of black lace that served as a bra.

'If I could be reborn, I would want to come back as your bra,' he said, his hands reaching out to cup her breasts as he straddled her again, his inner thighs gripping her hips.

'What about my knickers?' she asked, wriggling seductively. 'Surely you would prefer to be a pair of those?'

To her amusement he pretended to consider his options. Shuffling backwards down her legs, he paused to delve a thoughtful hand between her slightly parted thighs. Instantly, he felt the telltale wetness that signalled her arousal and on impulse he bent forward to bury his face in her crotch. For a moment he stayed like that, inhaling her musky scent as though it were the finest perfume in the world.

'Hm, yes,' he said, raising his head a moment later to grin at her lasciviously, 'perhaps you're right. I think your knickers could be my best bet.'

She laughed. What a ridiculous conversation.

Moving her body obediently this way and that, she allowed Mark to divest her of her underwear. It took no time at all. When she was completely naked he sat back on his heels, his buttocks brushing her shins, and contemplated her exposed body.

'I can't believe you are here,' he murmured, sounding completely serious for once. 'I can't believe you want me.'

'Oh, I want you.' Lisa reached out her arms to him and crushed his mouth against hers.

They kissed for a long time, his hands searching for her breasts, his fingertips tantalising her nipples as she moaned softly into his open mouth. She felt her desire rising, the flames of lust fanned by his caresses. For a large man, his touch was sublimely delicate – each caress as light as net curtains caught in the breeze – and inflamed her arousal to an even higher level than before.

'I want you, Mark,' she repeated, squirming her hips under him.

Taking a pert nipple between his lips, he nibbled gently, his eyes holding her heavy-lidded gaze. Further down her body, he sought the proof of her arousal once again, his fingers delving into the hot wetness between her legs. Spreading her sex lips apart, he began to stroke her clitoris methodically.

'Oh, Mark – oh, God!' she cried, churning her hips frantically.

All at once she felt as though she needed an orgasm more than life itself. She was tense without realising it. Even with two cocktails and a bottle or so of champagne inside her, she felt strung out. As though her body knew how much she craved it, her orgasm was elusive. She kept climbing and climbing, never quite reaching the peak.

Desperation made her touch herself. Her fingers drifted down her torso to join Mark's and she gently showed him exactly how and where he needed to be touched. She was thankful he didn't mind. Some men she had known had considered her guidance a personal insult to their prowess. Not so Mark. With a slight smile touching his lips and eyes he allowed her fingertips to guide him.

Both of them felt the hard nub of her clitoris and Lisa formed two of his fingers into a vee which she encouraged to stroke up and down either side of the throbbing bud. That was better. She could feel the heat rising again, passing the point which she had found so difficult to reach before.

All at once her mind was filled with a fantasy. One where Mark and Akira and Rio all watched her as she masturbated. In her mind's eye she saw the three of them, fully dressed, seated, their eyes intent only on her hand moving between her legs. 'Show us,' they said in unison, 'show us everything you've got, Lisa.' Humiliation shot through her, eclipsed by lust. A powerful, surging heat that made her helpless in the face of their demands. In her fantasy she spread her labia, opened wide and showed them the extent of her arousal, while all the time stroking the greedy nub of flesh that demanded more and more attention.

Relinquishing her body to Mark's capable fingers, she lay back, flung her arms above her head and began to churn her hips methodically as the video inside her head played out to its climax. Her climax. A long, almost unendurable lance of heat and sensation that speared her entire body and held it in the throes of erotic pleasure.

Gradually, she calmed down. The lance was withdrawn slowly and she felt her body slump with relief. Moving alongside her, Mark gathered her up in his arms and held her lightly, waiting for her shuddering breaths to subside.

'Thanks, I needed that,' she croaked hoarsely.

Mark laughed lightly. 'I'll say you did.' He continued to hold her but now one hand lightly caressed her hair and the nape of her neck.

Sighing, Lisa revelled in the comforting sensation of his caress, until she felt her strength returning and, along with it, a renewed surge of desire. With a light push against his chest, she rolled him onto his back, reached down and began to fumble with his fly. Her fingers were weak and she groaned with frustration.

'Here, let me,' Mark said, moving her hands out of the way and quickly removing his trousers and pants. Having taken off his socks and shoes when they arrived back at his room, all he had left on was a short-sleeved cotton shirt.

Lisa waited until he was ready, then reached forward and began to undo the buttons on his shirt, pressing a tiny kiss onto each portion of skin as she revealed it.

Mark allowed his head to drop back. He rested his weight on his hands as Lisa pushed the edges of his shirt away and began to lay a trail of kisses down the length of his torso before moving her lips up again and across his chest, sucking in each of his nipples in turn and biting them gently. He moaned, feeling the threads of desire begin to gather at the pit of his belly. His hardening cock stirred and grew a little more.

Lisa noticed the movement immediately, her eyes glowing with something akin to triumph as she watched his erection sway and move away from his body until it jutted out at right angles to his belly.

'I think you're ready for me,' she murmured softly.

Catching his shaft between both hands she held it tight and slipped her lips over his glans until he was fully enclosed. Her flickering tongue caught a salty droplet and smoothed it all over the taut flesh, loving the way that he moaned and arched his back, offering more of himself to her.

She sighed inside her head, loving her own ability to give pleasure. *To give is better than to receive*, she thought, then remembered the power of her recent orgasm and felt forced to refute the old saying. Giving and receiving were equally as good. Now it was time for both of them to take their pleasure.

Throwing one leg over his thighs she straddled him, her back arched slightly as she placed her hands palm down on the taut plain of his stomach. Through heavy-lidded eyes she watched him following the pendulum movement of her breasts as she leaned forward slightly and began to grind her hips.

His cock filled her, buried to the hilt, the rough bush of his pubic hair tantalising her newly awakened clitoris. She felt the flesh around the tender bud move in time with her rhythm – felt it pull this way and that, gently yet tantalisingly, like a spare pair of fingers at work.

She moved closer to him, the swollen buds of her nipples brushing the light covering of golden down on his chest until he reached up and cupped her breasts, squeezing them rhythmically in time with her gentle thrusts. It was wonderful to fuck him for once. On the two previous occasions he had taken control, plunging into her from above, or behind, holding her in a vicelike grip so that all she could do was take it. Now she had him where she wanted him and she was going to make the most of every moment.

She varied her rhythm, sometimes moving up and down, sometimes grinding her pelvis around and around. Glancing down, she noticed Mark seemed to be lost in his own private world. His eyes were closed, his lips moving as though he was reciting a silent poem. She would love to know what he was thinking. If lascivious fantasies ran through his mind, or if he simply gave himself up body and soul to the sensations coursing through his body.

'What are you thinking, Mark?' she ventured to gasp out as she slowed her movements to a gentle grind.

His eyes flew open with surprise, then he closed them again and smiled a secretive smile. 'If you must know, I'm imagining that I'm a horse and you're the jockey. You're riding me bareback of course,' he added with a slight chuckle.

'Cheeky!' Lisa said.

Urged on by the thought of participating in his fantasy she reverted to an up and down movement, her thighs gripping his hips as she bent low over him. Just like a real jockey would.

He reached out and tried to clasp her buttocks but she was moving too fast for him to get a proper grip.

'Leave me alone, let me ride you,' she ordered, her stern voice tempered by laughter.

'Okay, boss.' Mark allowed his hands to flutter away from her and he clasped them behind his head instead. With his eyes closed he missed her expression that said: 'I thought I told you not to call me boss.'

Chapter Eleven

The lure of Akira's king-sized bed did nothing to deter Lisa from spending the night with Mark. In fact, she realised the following morning, she had slept very well. Consequently she awoke with a smile on her face, feeling very rested and relaxed.

'Hi,' she murmured softly as Mark's eyelids fluttered open.

She watched him trying to focus his eyes and remember where he was and who he was with. When realisation finally struck his expression cleared, his whole face becoming animated.

'Lisa. Hi, yourself.' Cupping the back of her head he pulled her towards him, his mouth capturing hers for a sublime good morning kiss.

She was tempted to progress things, to turn their morning into one long lazy fuck but, in all honesty, after the night before she felt a little sore in her most delicate places and a sunny sky outside the window beckoned.

'Let's get up and do Greenwich Village,' she suggested, sitting up suddenly. The pale blue sheet pooled around her waist and she basked in his appreciative gaze for a moment before getting out of bed and padding over to the bathroom door. Glancing over her shoulder coquettishly, she added, 'Bags I'm first in the shower.'

Half of her regretted that he didn't try to follow her, but when she emerged from the bathroom, her torso and hair wrapped in soft white towels, she noticed that he was snoring gently again. With a slight shrug of resignation she decided to let him sleep on for a while and sat down in front of the dressing table to fix her hair and make-up.

When she had finished and was dressed again in her clothes from the night before she prodded him awake. 'Come on lazybones. There's a whole big wide world waiting for us out there.'

Mark groaned and struggled to support himself on his elbows. 'Why are you dressed already?' He glanced at his watch. 'Shit, it's almost twelve!'

'Precisely,' Lisa said, sitting down on the edge of the bed. Reaching forward she stroked a thoughtful palm across his chest. 'Look. I've got to get changed out of this stuff, so why don't I arrange to meet you somewhere at, say, one thirty.'

He caught her wrist, glanced at her and smiled. 'Sure, why not. If you come back to Greenwich Village I know the perfect place to grab a late lunch, then perhaps we can window shop along Eighth Street.'

Lisa liked the sound of that idea. She loved the enduring bohemian feel of 'The Village' and the prospect of spending the day wandering around there beguiled her.

'It's a deal,' she said happily. 'I'll hop in a cab and meet you – where?'

He named a place which she knew faced onto a green triangle of open space called Christopher Park. Trust

Mark, she thought, his choice was perfection.

'This time the meal's on me though,' he warned, planting a kiss on her lips as she rose to go. 'I don't want to start feeling like a kept man.'

She laughed, skipped away from him and bade him a cheery goodbye. All of a sudden life felt good again. Very, very good. And it was only when she was outside, seated in the back of a cab, that she realised that during the past twenty-four hours she had hardly thought about her forthcoming date with Akira at all.

The rest of the weekend passed pleasantly enough, although after a couple of hours' intense fucking on Sunday night, Lisa insisted on going back to Akira's apartment alone. On Monday morning she awoke feeling bright and breezy and greeted her new plane-load of clients with an infectious smile. As Mark was booked for the flight as well as Rio, she decided to forgo yet more sex and settled down with a new book instead.

On Thursday she greeted a passenger whom she recognised immediately. It was the woman with long, flame-red hair whom she had likened to Botticelli's 'Venus'.

'I couldn't resist taking my return flight with you,' the woman said, 'although I was a bit disappointed there was no way I could wait until next week so that I could take your orgy flight again.'

Lisa grinned. 'You enjoyed the orgy then?'

'Oh, yes. It was the first one I'd been to and it exceeded all my expectations.' For a moment the woman seemed transported to a different plane of thought. Then she glanced at Lisa. 'So I've done the next best thing and booked two men for this flight.'

Glancing down at the booking form, Lisa noticed that she had indeed booked two men. Any two, the woman had stated, as long as they've got the stamina to keep up.

As her eyes flickered over the instructions, Lisa laughed. 'I think you'll enjoy the choice I've made for you,' she said.

Raising her hand she summoned Gary and another of her 'boys' called Oscar. They made a nice contrast. Whereas Gary was tall and as red-haired as the client herself, Oscar was small and impish, with unruly dark blond hair. According to Michiko's notes, jotted down after their 'interview', both men had apparently limitless get up and go.

'Right, well, this is Gary and this is Oscar,' Lisa said, introducing them.

She turned her gaze to the woman who chipped in hastily that her name was Venetia. Not quite Venus, Lisa thought to herself with an inward smile, but near enough. As Gary and Oscar spirited Venetia away to a row of three chairs ready for take off, Lisa widened her outside smile and began to greet the other passengers.

Venetia Hammond was a woman who acted as though she knew exactly what she wanted, when in truth she wasn't quite sure what it was she sought to make her life complete.

Her career in music publishing was intensely rewarding – that wasn't the problem. She had countless men she could call on for a good time, or simply a good fuck, so that wasn't the problem either. Nor did she harbour any lingering desire to settle down into a permanent relationship and produce a tribe of squalling brats. In fact, the very thought made her shudder and, just to make certain, she had persuaded her gynaecologist to tie her tubes.

What she wanted out of life was something else. Something indefinably more*ish*. The trouble was, she had no idea what it could be and that bugged the hell out of her.

Instead of simply relaxing and following her own destiny, she threw all her spare time into creating a sexual nirvana for herself. A place in her life where men and occasionally women were allowed to enter but not linger. Sometimes she simply sought pleasure from her own hands, thinking lone sex had a lot going for it. But it was never quite enough.

As she entered her cabin a half-hour after boarding, the one called Gary gallantly holding the door back for her, she found her spirits were buoyed by the room's simple elegance. The thick fibreboard walls, painted in a soft eau-de-nil, were enlivened by watercolours by unknown but original artists and the furnishings were graceful and complementary to the rest of the decor. A quick glance in the en-suite shower room confirmed her positive feelings about the flight. Yes, here she could be happy for the next seven hours or so. Here she would be able to romp about on the wide double bed with her two elected companions and not worry about a thing.

Turning to Gary and Oscar who hovered uncertainly by the door, she instructed them to take their clothes off.

By some unspoken agreement, both men had come to the conclusion that their client would be the one making all the decisions and felt justifiably nervous. In all their combined years' experience they were used to taking the lead, of guiding anxious women of all ages along a path strewn with pleasure. Now they were both faced with someone entirely different to the norm, a woman who, though not quite a dominatrix, certainly made sure they all knew who intended to call the shots.

This was to be Oscar's first sexual encounter with an American woman. The prospect had delighted him, now the reality didn't. He was used to docile Englishwomen, grateful Italians and the happy-to-take-it-as-it-comes French. But although nearly half the clientele were American, during his time with Flights of Fancy he had never yet been called upon to service anyone from the other side of the Atlantic.

Watching and listening to the fiery-haired Amazon in front of him he felt anxious that, now the opportunity had actually arrived, he would not be able to perform to the best of his ability. Demanding women made him nervous, in any situation, no matter how innocuous. He invariably gave way to such women in queues, almost literally allowing them to trample over him. And on buses and trains, a single accusing glance from a woman who was standing up would be enough to encourage him to give up his seat.

Gary on the other hand was looking forward to the encounter. Girls like Bobo were fun but he could easily dominate them and often tired of having to be the one with the imagination. Giving up the responsibility to someone else was not only an enticing prospect, it was one he welcomed with open arms. Anxious to break the ice, he glanced down at the ice bucket on the dressing table and asked if anyone would like a drink.

It didn't matter to him that he and Oscar sat on the end of the bed and sipped their champagne, while the client reclined nonchalantly in a chair, still fully dressed. Nor did it bother him that she eyed them up and down so blatantly, her expression suggesting that she could possibly find one of them wanting in some way and demand a replacement.

Gary sincerely hoped that, if such thoughts were running through her head, she would not dismiss him. He wanted to get to know her – to get to grips with her, he supposed. She presented a challenge and it was a long time since he'd had one of those.

Venetia allowed her head to fall back so that she was able to gaze at the two men from under her thickly mascaraed lashes. The tall one was the most attractive, she decided, his colouring and therefore, no doubt, his temperament complementary to her own. Plus she liked the challenging stare he gave her. Here was a man who wasn't nervous about his own nudity, or the fact that he rented out his body for a living. Here was a man who could probably make her come.

The other one, though, she had doubts about. For one thing he was a bit on the small side and for another he seemed as nervous as hell. The more she stared at him, the more he rounded his shoulders and tucked his free hand firmly between his thighs, trying to obscure the fact that he didn't yet have an erection. In the dim recesses of her psyche she harboured secret fantasies about finding a man who could take control in bed but this one didn't look as though he could dominate a fly. Still, waste not want not, he was bound to be useful for something, even if it was only sucking her toes while the more promising Gary got on with the good stuff.

'What are we waiting for, boys,' she said suddenly, breaking the heavy silence between them. Putting her glass down decisively, she stood up and began to strip.

Both men stared on in awe. Her body was magnificent. Gary remembered her now from one of the orgies, although he hadn't actually had the pleasure.

Although she wasn't slim by any means, she had a certain voluptuousness about her. Her muscular arms and heavy thighs immediately incited thoughts in both men about what it would feel like to have them wrapped around their bodies. And her large, pendulous breasts, tipped with firm pink nipples, invited them to act on their most childish instincts and bury their faces in the soft, giving flesh.

Unpinning her hair, she allowed the red waves to ripple over her shoulders and down her back. It was in every way her crowning glory and for a moment she revelled in the feel of it as it caressed her naked flesh.

Surprisingly, Oscar was the first to respond. He stood up and walked over to Venetia, reaching out a questing hand to stroke her hair.

'Lovely,' he breathed, almost to himself, 'like liquid silk.'

Venetia gave an involuntary moan. Talk about say and do all the right things, this little guy had the measure of her alright. All at once she relaxed, allowing him to simply stroke her hair for what seemed like an age.

Presently she felt Gary's touch upon her thigh. More assured than Oscar's it provoked a primeval need inside her. Groaning with pent-up arousal she opened her legs, encouraging his fingers to leave her thigh and investigate the moist crevice that now beckoned to him.

'Yes,' she urged, 'yes, just like that.'

His fingertips set light to small sparks of desire, scattering them throughout her whole body. She opened her legs wider still, wanting more of him yet anxious not to disturb Oscar's caresses which had now moved more purposefully to her breasts.

Oscar's palms skimmed over the full globes, his touch light yet stimulating in a way she had never thought possible. Most of the men she went for of her own volition were easily as large as her, with heavy-handed caresses to match. In comparison this young man was a revelation.

'Please, yes,' she urged him in a voice so soft it didn't sound like her own.

He grinned, warming to the way she responded to him. Where was the dominating attitude now, he thought, could it all have been an act? Whispering in her ear he told her to kneel.

Trembling with renewed excitement she obeyed, careless that her hurry to do so dislodged Gary's hand from between her thighs.

'That's it, bitch, now suck me,' Oscar said.

Gary paled at Oscar's words. What the hell did he think he was playing at? But to his surprise he saw the smouldering desire in Venetia's eyes and the way her hand shook as she reached out to grasp the other man's impressive erection and jam it into her mouth. He winced on Oscar's behalf. Their client's approach was by no means delicate.

As far as Oscar was concerned a lack of finesse was neither here nor there when he was having his cock sucked so thoroughly.

'More,' he urged, 'take it deeper. Take all of it.' It thrilled him that she complied immediately, sliding her full, fleshy lips down his shaft, further and further until he felt his glans nudge the back of her throat. Throwing a bewildered-looking Gary a sly wink, he cupped the back of Venetia's head with both hands and urged her on. 'That's it, bitch, more, more.'

As Venetia sucked, she trembled, the shivers becoming more and more violent until she felt as though she could hardly breathe. It didn't help to have her mouth stuffed full of cock but it was his words and the way he rapped them out that did her in. Bitch, he called her, bitch! How dare he? A wet trickle ran down the inside of her thighs. God, she loved it!

She had never been debased before. No one but no one had ever dared to try and humiliate her. Now here she was, turning to jelly at the forceful commands of a guy who looked as though he couldn't beat an egg. As she continued to suck hard on Oscar's cock, she sensed Gary kneeling down behind her. A moment later, his hands reached around her and began to caress her breasts.

Wriggling slightly, she gave herself up to the sensation of Gary's knowing touch. She felt her nipples harden all the more as he rolled each of them between thumb and forefinger, occasionally pulling at them so that they stood proud from the fleshy mounds of her breasts. Glancing up, she noticed that Oscar was staring at her breasts intently, his eyes glittering with something that she couldn't quite define.

Mouthing him with increased fervour she felt compelled to cup his balls in her hand and juggle the hard, hairy globes in her palm. It excited her that the caress elicited a groan and encouraged her to rasp a long crimson nail along his perineum and up between his taut buttocks to his anus. Scraping delicately at the tiny puckered hole, she whimpered with pleasure as she felt his hot, salty come jettison into the back of her throat.

She licked him completely clean, covering every millimetre of his long shaft with her tongue before sliding it over the bulbous glans which bore the sheen of her own saliva.

'What a good little whore you are,' Oscar murmured thickly, his eyes now moving from her breasts to her face which she raised in supplication. 'Now Gary is going to fuck you and I'm going to sit back and enjoy the show. I'm going to watch his cock pumping in and out of your juicy cunt until I tell him to stop.'

Gary flashed Oscar a look of pure amazement. Where did he get off trying to dictate the pace? He had his own way of doing things and he certainly wasn't planning to fuck this lady for a long time yet.

'Oscar, I—' he began but his colleague flashed him a look which said: 'Do it!' in no uncertain terms.

Glancing at Venetia, he saw how excited she looked. Her eyes bright with anticipation, her full breasts heaving with barely contained emotion.

'Okay, pal, whatever you say,' he concurred, feeling helpless in the face of such determination.

Placing his palm flat against Venetia's forehead, Oscar pushed her away from him slightly, his action almost disdainful. Totally lost in a realm of awakened fantasies, Venetia whimpered. In that brief moment, as Oscar glared down at her with an expression that screamed his contempt, she felt as though she had finally discovered the meaning of life.

'On the bed, Venetia, and spread those legs wide,' Oscar ordered, his stern expression unchanging as she scrambled to her feet and half fell in an ungainly heap on the bed.

Rolling over onto her back she opened her legs, just as he had ordered, and lay upon the soft, satin quilt, quivering with anticipation as both men simultaneously glanced down at her desperate flesh before exchanging a pointed look.

God, she felt ashamed. Ashamed of herself and of her lack of self-control. Her body was betraying her, her sex flesh swelling and opening up under the power of their stereo gaze. *Don't!* she longed to cry out. *Don't look at me like that.* But she felt robbed of the power of speech, her throat closed up tight against the possibility of rebellious speech.

'I didn't say you could just lay there,' Oscar commanded, 'touch yourself.' His tone dropped to a seductive level. 'That's it, baby, open up for us. Show us what you've got. All of it.'

She didn't know what was worse, his stern tone or the one he was using now. Both filled her with a profound sense of shame which excited the hell out of her. As though she had never dared to touch herself intimately before, her fingers fumbled, the tips eventually landing on her fleshy outer lips and spreading them wide apart so that every little bit of her was cruelly exposed. A draft of cool air from the ventilation unit wafted over her moist flesh, lingering and swirling around her clitoris which strained toward the two men who stood impassively at the end of the bed.

Raising her head slightly she gazed back at them through heavy-lidded eyes. Her whole body seemed to pulse and throb to a rhythm that was charged with eroticism. How could she bear it, the way they examined her with their eyes, so candidly, so knowingly. Their secret smiles as poignant as a caress. *Touch me!* she wanted to scream. *Cover me with your hands, your mouths. Take my flesh and devour it, kiss it, suck it. Taste me!*

The pleas screamed in her head but emerged from her parted lips as whimpers, agonised little sounds that could have come from a wounded animal.

'Take her,' Oscar said, nodding to Gary who seemed transfixed for a moment. Then he seemed to come to and began to climb onto the bed.

His hands either side of her legs, he crawled towards her, until his knees were between her splayed thighs, the pale skin almost brushing the outer limits of her sex. She saw his erection was as impressive as Oscar's, swaying to and fro at right angles to his body. It emerged from a thick bush of red gold curls like a stout rod, a pleasure stick, she thought wildly.

He murmured to her to move her hands and in the next moment grasped her thighs and pushed them back towards her chest. Pulling them apart he glanced down at her pouting sex, noticing the way creamy trickles of nectar snaked their way down over the fleshy mounds of her buttocks.

Oh, Jesus H Christ! Venetia screamed inside her head. She felt so suffused with shame that her throat and cheeks glowed as brightly as her hair. *How could you do this to me, you bastards – how could you humiliate me so completely?* There was no hiding her arousal now. Her sex flesh felt so diabolically stretched that she quaked, wanting to break free of Gary's vicelike grip on her thighs and run for cover. She imagined herself cowering in a corner, scrunched up in a foetal ball, her nipples aching, her clitoris pulsing with unsatisfied arousal.

She had no more time to think, she could feel the tip of Gary's cock describing tantalising circles around the lips of her vagina, skating around and around the dewy flesh on a film of her own moisture.

Oscar moved and sat on the edge of the bed just a few inches away. Venetia felt her breath catch as his hand reached out and cupped her mound, his palm pressing against her exposed inner flesh with a slight up and down movement that tantalised her clitoris to an unbearable degree.

She could feel her orgasm building, the slow spread of heat that engulfed the unprotected portion of flesh between her thighs, the fiery tongue that licked at her helpless clitoris.

'Mm, oh, yes,' she mumbled, barely coherent.

Gary and Oscar exchanged glances, Oscar keeping his hand in place as Venetia tried to squirm and churn her hips.

'Stay still,' Oscar said evenly, his palm resuming its slight up and down movement.

'I – I can't,' Venetia gasped.

'Oh, but you must.' Oscar was uncompromising and in truth she had very little choice in the matter because Gary was holding her so firmly.

Serpents of desire uncoiled in the pit of her belly and began to move about inside her, plucking at her taut nerves until she felt herself ascending beyond the limits of her endurance. Just as she began to peak she felt the surprise intrusion of Gary's cock inside her, thrusting deeply up to the hilt. It was her undoing. Screwing up her face and opening her mouth wide she let out a protracted scream. At least, in her head it sounded like a scream, to the outside world it was a harsh, anguished grunt.

With the release of tension came the power to speak again, to urge Gary on, faster and faster, harder and harder. She rocked her hips, all the time watching Oscar watching her. His uncompromising gaze was concentrated on her sex, on the sight of her secret flesh now red and swollen, grasping at the cock inside her as though it were a lifebelt.

It was true she was drowning – being sucked down into the filthy mire of lust and depravity. She cursed herself for being so wicked, so utterly debauched and then came Oscar's confirmation.

'You slut,' he said, 'you dirty whore.'

She growled again, an unintelligible sound that was supposed to tell him to shut up, to keep his nasty accusations to himself, and yet she found herself nodding helplessly – her mouth saying, 'Yes, yes. I'm a whore. I'm a slut. I'm a dirty bitch. Now fuck me.'

Although she hardly believed it possible, Gary increased his pace, his cock nudging the small spot inside her that always caused white lights to explode in her head. And explode they did, like cannonfire, ricocheting against the backs of her closed eyelids, the heat of lust consuming her.

Gary shuddered, groaned and came. His grip loosened but she replaced his hands with her own, clasping the backs of her thighs just behind her knees so that both men could clearly see the moment when his cock slid out of her gaping vagina. As Gary half fell, half reclined across the width of the bed, she kept herself exposed.

'I want more,' she said, surprising herself by the normality of her voice. 'I want another fuck.'

Oscar reached out and slapped her wet sex with the flat of his palm. 'You don't give the orders,' he said. 'I say what you get and when you get it.'

She cringed at the slap, her whole body seeming to fold in on itself and then she felt another torrent of arousal and cried out as another quick, yet no less intense, orgasm wracked her body. He slapped her again and again, smacking her swollen, reddened flesh until he was satisfied that her climax was abating.

Then he turned his attention to the exposed part of her buttocks. Flexing his wrist first he delivered a stinging blow to each fleshy cheek, watching as they wobbled and blushed in the shape of his handprint.

'Don't hit me,' she gasped, wondering why she didn't just lower her legs and therefore make it impossible for him to get to his target. 'I don't like it.'

His eyes narrowed. 'Liar,' he snapped. 'Lying little slut. You love it.' He lowered his tone to one that was almost questioning. 'You do love it don't you? Tell me you love it, bitch.'

Venetia gulped, thrilling to the timbre of his voice and the dark, dangerous expression on his face. 'I – I love it,' she whispered. 'Oh, God help me, I love it!' Throwing her head back she cried out her wants, her needs. 'Do it again. Harder. Faster. Beat me till I come. Tell me what a dirty girl I am.'

A knowing smile flickered across his face, victory and desire turning his hazel eyes to black. 'You are a dirty girl,' he said, delivering two more stinging blows to her reddened rump. 'You need to be punished. You need to be humiliated. Don't you?'

Venetia fought for breath. 'Yes,' she gasped, 'yes, please.'

Oscar nodded. 'On your hands and knees. Do it, bitch. Quickly.'

Anxious to please him and to taste the delights yet to come, she let go of her thighs and rolled over onto her fleshy stomach before pushing herself up onto her hands and knees. Her sweaty palms slipped on the delicate satin quilt, earning herself another couple of slaps.

'Stay,' Oscar ordered as if she were a recalcitrant hound, 'stay right where you are or I swear I will walk out of this room.' He knew that threatening her with anything physical would only thrill her all the more and he wanted her to remain obedient to him.

Hanging her head in shame, Venetia nodded and

struggled to right herself, the ends of her fingers digging into the quilt and hanging on for dear life.

Gary lay, sprawled on his back, across the bottom of the bed. He turned his head. From that angle he could see the pouch of Venetia's sex oozing between her parted thighs like a ripe plum. He had ceased to wonder at Oscar's methods. Whatever prompted him to behave in such an out-of-character way was obviously having the desired effect.

Oscar glanced at him. 'Suck her breasts.'

With a shrug of acceptance, Gary moved up the bed to lay alongside Venetia, angling his head so that he lay under her, her hugely swollen nipples brushing his face. Gathering up the pendulous flesh in both hands, he pressed his lips to her nipples, mouthing first one then the other, delighting in her soft moans and the succulence of her flesh.

Arching her back, Venetia urged her breasts down into Gary's hands and her desperately aching nipples deep inside his mouth. Like the rest of her body they felt aflame, burning with the desire to be touched and held, stroked and fondled, massaged and licked. Her nipples had never felt so swollen, she thought, as though all the lust that couldn't be squeezed into her throbbing clitoris had forced itself into those tender buds.

She remembered how, as a child at a birthday party, she had taken an inflated balloon and compressed it between her hands, forcing the air into a tiny bubble at the end until it seemed on the point of bursting under the pressure. Now her breasts felt that way. Hugely inflated, hopelessly trying to resist the pressure of Gary's hands as he moulded them together. The image in her mind's eye and the insistent suction of his mouth drove her to distraction, inciting another wave of moans and encouraging her to arch her back even further.

It no longer mattered to her what she looked like – if Oscar was witnessing the conspicious desperation of her aroused sex flesh. It didn't matter that her beautiful hair hung in clumps, the fine tendrils matted together with her own perspiration. It wouldn't even matter if she opened her mouth in the next minute and begged him to touch her, to bring her the utter relief she was sure was beyond her body's capabilities.

She'd always thought that arousal was a bodily reaction and not a state of mind. Now, faced with the stern orders of a pale little guy, her body no longer felt like her own and in her mind – for the next few hours at any rate – she felt compelled to cede to him. Total surrender was the option facing her and, beyond all the boundaries of her rational self, she knew it would be her only way forward.

Glancing over her shoulder she saw Oscar, his hair brushed back from his forehead to display a determination she had never seen in a man before, his naked body worn with the confidence of a suit of leather and chains.

'Touch me, please,' she gasped, surprising herself even though she knew the die had already been cast. 'Slap me, finger me, do what the hell you like to me, only please, God, make me come again.'

Chapter Twelve

Lisa was sorry to lose Oscar. Not only had his resignation come as a complete surprise but she was amazed that he and one of her clients, the overpowering Venetia, had apparently come to some sort of romantic understanding.

Later Gary told her the whole story. Starting with the way Venetia had initially taken full command, he ended with a description of her laying spent and awash with tears of gratitude, literally pleading with Oscar to go and live with her in America and become her lord and master. Or words to that effect.

'Venetia did?' Lisa still couldn't believe her ears.

Gary nodded, a bemused grin suffusing his face. 'Yup, absolutely. And she even offered to pay him, although he wouldn't hear of it. Apparently he has ambitions of playing bass guitar with a rock band and Venetia has promised to find him a suitable slot. She's in the business you know?'

'No, I didn't but it doesn't surprise me,' Lisa said. 'Most of our clients seem to be involved in one area of showbusiness or another. Particularly the American ones.'

Returning to her cabin, she quickly drafted out an official acceptance of his resignation and, as an afterthought, tucked a cheque for one month's salary inside the envelope. Sealing it, she sent it to Oscar via a steward who was hovering about in the passageway outside her door.

'Make sure he gets this straight away, before he disembarks,' she said, 'and tell him I said good luck and to keep in touch.'

Walking back inside the cabin and closing the door behind her, she sat at her desk which stood in place of a dressing table. Oscar's leaving posed a bit of a problem which she had been reluctant to face, namely the necessity to recruit a few extra 'boys'. During the past couple of weeks several had called in sick at the same time, leaving her with barely the twenty minimum that she needed for every flight.

At the moment she didn't operate the flights at weekends but lately she had received a number of enquiries about just such an extension to the Flights of Fancy service. All things considered it made her think that perhaps she should give it some serious thought. And a manager who could deputise for her occasionally wouldn't be a bad idea either. Even countless years' experience as a stewardess had not been enough to prepare her for the sheer exhaustion she felt by the end of each week. Constant changes in time-zones and the consequent jet lag could certainly take their toll.

It was something she resolved to talk to Akira about that coming Saturday – if they could spare any time to actually indulge in intercourse of a non-sexual nature. She laughed inside. Thinking about Akira made her feel extraordinarily warm all of a sudden and she found herself looking forward to Saturday evening with even more fervour than before.

All at once she felt tempted to lay down on her bed and pleasure herself for a while. She hadn't had any sex at all since the Sunday evening she had spent with Mark and was now beginning to realise that her body was on full alert. Being celibate, even for a few days, did not suit her. She needed sex almost as much as she needed food. It was one of life's essentials.

Friday seemed interminable and she slept most of Saturday away. It was easier to cede to complete oblivion than spend the whole day awake and thinking – anticipating the evening to come. And come she would, she was certain of that. It was where or how she might find herself coming that sent tingles of anticipation running through her. Akira was as unpredictable as he was inventive. Whatever happened tonight, she was sure it wouldn't be a simple case of eating dinner and then going to bed.

She finally roused herself at four o'clock, forced down a small prawn salad and then filled the bath to the brim with heavily scented bubbles. Immersing herself in the warm, soapy depths she allowed her head to drop back and her eyes to close. Surely she couldn't still be sleepy?

An hour later she awoke, the water around her cold, the bubbles hardly more than a thin film which floated around her like little islands. Shivering, she stood up quickly and enveloped herself in the comforting warmth of her bathrobe. Then, stooping over the bath to let out the water, she grabbed the shower head and began to quickly wash her hair. It wouldn't do to be late for Akira.

Back in her bedroom, her dark, wet tresses be-turbaned, she proceeded to apply her make-up. Dark smoky shadow around her eyes, only a thin coat of mascara, as her eyelashes hardly needed any cosmetic help, and several coats of bright red lipstick. The dress she had chosen to wear was red – a simple shift that ended halfway down her shapely thighs – and she had a new pair of high, strappy sandals to match which she had bought during her whirlwind shopping spree in New York.

Small gold knot earrings and a matching necklace completed the ensemble and, as she paused to cover her throat with a fine mist of perfume, she found herself studying her reflection. Not bad, she mused, not bad at all, girl.

The certainty that Akira would be pleased with her appearance made her smile a smile which lit up her eyes, revealing every ounce of excitement and anticipation that she felt inside. Life was good. It ran along on a more or less even keel, bringing with it a host of delights, some sexual, some equally rewarding because they were the result of her own hard work. It made her realise how lucky she was – and how lucky Akira should consider himself to be getting her tonight.

She was surprised to find that Akira wasn't waiting for her by the lift when she arrived. He often did that, or sent his manservant – a dour Englishman of indeterminate age who looked and acted as though he were an ex-Colonel, or someone of equal military standing. In a way she felt sorry for the man. After half a lifetime serving Queen and country, he was reduced to living out his days in the service of one man who was hardly ever there.

The lift opened straight into a small lobby which comprised part of Akira's apartment. He owned the whole floor, the penthouse suite, giving him far more space and privacy than any of the other residents in the Mayfair tower block. The door to Akira's inner sanctum was slightly ajar, she noticed, which struck her as odd. No one to greet her, the door left open and what was this – a note?

The yellow Post-it note affixed to the door bore only three words: Come In Lisa.

Feeling excited she pushed the door open and stepped over the threshold. This was yet another new scenario – Akira being inventive and playing his little games again. Well, if that was the case, considering her past experiences with him, she was bound to enjoy taking an active part in the game, whatever it might be.

The inner lobby was in near darkness, the only light supplied by a fat white candle which flickered in a wrought-iron wall sconce. As she cautiously closed the door behind her, she thought she detected a movement in the shadows. Correction, two movements, one to either side of her. In the next instant she found herself being grabbed from both sides, strong, broad fingers closing over her upper arms and gripping so tightly that she almost cried out.

Fear thundered through her, pumping a rush of adrenalin into her brain with such intensity that she felt faint. *Burglars!* she thought wildly. *Akira's apartment is being burgled and I've just walked into the middle of it.*

A deeply masculine voice spoke in her ear. 'Don't panic, Mr Tanaka knows you're here.'

Her involuntary sigh of relief was tempered by a fresh surge of alarm. If Akira knew she had arrived what the hell was going on!

Turning her head swiftly in the direction of the voice, she saw that the man holding her was the chauffeur who had driven Akira's limousine in New York. Glancing to the opposite side, she noticed that her other assailant looked just like the chauffeur – equally tall, blond and muscular they could have been twins.

One of the men produced something from his pocket, something black and silky. He raised it to her face and in the brief instant before he pressed it over her eyes she realised that it was an eye mask, of the kind that she was used to dispensing on planes to weary travellers so that they could blot out the bright world around them and sleep.

'What the hell's going on!' Lisa shouted angrily.

She heard her voice, so strident in the hushed darkness. Now she was wearing the eye mask everything was totally black. She tried to wrench it from her eyes but the men still gripped her arms. Squirming wildly, she tried to break free of their grasp but their fingers held her tight, their grip uncompromising. To her horror she felt her zip being pulled down at the back and in the next instant her arms were liberated and her waist grabbed instead.

The dress began to slip, lower and lower until she felt the soft caress of warm air on her naked breasts. True to form, she wore no underwear. With Akira it hardly seemed necessary. Clothing played very little part in his games. Oh, God, this was awful. She didn't know if the two men were staring at her naked breasts but felt certain that they were. Unless they were gay they would be extremely interested in her bare flesh.

She felt compelled to cry out again. 'How dare you, let me go!'

'Mr Tanaka's instructions,' the one to the right of her said.

It took a few moments for his words to sink in. And as she pondered the implications of the situation she felt her dress slip lower, over her hips, whispering down her thighs until it pooled around her feet.

Again she felt a slight loosening of the grip around her waist as one of the men obviously bent down to pick up her dress. In the blackness she heard movement and felt the slight brush of fingertips on her ankle.

'Please lift your foot,' the man said.

Hesitating for just a moment, Lisa did what he asked. She hardly liked to think about this latest development – the fact that she now stood completely naked save her necklace, earrings and shoes. Raising one foot and then the other with extreme care, lest she display far more of herself than she intended, Lisa stepped out of the dress.

'Beautiful,' one of the men said, 'gorgeous.'

There followed a brief moment of silence during which she imagined his companion nodded, then he spoke.

'Lovely body.' She felt a hand travel across her right shoulder and down over her breast. A broad palm cupped one firm mound and massaged it lightly, the fingers tweaking her nipple. 'Great tits.'

She cringed then found her voice again. 'How dare you touch me, let me go.'

'I'm sorry, miss, we can't do that. We have our instructions.'

'What—what instructions? I don't like this. Leave me alone.' She knew her voice was starting to lose its hard edge. It was beginning to sound plaintive and she hated the fact almost as much as the degrading situation itself. Trying to assert herself she added, 'I'm warning you. Mr Tanaka will be furious when he finds out and believe me, I intend to tell him.'

Stereo laughter touched her ears, the sound making her blush with shame.

'I thought we already told you. Mr Tanaka knows. Mr Tanaka told us to do this.'

It couldn't be true. How could she possibly believe that Akira would deliberately do something like this to her?

The hand which held her breast moved to the other one, massaging and fondling in the same way. Then moments later, she felt another hand slide over her buttocks and insinuate itself between her tightly compressed thighs. Oh, God, not that!

She moaned. It was too awful. Too shameful to bear. She hated the fact that she was totally at the mercy of two complete strangers – she didn't think saying a brief 'hello' and 'thank you' to the chauffeur counted as a proper introduction.

'Open your legs,' one of them said.

Lisa retorted quickly, 'Fuck off!'

One of the men *tut-tutted*.

'Feisty little thing,' the other murmured in a mocking tone. 'We're not interested in playing games. Now open your legs.'

Shaking her head furiously from side to side, Lisa remained defiant. 'The hell I will, you bastards.'

There was a moment of silence, then one of the men said to the other, 'If she won't cooperate it looks as though we'll have to use force.'

Before Lisa could even begin to wonder what he meant, she felt strong hands prising her legs apart. Her heart began to beat wildly. God, the shame was unbearable, almost as poignant as her fear.

Just as she dreaded, a hand slid between her legs, an insistent finger sliding into the furrow between her outer labia. Again she tried to wriggle. All she could think about was getting away. Fuck Akira, fuck everything! She just wanted to get the hell out of there.

The finger slid into her vagina, aided by the slickness of her own moisture which her body created regardless of her anxiety.

'Hell, she's wet,' the man exclaimed.

Whimpering with shame, Lisa felt her knees sag. Perhaps she should try to make her mind go blank, just let them get on with it until they'd had enough. Just then another terrible thought struck her. What if they didn't stop at touching, what if they tried to rape her?

Never before had Lisa been in a sexual situation that was not of her own making. She was used to calling the shots, or at least being a willing participant. This was all so horrible she didn't think she could bear it. *I want to die*, she thought dramatically, *I want to simply expire right here and now.*

No such luck, she realised. The men were intent on discovering her body, it seemed, their fingers travelling everywhere, into every little crease and crevice. She felt her buttocks being forced apart and a questing finger probe her anus. The other man still continued to finger her vagina, probing deeper and deeper, adding a second finger, then a third, twisting and turning, scissoring apart.

Despite her fear and loathing she felt a familiar warmth creep over her. *Oh, please God*, she moaned inside her head, *don't let my body betray me.*

'Don't try to pretend you're not enjoying this.'

She wasn't sure which man spoke, although by now she thought it hardly mattered.

'I'm not. I told you to leave me alone,' she said through gritted teeth.

Both men laughed harshly and she fumed at their arrogance. A thumb brushed over her outer labia and wriggled between them. It began to stroke her clitoris. Almost immediately she felt herself responding, the treacherous little pleasure bud swelling and hardening.

'You can't pretend you don't like that.'

Lisa shook her head from side to side in dumb protest. The finger left her anus but her sigh of relief was quickly tempered by another whimper of shame as more fingers pressed open her labia and began to stroke her soft inner flesh. They were both touching her sex now, probing, fingering, stroking – oh, God!

A shameful wave of heat engulfed her, the waves of her climax leaving her sobbing and trembling in their grasp which was the only thing that kept her upright. Her legs were like jelly, her bones soft as though the heat of her orgasm had melted them completely. She felt so totally bereft of her senses that she hardly heard the words spoken next, or felt the fingers slide away from her pulsating sex.

'I think it's time we took her through to Mr Tanaka.'

Only vaguely aware of what was happening, she felt the same strong hands grasp her under her armpits and beneath her thighs, holding her legs wide apart as they raised her off the ground. She heard the sound of a door opening, felt the movement of the men carrying her forward and then the distinctive sweet perfume of burning joss sticks touched her nostrils.

The aroma seemed to clear her mind and in the next instant she gasped with relief as she heard Akira's voice. He was speaking Japanese and she heard another voice answer in the same language. It was a much older voice, with a singsong quality about it. Her blushes returned with a vengeance as she realised yet another person was there to witness the shameful display of her body.

Soft lips touched her forehead, her cheeks and finally her mouth.

'Akira!' She almost sobbed with relief.

'Yes, little one.'

His presence gave her the wherewithal to speak properly for the first time in what seemed like an age.

'Please, Akira. Tell your men to let me go. They grabbed me as soon as I arrived. They assaulted me. They . . .'

Akira interrupted her smoothly. 'Hush, Lisa. I know. I have been watching everything.'

It was then she remembered his apartment was equipped with a closed-circuit surveillance system.

She began to squirm again. 'How could you, Akira – how could you let them?'

225

His soft laugh filled the darkness that kept her at an unbreachable distance from him.

'Was it that bad, Lisa?' he said evenly. 'You still came, remember.'

An anguished sob tore from her throat. 'I couldn't help it. That wasn't me. That was my body.'

A finger stroked the length of her torso, from the base of her throat to her navel. 'Your mind and body are not independent of each other, Lisa. Surely you realise that?'

'You don't mean to suggest I enjoyed it?' Feeling angry and horrified at the possibility that what Akira said might be right, she spat the words out. Her imagination picked up the inscrutable smile on his face. 'Don't look like that,' she said, still angry.

He laughed again but his laugh was more loving than derisory and Lisa felt the fight seep out of her, leaving her bereft and helpless.

'Can you ask your men to put me down now?' she asked.

Again, Akira said something in Japanese and she felt herself being carried and then lowered onto something soft and wide. Something covered with rubber.

She felt around her with her hands. 'What is this?'

A movement beside her and then Akira's soft caress comforted her as he stroked his hands across her breasts and down over her stomach. As she straightened her legs, her thigh muscles began to protest.

'I don't want you to close your legs, Lisa,' Akira said, his gentle hands parting her thighs again.

'But—'

'I have another little surprise for you.'

Her stomach knotting tightly, she gazed in the direction of his voice. 'What?'

She trembled as his hands moved to the thatch of thick, black curls which covered her mound. One hand slipped lower, between her legs, cupping her sex. Almost against her will, she moaned.

'This has got to go, Lisa,' Akira said, the fingers of his free hand plucking at her pubic hair.

It took a moment or two for his words to sink into her brain. 'Go?'

'Yes,' Akira said softly. 'I have asked a good friend of mine. My barber, Yamamoto San, to denude you of this silky bush.'

Sometimes she really enjoyed his flowery way of speaking, at other times it really annoyed her. This was one of those times.

'Do you mean shave me?' she demanded angrily. 'Well, no thanks. I don't want to be shaved.'

Akira's fingers sank into her vagina, the surprise action eliciting an involuntary whimper.

'But I want it,' he said. 'Surely you would not deny me the pleasure of seeing your gorgeous body unadorned – open to me in all its glory?'

She thought hard. It had crossed her mind in the past to try shaving herself, or at least trimming her pubic hair into a more pleasing shape – perhaps a heart. Nevertheless, she didn't welcome the prospect of a complete stranger attacking her most secret flesh with a razor.

'I will take your blindfold off so that you can watch,' Akira said. 'You will see there is nothing to worry about. Yamamoto San is a master of his craft – an artist.'

Lisa felt his fingers leave her body and in the next instant they were pushing the eye mask up, away from her eyes. As Akira removed the scrap of black silk, she blinked several times, trying to focus. Again the lighting in the vast living room was subdued, provided by small clusters of beeswax candles which stood grouped together on several side tables.

Glancing down, to the left and right of her, she found that she was sitting on a low examination table, of the kind doctors use but wider. Across the room on one of the leather couches sat an old Japanese man, his face etched with numerous deep lines from the depths of which glittered a pair of surprisingly alert eyes. It was then she remembered that she was completely naked and sitting with her legs apart.

Hurriedly moving to close them again, she sighed with relief when Akira didn't try to stop her. Nor did he protest when she placed her palms flat on her thighs so that her arms obscured her breasts.

Akira nodded in the direction of the old man. 'Lisa, Mr Yamamoto.'

The old man nodded. '*Dozo, yoroshku. Hiroshi desu.*'

'He is inviting you to call him by his first name, Hiroshi,' Akira said.

Feeling very inscrutable herself all of a sudden, Lisa remembered her manners and bowed her head.

With a sudden change in demeanour, Akira clapped his hands together briskly and issued a few words in Japanese to which Hiroshi stood up and hurried over to stand at the other side of the examination table.

'Do you agree to this, Lisa?' Akira asked, his dark eyes compelling her to agree.

Silently, she nodded. The idea of being shaved by this wizened old man filled her with trepidation but she trusted Akira and if he thought it was a good idea then who was she to argue? It might be nice, she thought, and especially nice for her lover whose tongue and fingers would be given instant access to her most sensitive parts.

Thinking as much of her own pleasure as Akira's, she didn't protest as Hiroshi picked up a low stool and placed it by her feet. It was then she noticed that another side table was already laid out with the tools of his trade: a bowl of water from which rose a curl of steam, several thick hand towels, a shaving brush, an oblong bar of white soap and lastly a wicked-looking cutthroat razor. She paled as she saw it lying there, its mother-of-pearl handle and steel blade shimmering against the background of the black velvet drawstring bag on which it rested.

Hiroshi muttered a few words in Japanese to Akira who, in turn, translated them for Lisa's benefit.

'He wants you to sit right at the very edge of the table,' he said.

Trying to ignore the surge of anxiety that gripped her, Lisa shuffled forward on her bottom obediently.

'Now lay back,' Akira said.

She did as he asked.

Hiroshi said a few more words and Akira said, 'Now don't be shy, Lisa. He wants you to open your legs as wide as you can.'

While she allowed the shocking suggestion to sink in, Akira walked away and returned with two hardbacked chairs. Positioning them either side of Hiroshi, Akira told her to put her feet on the chairs.

'No, Akira, I can't do this,' Lisa said plaintively. Now it came to it, she really couldn't bear the idea of the old man sitting between her widespread thighs, his wizened face exactly level with her naked sex.

Akira squatted down beside her and took her hand. 'Please, Lisa. Do this for me,' he said beguilingly. 'Pretend you are having a medical examination or something. Imagine Hiroshi is your gynaecologist.'

Oh, God, how can I? Lisa thought. The location with its subdued lighting and flickering candles, the scent of jasmine and patchouli, and the presence of Akira and this strange old man were not conducive to imagining that she was in the stark, impersonal setting of a doctor's surgery.

Then again, how could she not? She wanted to please Akira. She wanted to see and feel what it was like to be denuded of her pubic hair – the thick bush she had worn since puberty. And most of all, she longed to discover the difference this new dimension would add to their lovemaking.

With a small sigh of resignation she said, 'Okay, why not?' and slowly opened her legs, her feet fumbling for the seats of the chairs.

For a moment she concentrated on staring at the ceiling, or rather into the blackness that seemed as deep and everlasting as the night sky. Then she glanced down, along the length of her body to the point where Hiroshi sat, his beady eyes trained on the triangle of hair covering her mound.

Shuffling his stool forward a little, the old man reached out and stroked an assessing palm over her mound. Cringing with embarrassment, Lisa watched as he fingered the glossy curls, rubbing them between thumb and forefinger as though gauging their quality. *What does it matter?* she thought. *The hair will not exist in a minute, it will lay in a little pile on the floor.*

At regular visits to her hairdresser, she often watched in fascination as the ends of her hair were trimmed – the dusky curls falling, making little question marks on the white floor tiles. Now she noticed that strewn around the end of the table were large sheets of white paper. It was easier therefore to imagine that she had gone along to the salon for her usual trim – but without the customary blow dry afterwards, she chuckled to herself despite her trepidation.

Hiroshi's fingers smoothed the curly hair, the bony tips brushing the curls this way and that. He explained, via Akira, that he was just ascertaining their natural direction of growth. Then his fingers slipped lower, brushing over her outer labia and sliding into the cleft between her buttocks.

'Remove all of it,' Akira instructed as he stood up to watch the path the old man's fingers took.

Lisa flinched from Hiroshi's touch. She was loath to consider the exhibition that her body provided in such an ignominious position. Every millimetre of her private flesh was exposed, every tiny, blushing part. And there was Hiroshi, his face between her legs, his fingers busily engaged as he explored and appraised her sex.

To her shame, he ran his fingers up the sides of her sex,

where her thighs met her groin and in the next instant they pinched her fleshy outer lips and pulled them apart. Rubbing them between the thumb and forefinger of each hand, he said a few words to Akira.

'He said you have much hair,' Akira explained, with just the slightest hint of amusement in his voice.

Lisa immediately felt her stomach knotting. 'Does that matter?' she asked. 'Does it mean he can't shave me after all?'

Akiras shook his head. 'Of course not,' he said lightly, 'it was merely an observation.'

'Well, do you think you could ask him to stop fondling me and just get on with it?' she retorted, feeling quite annoyed at being treated like an object rather than a person.

At that Akira laughed aloud and reached out to stroke the backs of his knuckles along her cheekbone. 'Don't get so het up, Lisa,' he admonished. 'I can assure you Hiroshi is not looking at you sexually.'

She sincerely doubted that but held her tongue. Instead she closed her eyes and concentrated on Akira's caress which still continued – his knuckles brushing back and forth across her cheek in a soothing gesture. For just a moment or two it helped her forget about the other man's hands between her thighs.

Chapter Thirteen

Soothing music flooded the room – a light oriental melody that made Lisa think of water gardens complete with tinkling waterfalls, giant floating lily-pads and a woman in traditional costume leaning over the rail of a small humped bridge, perhaps waiting for her lover.

It was a romantic image but try as she might she couldn't put herself in the woman's place. It wasn't in her nature to wait around for anyone and it was far removed from the reality of her situation.

Akira had gone to sit on the sofa where he had been seated earlier. Picking up a black remote-control handset, he had pressed a button which operated a hidden music system. Then he had reclined upon the sofa, a soft, inscrutable smile suffusing his face as he prepared to watch Hiroshi perform his art on Lisa's body.

She felt tense but the music was gradually calming her. Hiroshi had worked up a lather with the bar of soap and now he was gently brushing her pubis in a circular motion, piling it up with thick, creamy bubbles. Before he sat down Akira gave her a small pillow so that, with her head raised slightly, she could watch the old barber at work. Now, when she saw him pick up the cutthroat razor and test the blade against his middle fingertip, she felt a twinge of anxiety.

Glancing across the room to Akira she noticed he gave her a slight nod which she supposed was intended to reassure her. It would take a damn sight more than that, she thought ruefully – allowing a complete stranger to attack her most delicate parts with a razor was not, to her mind, exactly conducive to relaxation.

As she watched the blade cut a swathe through the lather coating her pubic mound she tensed, but to her surprise felt nothing at all. Not the slightest nick nor scrape against her newly bared flesh. Hiroshi paused to rinse the blade and, as he raised it over her for the second time, she noticed how it reflected the flickering candlelight. Bony fingers held her flesh taut and another pale path was sliced through the thick black bush.

Already there seemed to be very little of her pubic hair left on her mound. From where she lay it looked pink and vulnerable, reminding her for an instant of new born mice, their shivering bodies pallid, almost translucent without the benefit of fur.

'How often will I have to shave myself?' she found herself asking, in a voice that sounded too matter of fact to belong to someone who was still quivering inside with a mixture of shame and trepidation.

To her surprise Akira answered straight away, leading her to wonder how many times he had experienced the shaving of a woman before.

'Ideally, once a day,' he said, 'if you do it that often it will only take a minute or so.'

This prompted her to ask another question. 'Why, Akira?'

'Why shave so often?'

'No. Why do you want me to be shaved at all?'

The inscrutable smile didn't falter. 'Because I prefer it.'

'But why – what difference does it make?'

He sighed softly. 'You'll see.'

The words were loaded with such promise that Lisa trembled visibly.

Hiroshi clicked his tongue impatiently against the roof of his mouth and raised the blade. He spoke a few curt words in Japanese which Akira immediately translated.

'He says if you want to keep all your feminine parts intact you must try not to move.'

Lisa muttered, 'Sorry,' and willed herself to relax again.

Now her head was filled with the prospect of herself and Akira afterwards – once this ordeal was over and it was just the two of them alone. Despite the fact that the old man sat between her legs, she felt her vagina moistening in anticipation, her clitoris rousing itself.

The barber noticed the signs of her stimulation and spoke to Akira again.

'Hiroshi tells me you are becoming sexually excited,' Akira said bluntly, as though the old man had commented on the weather and not her body.

Lisa blushed. 'I— I,' she stammered.

Hiroshi interrupted with something.

'Don't be embarrassed, Lisa,' Akira urged. 'He says he is used to women responding in such a physical way to the shaving process.'

She wanted to put him right, to tell him the real reason

for her excitement, but the words died on her lips. Let the old man think what he liked. Perhaps the occasional job like this made his career worthwhile. After all, there were precious few areas of employment which involved looking at and touching a strange woman's sex. Hiroshi should consider himself lucky and probably did.

Whirling the soapy brush around and around, Hiroshi covered one side of her groin with lather. Then he began the swiping and dipping process again, cleaning the blade each time after a little bit more of her had been shorn.

Feeling slightly more uncomfortable, Lisa had to fight the urge to move. Hiroshi's fingers seemed to be all over her sex now, smoothing out the skin, holding it taut as he practised his craft. He was working his way gradually lower, closer to the vulnerable area around her vagina. Now she worried that he might nick her most sensitive flesh and consequently felt her arousal die a little.

Having finally attended to both sides without accident or injury, Hiroshi sat back and smiled, a hand smoothing the bare skin thoughtfully. Turning his head, he directed another comment at Akira who slowly got to his feet and came over to inspect the result.

Glancing up at Lisa's face – which was wide-eyed and curious – he smiled right into her eyes, melting her from the inside out.

'You look beautiful,' he said soothingly. He too ran an assessing palm between her legs, his gaze unflinching. 'Now there is just the last little bit to be done and then we can have some fun.'

Tearing her gaze away from his, Lisa struggled to sit up and peer between her own legs. It seemed so strange, the flesh so pink where it was normally shadowed with hair, and she could clearly see the folds of her inner labia nestling between her outer lips like a closed bloom waiting for the moment to blossom.

'Isn't that it then?' she asked.

'No, Not quite,' Akira said in answer to her question. 'There is still the small amount of fuzz which runs up the cleft between your buttocks which needs to be removed.'

Lisa quaked at his description. Of course, she knew there was hair on that part of her body. Only a light fuzz, as Akira described but surely that didn't need to be shaved off as well.

'I want you completely denuded,' Akira said evenly, when she voiced her objection.

Pausing only to drop a light kiss on her lips, he moved down to the end of the table. He and Hiroshi exchanged a few words in Japanese and in the next instant, Lisa saw Akira's hands dive between her legs and felt her buttocks being pulled apart.

All her old feelings of shame, which she thought she had managed to overcome by now, came flooding back with a vengeance. Some things were just too private to be displayed to all and sundry, she thought anxiously as Hiroshi's gaze immediately became transfixed by the new area of her body to be shorn.

Again his fingers stroked and smoothed her flesh. Then he glanced away, picked up the razor and the whole process began again. This time Lisa concentrated on staring at the ceiling. She couldn't see anything properly anyway, Akira's slight body obscured her view and she wasn't sure she wanted to watch even if she could. Finally she heard a couple of satisfied sighs. Firstly from Hiroshi as he rinsed the blade for the last time, folded the razor and placed it carefully in its velvet drawstring bag. And then Akira sighed – a pleasurable sound that indicated his satisfaction with the end result. His fingers stroked up and down her cleft for a moment or two and then he let go of her buttocks and gave them an indulgent smack. Despite her discomfort at the situation, Lisa heard herself moan faintly.

Now that it was all over she felt her anticipation growing by leaps and bounds. As soon as Hiroshi left, she and Akira would be able to examine her newly exposed body parts at their leisure – especially Akira, with his clever fingers and expert tongue. She shivered.

In the next instant she shivered again as something cold and wet dripped onto her denuded mound and slowly trickled between her thighs.

'A little oil to moisturise your skin,' Akira explained, when he saw the surprise she felt reflected in her eyes.

She hoped Akira would massage her body with the oil but it seemed that was still part of Hiroshi's job. Trying not to think too hard, she felt his fingers smoothing the unctuous liquid into her flesh. He seemed to take a long time about it, massaging the oil in tiny circles, covering every portion of her sex. She winced as the tips of his fingers brushed over her clitoris and skated around the slick rim of her vagina.

All of a sudden, one finger slipped inside her. It took her by surprise and she assumed it was an accident, the fingertip slipping on the oily surface of her skin. But the finger stayed and finally she had to give Akira a pleading look before Hiroshi removed it with an overt look of regret.

He murmured something to Akira which made the other man laugh aloud – a sound she seldom heard – and then the old man began to rummage in a bag by his feet.

'What's going on – what is he doing?' Lisa asked anxiously.

Akira turned and smiled at her, one hand coming to rest protectively on her stomach, the other reaching out to stroke a stray tendril of hair away from her face.

'Relax, Lisa,' he said. 'Hiroshi has a little gift for you. Something a bit different which we both think you will like.'

Wanting so much to be alone with Akira at long last, Lisa doubted his promise but her lover added, 'Hiroshi said if he were twenty years younger he would take great delight in fucking you. He has been very complimentary about your appearance, your body, especially here.' The hand that rested on her stomach moved to pat her sex.

She flinched. Thank God the old barber wasn't twenty years younger, what was Akira thinking of letting him talk about her in that way? Despite the fact that she thought she had a handle on things, her cheeks flushed with mortification.

Glancing at Hiroshi's hands she saw him raise something long and white, something that looked suspiciously penis-shaped.

'It is a dildo,' Akira said in reply to her unasked question. 'Hiroshi said he had it specially hand-carved from an elephant tusk – before the practice was outlawed of course,' he added unnecessarily. Lisa couldn't have cared less about the aesthetics of the instrument, or the fact that the ivory trade was now illegal.

Akira took the dildo from Hiroshi and handed it to Lisa for her to examine. About eight inches long and a good inch and a half in diameter, it felt cool and smooth, totally unlike any similar item she had handled before.

'Please, Akira,' she said, 'tell him his job is finished now. I want us to be alone.' She hated the pleading note in her voice and the fact that her lover seemed to find her request amusing.

'You English have a saying, don't knock it till you've tried it, I believe?' he murmured, taking the dildo out of her hands.

'Akira!' The pleading note was replaced by a warning tone.

His response was a darkening of his expression: his eyes becoming as hard and dense as black marble and his mouth settling into a determined line.

Lisa knew when she was beaten.

She watched wide-eyed with trepidation as Akira handed the dildo back to Hiroshi. The old man bowed his head briefly and muttered a few more words in Japanese. Akira bowed back and in the next instant Lisa felt something cool and smooth nudge the slick entrance to her vagina. Forcing herself to relax, she felt the ivory wand slide effortlessly into her honeyed channel.

At once she began to squirm and buck, her vaginal muscles contracting, bearing down against the intrusion. She heard Akira draw in his breath sharply and watched as he walked across the room, opened a drawer in a black lacquered console and withdrew something which he concealed from her as he walked back to the table.

'What have you got, Akira?' she asked, trying to sound calmer than she felt.

With increasing anxiety she watched as her lover sank to his haunches, only the top of his glossy black head visible from the position in which she lay. Then she felt his fingers brush her left ankle followed by the soft caress of silk. All at once realisation struck her as the silk wound tightly around her ankle. He was tying her to the table leg. A moment later the same was happening to her right ankle and when she tried to kick out she found, just as she expected, that she couldn't move her legs.

He came to stand by her head and ignored her questioning expression as he slowly unwound another long strip of black silk and drew it thoughtfully through his fingers. All the words that screamed inside her head and longed to tumble to her lips died instantly. He reached for her wrists and she let him, acknowledging that in a moment she would be truly helpless and there was not a damn thing she could do about it.

'Please, Akira,' she tried one last time but he kept his inscrutable gaze averted from her pleading one and proceeded to tie her wrists.

As he tied the silk, he and Hiroshi spoke in low murmurs. Then she felt the dildo move inside her with a slow in and out action that stimulated the sensitive walls of her vagina. Almost against her will, she felt her body respond with a slow warmth that crept up the exposed flesh between her labia and suffused her whole pelvis.

Glancing down the length of her spread-eagled body, she saw Hiroshi, still seated between her widespread thighs, his right hand working the stick of ivory inside her. A powerful feeling of shame flooded her as his left hand moved up to her clitoris and his fingers began to gently stimulate her.

'No, please, no,' Lisa moaned quietly.

The atmosphere around her was tense with expectancy, the hushed room with its flickering light filled only with the echo of her whimpers and the slick, wet sound of her desperate body as the dildo slid in and out.

Akira's hands cupped her breasts, his deft fingers plucking at her distended nipples until they felt as though they were on fire. Her arousal was mounting, despite her efforts to fight it as hard as she could. Gradually her whimpers turned to groans of encouragement. It no longer mattered who or what stimulated her body, all she craved was the pleasure and release that orgasm would bring to her body.

'See, Lisa,' Akira said gently, the old light of desire returning to his eyes, 'I told you that you would enjoy it.'

Instantly, she wanted to deny it but she knew it was useless to even try. Her clitoris felt as hard and as close to bursting point as her nipples. Her pelvis ached with desire and her sex screamed silently for release. Moments later, her body conceded, tightening up and then exploding in a surge of heat and lust that left her trembling and covered with a thin sheen of perspiration.

Akira leaned forward and planted a gentle kiss in the middle of her forehead, then he kissed her closed eyelids and finally his lips commanded her mouth for a long, searching kiss. As his tongue jousted with hers, Lisa felt the dildo slide from her body. Slowly, Akira took his mouth from hers and stood up, his expression one of pleasure and contentment, as though he had been the one who had just reached nirvana.

Hiroshi sat back and wiped the stick of ivory on a small white hand towel. Then he replaced the dildo almost reverently in its box, packed away the last of his things and stood up. Bowing formally to Akira and then to her, he bade them both goodnight in English.

Lisa smiled back at him wanly, she wanted to say something – to thank him perhaps – but she didn't feel as though she had the strength to open her mouth. Instead, she inclined her head forward and allowed just the faintest of smiles to touch her lips and eyes. Although it wasn't much it seemed to satisfy the old man and he smiled down at her as he reached out to take Akira's hand and shake it.

The two men moved away from the table and Lisa heard them talking as Akira showed Hiroshi to the door. A moment later she heard the door open and close and then Akira was back beside her, his expression inscrutable once more. To her relief he didn't repeat the words, 'I told you so,' but proceeded to untie the knots that had kept her bound and helpless to his will.

With some difficulty, Lisa sat up. Reaching behind her she rubbed the small of her back and was gratified when she felt Akira's fingers, and then his lips, touch her there.

'You pleased me tonight, Lisa. You really pleased me,' he said, whispering against her back.

Suffused with pleasure at his compliment, the shame of the past couple of hours already receding, she smiled like a cat and arched her neck to allow the ends of her hair to tickle his cheek.

'I didn't want it though, Akira,' she murmured, still moving her head slowly from side to side, the movement easing the tension in her neck and shoulders. 'I did tell you but you wouldn't listen. I don't know how I feel about that.'

Akira straightened up and stood by her side, his hand sliding down the length of her throat, her torso, her belly, until finally his fingertips rested lightly on her hairless mound. He stroked her softly.

'You enjoyed it.'

'Not all of it.'

'Yes. You did.'

'No.'

She sighed as his middle finger slipped between her labia and began to stroke her clitoris. Still hypersensitive from the powerful climax she had experienced, this tiny part of her body seemed to recoil from his touch.

'You like this?'

She nodded. 'Yes, but that's because it's you and I want you to do it.'

'Sometimes we don't know what we want until we try it,' he persisted, his finger making small circular movements. 'We all need to learn and usually that means we need someone to show us the first time.'

Lisa raised her head and stared straight into his eyes. She hoped to see something there, although she didn't quite know what. Compassion? Desire? Love? Try as she might she couldn't see any of those things and of all of them the latter was the one she least expected. All at once she felt restless again, the sense that she was missing out on something vital beginning to gnaw at her mind.

She couldn't help wondering why she couldn't just be content with what she had: success and pleasure high on the list. Akira was a good lover, she enjoyed their times together – usually – and he made no demands on her. He gave and gave, asking very little in return, and yet she felt as though he had somehow demanded too much of her that evening. What he wanted, he had just taken, without truly considering her objections – and that rankled. What's more, it really hurt.

Ignoring his fingers which still worked between her legs, she moved to get off the table. To her relief, Akira removed his hand and waited until she was standing upright before reaching out and gripping her by the shoulders. He pulled her to him and held her but Lisa felt wooden. She stood stiffly in his embrace, accepting his kiss but not making any effort to return it.

Eventually Akira sighed and broke away. 'It's no good throwing a tantrum, Lisa,' he said in a condescending tone that made her want to scream abuse at him. 'You know you enjoyed it and you know you want me.'

Staring at him levelly, Lisa tried to unravel the jumble of conflicting thoughts that jostled in her head, all anxious to become words. Finally, she gave up and walked across to the sofa where Akira had been seated earlier. With a sigh of defeat she sat down heavily, crossing her arms and legs simultaneously, her expression grim.

As though he intended to deliberately ignore her, Akira began to tidy away the few things that Hiroshi had left: a couple of white hand towels, the bowl of warm water which had now turned as stone cold as Lisa's face. He took the things into the bathroom and a few moments later returned and began to blow out the candles. When only the group on the side table next to Lisa remained alight he went into the kitchen and came back carrying a bottle of champagne and two crystal flutes.

Apparently concentrating on pouring the champagne he said nothing but as soon as Lisa had grudgingly accepted a glass from him he sat down on the edge of the coffee table, took one of her feet and began to massage it slowly, his eyes fixed on that small portion of her body.

Despite her anger, Lisa felt the tension slowly ebbing away, to be replaced by a vague feeling of remorse. For a few more minutes there was silence and then she spoke.

'I want you to make love to me, Akira.'

He glanced up then and she registered the look of surprise on his face. In the past they had never made love, only fucked, but it was clear that he recognised the distinction she had made.

With just the slightest incline of his head he put down her foot, stood up and stretched out his hand to her.

'Come,' he said, 'I think the bedroom would be the best place for us.'

The room was in complete darkness, the curtains drawn against the night. Akira didn't bother to switch on the light, or set a flame to any candles which she knew were grouped in small clusters around the room. All she could sense was the sound of their breathing – hers shallow and rapid, his smooth and even. Even though she had been in his bedroom many times before, the darkness disoriented her and she was grateful that Akira led her by the hand to the bed, then urged her gently down.

Feeling unaccountably nervous all of a sudden, she perched on the edge of the bed, one hand feeling the soft cotton of his black duvet, the other still resting lightly in his. He let go of her hand and she sensed him sit on the bed beside her, felt it give slightly under his body weight. Then she felt just the lightest of touches on her head as he began to stroke her hair and speak to her so softly that she had to strain her ears at times to catch all his words.

'Lisa, Lisa. Do you think that I don't love you, darling? Do you imagine that I wanted to humiliate you solely for my own pleasure? Can't you allow yourself to admit that there were at least parts of this evening that you enjoyed? I thought you were a sexual woman, Lisa. A truly sexual woman. Why do you deny yourself? Why can't you accept pleasure as it comes? There is no shame in what happened tonight, my darling. Only pleasure. Can't you see that? Didn't you feel even the slightest excitement?'

Although he couldn't see it, she knew he felt the movement of her head as she nodded slowly.

When she didn't speak he continued in the same soothing tone, one hand stroking her hair, the other her thigh. 'You are a beautiful young woman, Lisa. Very beautiful. You know that. You know how much I think of you. Desire you. Always. Being apart from you for so much of the time is often torture. I stand alone at the window in my apartment in Tokyo, or New York, when you are here in London and I think of you – imagining you out there, somewhere. I ache inside because I can't have you with me. I can't touch you. And, oh, how I long to touch you. You have the most exquisite body, Lisa. So firm, so voluptuous. Your skin so smooth, like satin. My nostrils fill with the memory of your scent and I feel like crying out my need for you. It pains me, Lisa. It hurts. I want you so badly I feel as though I am being ripped in two.'

His words floated around her like a mist, shrouding her naked body with a fine layer of awakening desire. He meant them. She knew that without a doubt. Akira wasn't a man to mince words, neither did he pour out his heart for no reason.

Turning her head in the direction of his voice, she felt a surge of happiness as her lips met his. His mouth opened under hers and his hands moved to cup her face. Then one slid around to the back of her head and began to gather up handfuls of her hair. Bunching it. Holding it in a tight grip that pulled at the roots.

Lisa gave an involuntary moan. This was what she and Akira were all about. Slow, sensuous sex. Not the blatant humiliation of earlier. For a moment or two she allowed her mind to dwell once again on the evening's surprising chain of events. Then, unaccountably, remembering the way Akira's two bodyguards had grabbed her, the way they had spoken about her body and the secret places they had touched, suddenly sent desire zinging through her. Feeling helplessly wanton, she groaned against Akira's lips and turned so that she could press her naked breasts against him.

There was an unmistakable urgency in her movements that transmitted itself easily to her lover. That much was obvious as he groaned too, an uncharacteristic response for him. And he pulled her sideways, so that she fell with him onto the wide, black bed.

The hand that had cupped her face now slid down the

length of her arm, stroking the skin so softly that she felt an answering tingle in her toes and then in the pit of her belly as he nibbled her bottom lip so gently, ever so gently.

Lisa gasped, 'Akira!' as she felt herself slipping into the hazy realms of ecstasy.

His touch was so light – barely there. His fingers skimming her shoulders, her arms, her torso, before finally coming to rest lightly on her breasts.

She felt them slide across her skin, around and around, describing circles that became smaller and smaller until his fingertips simply traced a continuous path around each nipple. The buds hardened immediately, straining towards the unseen fingers, aching for his touch.

Pushing her gently so that she rolled onto her back, he lowered his head and she felt the silky, soft caress of his hair upon her breasts as he took each nipple into his mouth in turn and sucked them gently. Gradually, the despair and confusion that she had felt earlier began to dissipate, to be replaced by the slow, inexorable growth of desire.

'Yes, Akira. Yes,' she found herself moaning, arching her back so that she could press her breasts against his mouth.

In answer to her plea he cupped them, forcing them up and together so that he could flick his tongue remorselessly over her nipples. To Lisa, they felt as though they were on fire, aching to be touched, to be sucked.

'More,' she gasped, her own hands reaching for her breasts, replacing his so that he was free to explore the rest of her body.

For a few more minutes he continued to lathe the taut buds with his tongue, his fingers delving between her legs and exploring her sex. Then all at once he sat up and then stood. Lisa couldn't see him in the all-pervading blackness but she could sense his movements and she could hear the soft padding sound his feet made on the thick carpet as he moved about the room. There followed the sound of a cupboard opening and closing. Then another. Then the clinking, jangling noises of objects being assembled.

'Lie back, Lisa,' Akira said, his voice sounding strangely compelling in the darkness. 'Lie back and spread your legs.'

Thinking he was probably undressing and planned to fuck her straight away, she complied eagerly. Stretching her arms above her head and her legs wide apart, she waited.

Suddenly a light went on, piercing the blackness and momentarily blinding her. It shone between her legs, or rather the beam of light was trained directly on a certain place between her legs. Her recently shaven sex.

'What are you doing, Akira? What's going on now?' Her voice wavered as all her previous fears resurfaced.

His response was soothing but firm. 'I want to photograph you, darling.'

'But—' she started to protest. He silenced her with soothing words.

'Hush, Lisa. Don't worry. Relax. Your cunt looks so beautiful without its hair. I can see everything. Everything, Lisa. Every tiny feminine fold. And I want to have something to look at when you're not with me.

Something exquisitely personal. I want this, Lisa. I want it. Please don't deny me the pleasure of your body.'

She sighed. It was hard to resist him. Impossible to ignore the persuasiveness of his words. At that moment she felt as though he truly loved her and she him, but would she feel the same way later, she wondered? If she let him photograph her now, like this, would she regret her acquiescence in the cold light of day?

He took her silence as acceptance and she heard the rapid whirr of the camera as he took a series of shots just as she was. Then he began speaking again in the same low, hypnotic tone, asking her to move this way and that.

'Please, bend your knees, Lisa,' he urged. When she complied he added, 'That's it. That's beautiful. Oh, so beautiful, darling. I can see everything. Let me bring the camera a little closer.'

Glancing down she saw how close he held the camera to her sex. As far as she was aware, that was the only part of her he had photographed.

'Are you sure these are just for your own enjoyment, Akira?' she asked tentatively, despising herself for not trusting him implicitly.

He was quick to reassure her. 'Of course, my darling. How could you think anything else? Do you believe I want others to see your gorgeous body? No. These photographs are just for me.'

It occurred to her that he hadn't so far shown any reticence about allowing others to see and even touch her body but under the circumstances – in the warm, seductive darkness – it was the easiest thing in the world to believe him.

Then he adjusted the light so that it shone upwards. He urged her to sit up and she found herself forced to look away from the piercing beam which now flooded her face and breasts with a brilliant wash of light. He knelt in front of her and the camera began to whirr again, capturing all of her for posterity. When he was apparently satisfied, he turned off the light and put everything away again before lighting a small cluster of candles that stood on a table by the bed.

Now she could see him as he moved. Watch him as he undressed completely and climbed onto the bed beside her.

'Now we make love,' he said, sliding a determined hand over her torso and down between her legs.

For a moment he cupped her hairless mound. His lips moving as he made appreciative noises. Then he began to stroke and finger her very gently until she found herself whimpering with barely restrained desire.

Chapter Fourteen

Grinding her pelvis gently at first and then more urgently, Lisa worked her hot sex against his fingers, desperate for the orgasm that teased her. Time and again it flared then died before actually peaking and she felt certain that Akira was controlling her body with the same assured efficiency that he used when managing his global business empire.

She didn't want to beg. She wouldn't. This time she would make sure she took her pleasure as and when she wanted it. Urging her body violently against his, she manged to roll him over onto his back and then reached for his cock. Ignoring the fingers at work deep inside her, she manoeuvred herself around so that she could take his hardness in her mouth.

For a moment Akira protested and then conceded just as quickly as Lisa wet her lips and slid them expertly over his glans and down his shaft, taking as much of him as she could possibly manage. As she concentrated on relaxing her throat and sucking hard, she felt him rise inexorably towards orgasm. She knew him well enough by now to be able to distinguish the little sounds, the slight arching of his back and other body movements that heralded crisis point.

Then she stopped and raised her head.

'Lisa!' Akira's voice sounded desperate.

Burying her face in the crook of her arm, she smothered a wicked smile. For a few moments she stayed like that, then she returned her mouth to his cock, bringing him once again to the point of climax before stopping and raising her head to gaze ingenuously at him.

It seemed her lover was no fool. By the expression on his face she could tell he knew exactly what she was doing.

'Bitch,' he murmured harshly before softening his tone, 'clever little bitch. You want to play games do you?'

Shaking her head determinedly, she forced herself to stare straight into his eyes without wavering.

'No,' she said softly, 'but what's sauce for the goose is sauce for the gander.'

'Is that another one of your strange English expressions?'

'Yes. But it seems appropriate under the, er, the circumstances.' She was smiling now. A broad grin that was reflected by the glint in her eyes.

He smiled back and at once she realised that somehow, during the course of the evening they had overcome the last invisible barrier that had existed between them. There was nothing inscrutable about him now. His desire was evident, his expression a veritable open book. All at once she realised how much she preferred him like that. She was a straightforward person. Straight talking. Straight thinking. All their previous game-playing had put her on edge and kept her there, she realised. And she liked this new development in their strange relationship a whole lot better.

Deciding that honesty was the best policy she told him what she was thinking.

Leaving his fingers inside her, he manoeuvred himself and her so that he was laying full length on top of her. There was a long pause when time seemed to stand still, the only things connecting them his fingers, the simultaneous gaze that held them both transfixed and an undeniable thread of sexual tension. He was the first to break it.

'I feel different too,' he said at long last. 'Calmer, more relaxed. I really believe I love you, Lisa. And you can rest assured, that's not an easy thing for me to admit. Everything I said before – all of it – is true.'

He paused, during which time she held her breath, then she felt his fingers leave her body to be replaced straight away by his hard cock. Slowly, ever so slowly, he began to move inside her and she exhaled with a deep sigh of pleasure.

'This feels so right, Akira,' she murmured.

He nodded gently, the soft ends of his hair brushing her face. 'I know. I can't explain what's changed. Or when it changed. I just know I can't let things carry on as before.' He paused again then added, 'I want you to marry me, Lisa. Lisa. *Lisa!*'

When she opened her eyes she realised straight away that she must have fainted. She remembered Akira moving inside her, remembered the sudden all-consuming heat of her orgasm and then the shock of his words. Then it seemed, at the moment of climax, she had passed out. The realisation made her laugh, albeit weakly, and he joined in her laughter.

'My lovemaking has never had that effect on a woman before,' he joked.

Shaking her head, Lisa smiled up at him. 'You know full well it wasn't that which made me faint, you arrogant bastard,' she replied fondly. 'Oh, God. This is incredible. What am I going to do?'

Akira started to move slowly inside her once again. 'Say yes,' he said simply. Pushing himself up onto his hands he began to thrust more urgently. 'Say yes, Lisa.'

She stayed silent for a moment but she couldn't ignore the movements of his body and wrapped her legs around his waist, the insistent thrusting of her pelvis urging him deeper and deeper.

For the duration of their lovemaking he seemed content with her silence. Perhaps he took it once again as acquiescence, she thought, remembering all the other times when he had done just that. But she hadn't agreed to his proposal, not literally or even inside her head. It seemed too much of a momentous decision to make on the spur of the moment.

All of a sudden Akira cried out and he came. After a few minutes he apparently gave up trying to coax a second climax out of her and slumped forward before rolling off her to lay on his back by her side.

'You haven't answered me,' he said finally. 'I must admit I feel a bit concerned about that.'

Lisa took a deep breath. 'I'm not quite sure what to say in all honesty,' she whispered softly, as though they could be overheard. 'Your proposal has taken me by surprise to say the least.' She rolled over onto her side, propped her head on her hand and gazed lovingly down at him. 'Do you mind if I say I want to think about it?'

He seemed genuinely surprised by her reticence. 'No, I don't mind,' he said. 'But I must admit I am surprised. I thought you would agree straight away. I am an excellent catch, you know?'

'I know,' she admitted. 'I know. But it wouldn't matter to me if you were dirt poor and had no prospects. That's not what love is all about as far as I'm concerned.'

'I'm aware of that.' Akira sat up and reached for a box of tissues. Handing a couple to Lisa, he proceeded to clean his wilting cock as he spoke. 'That's one of the things I love most about you, darling. You're one of the very few people I come into contact with who doesn't expect something from me all the time.'

She laughed then. 'How could I – you've already given me so much?'

Akira shook his head. 'Not *given*, Lisa,' he said firmly. 'The money and support I provided for Flights of Fancy was a business deal, nothing more. That wouldn't alter. You could go on running it just as you have been doing.'

'And you wouldn't mind?' she asked, unable to conceal her amazement. 'It wouldn't bother you that once a week I would be taking part in an orgy and in between times recruiting other men to join the team?'

'No.' He shook his head again, then sat up. Balling the used tissues in his hand he glanced down and added, 'That's just work, Lisa. It means nothing. Or at least, I assume it means nothing?'

For a moment her mind flickered over recent events and she found herself dwelling on the image of Rio. His hair, his eyes. The way he looked at her. The way he made love to her.

Reverting to form, Akira took her silence as agreement.

'Then where's the problem?' he said simply.

All at once Lisa began to struggle to her feet, her eyes scanning the room for her clothes. Then she remembered she had been stripped in the inner-lobby.

'I don't know,' she muttered. 'I don't know if there is a problem. I feel confused. I think I'd better go.'

'No, don't. Lisa, darling.' At once Akira was beside her, reaching out to her, trying to draw her back into the circle of his arms.

She shrugged him off. Then, feeling guilty, forced a smile. 'Look. It's late and I'm tired,' she said as evenly as she could. 'This has come as quite a surprise and I think I'd be better off back at my own place. I need to be alone for a bit. To have my own space where I can think.'

For a moment she thought he was going to protest. To try and persuade her to stay. But instead he gave a small gesture of defeat and moved toward the door. Opening it he let her pass and then went into the lobby himself to collect her clothes.

As he handed them to her, he gave her another one of his compelling smiles which this time she had no difficulty returning.

'I understand,' he said. 'Think about it. Take all the time you need. Then call me, okay?'

'Okay.' She pulled on her dress and waited while Akira helped her zip it up. Slipping on her shoes she leaned forward and planted a light kiss on his mouth. 'I promise I won't take too long about it, Akira,' she said. 'Just give me a day or so.'

'Alright, whatever.' He shrugged, a mite too nonchalantly, she thought, and then saw her to the lift. 'Just remember, I'll be here in London all week. You can reach me anytime.'

The lift was already there waiting for her to step inside. As the wrought-iron doors closed Lisa smiled back at Akira and raised her fingertips to her lips. At that moment, ridiculous though it seemed, she had the distinct impression that she might never see him again.

The next few weeks were extremely busy ones for Lisa. A fact for which she felt inordinately grateful. She was no closer to making a decision about whether to accept Akira's proposal and was thankful when he had rung her briefly to say that he had to go back to Tokyo unexpectedly and didn't know when he would be able to get back to either London or New York.

She was surprised but relieved that he made no reference to their last night together, nor did he press her for an answer. Instead he had sounded strangely businesslike but then he *had* opened the conversation by saying that he was due to rush straight out of the door to catch his flight.

Lisa made up her mind to try and stop thinking about Akira and concentrate instead on Flights of Fancy which was now doing so well that they were not only fully booked for every flight but having to turn potential clients away. The orgy flights were the most popular by far – obviously word had got around fast, she realised. And it was this, more than anything, which strengthened her resolve to throw a special orgy to mark the company's first three months of successful trading.

She knew it would take a lot of planning and in some ways wished she had more time. Perhaps a party to celebrate the first *six* months' trading would have been a more astute decision but she was a determined person and didn't like to alter her original plans.

The orgy was to take place on the ground. In a suite which she had booked in one of Akira's own London hotels. It had been his suggestion and it made sense. There would be no problems using the suite for the purpose for which it was intended. No awkward questions asked. Akira had already said he would see to it personally. Furthermore, he had offered unlimited assistance from his own staff to help organise the event. It was one offer from Akira that she had no hesitation in accepting.

With initial preparations underway, she set about drawing up a guest list. Her regular orgy clients were the first to be added, followed by others who had expressed an interest in the special flights but so far hadn't dared to make a booking. Perhaps this event would change their minds, she thought hopefully. The probability of having to launch additional flights was looming ever larger and this helped to push her towards making a decision about who to appoint as her deputy.

In the end, the answer to her plight came from an unusual source.

One morning, just as Lisa was agonising over that very subject, the phone rang. She was delighted to hear Michiko's voice at the other end of the line. It seemed like ages since she had last spoken to the young Japanese woman and could only assume that her visit to Chun's parents had gone better than expected. It was an assumption which Michiko was quick to confirm.

'Yes, everything went brilliantly,' she trilled brightly. 'Much better than I could ever have hoped.'

'Did they raise any objections to your marriage plans?' Lisa asked.

For a moment Michiko seemed to hesitate. 'Well, sort of,' she said. 'It seems they would prefer a traditional Chinese wedding – in Hong Kong. It seems Chun has about a thousand relatives there who will all expect to attend the ceremony.'

'Wow!' Lisa let out the exclamation on a long breath. 'Won't that cause you some problems – what about your family, for instance?'

A musical giggle came down the phone line. 'No. Not at all,' Michiko replied. 'My family are not that religious and are ultimately far too materialistic to care all that much.' She sounded slightly depressed for just a moment, then her tone brightened again. 'I think I explained all that to you,' she said. 'And just this once, I'm grateful that that's the way they are – espcially if it means a hassle-free wedding for me and Chun.'

'I take your point,' Lisa chipped in, 'trying to combine

261

two completely different religions and their attendant rituals could have been a nightmare.'

As she said the words it struck her that she had her own concerns about Akira's proposal for very similar reasons. Although neither she nor her family were particularly religious she wondered what her ageing C of E aunts and uncles would make of his background. Nothing had been said – even when she mentioned to her mother that she was seeing a Japanese man – but then marriage had never been mentioned. Nor the fact that their future grandchildren could possibly end up with oriental features.

'So how are things with you, Lisa?' Michiko asked, disturbing her lateral train of thought.

Lisa couldn't disguise a smile. 'Oh, so, so,' she said. 'Right at this very minute I'm trying to draw up a guest list for Flights of Fancy's first-quarter celebration. And decide what to do about appointing a deputy.'

Michiko giggled again. 'I thought so,' she said. 'That's one of the reasons I called today.'

'Really, why?' Lisa swapped over the receiver to her left ear and leaned her corresponding elbow on the desk top to make herself more comfortable.

'Well,' Michiko began, 'Chun wants me to carry on working after we're married. He knows all about Flights of Fancy and the ways I've already helped you and it was he who suggested that I contact you to see if I can come and work for your company in some capacity.'

Lisa was almost struck dumb. 'What about Akira?' she gasped out finally. 'Won't you be leaving him in the lurch?'

Michiko cleared her throat. 'That's been the only sticking point between myself and Chun. He doesn't want me to carry on working for Akira. In fact, I've already resigned.'

Michiko's disclosure didn't come as any surprise, Lisa realised quickly. The young woman's relationship with Akira had obviously been far more than simply that of boss and employee. It was natural that her future husband wouldn't be too happy about allowing that situation to continue.

'You know I'd be delighted to have you on the team, Michiko,' Lisa said without hesitation. 'In fact, your offer is the answer to a prayer. How do you feel about becoming my deputy?' She went on to explain exactly what the position would entail and about her plans to launch a second service in the near future. 'Of course that would mean you working almost full-time. How do you think Chun would react to that?'

Again, Michiko giggled. 'I can't see any problems and the money will be more than useful. The only thing is—' Here she paused for a moment but Lisa had already second guessed the reason for her hesitation.

'The only thing is, he wouldn't be happy about you taking part in the orgies?' she filled in.

'Yes, that's about the size of it,' Michiko agreed. 'I don't know how we'd get around that. Is it too much of a problem?'

Although she knew Michiko couldn't see her, Lisa shook her head. 'No. Not at all. In fact I'd already decided to stop taking an active part myself. I don't think my clients need any encouragement from me. From now on the managerial role will be strictly hands off. And all other body parts come to that,' she added with a low chuckle.

Michiko's response was the last one she expected. 'Is that because of Akira's proposal?'

For a moment Lisa felt stunned, then realised that the young woman was probably the closest friend Akira had. 'Believe it or not, no,' she said. 'I've been thinking about the situation for some time. In all honesty I'm feeling a bit jaded with regard to sex.'

'No! You of all people?' Michiko laughed to show that she was only joking but Lisa felt therein lay more than a grain of truth.

She had promoted herself as an independent, let-it-all-hang-out type of woman. It was no wonder that Michiko was surprised by her confession, even if she chose to make light of it.

'Yes, me,' Lisa said. 'I can't – well, I can't really explain how I feel. It's just that sex doesn't seem that important to me anymore.'

'Only people who are getting plenty of it say that,' Michiko cut in incisively.

Lisa sighed and attempted another faint laugh which didn't quite come off. 'I daresay. But it's the truth. Just lately I've been hankering after something more meaningful. I really envy you and Chun.'

'So you're going to marry Akira?' Michiko said excitedly. 'How wonderful. I know you'll be really perfect for each other.'

Quick to put the young woman right, Lisa said, 'I don't know if that's really the case, Michiko. Akira and

I, well, we don't exactly see eye to eye on everything. Some of the things he likes to do sexually are not strictly to my taste if you know what I mean?'

Michiko said she did but Lisa wasn't so sure. To put the record straight she decided there and then to tell her all about her last encounter with Akira.

'Boy, oh, boy,' Michiko said when Lisa had finished describing every last detail. 'I feel hot and cold all at the same time.'

'You and me both,' Lisa said. 'And I don't know if I can cope with his games on a permanent basis. I mean, who knows what to expect with him?'

'But isn't that part of his charm?' Michiko asked.

Again Lisa nodded. 'I suppose so,' she admitted. 'But I can't see me accepting his behaviour on a permanent basis. It's not really the proper way for a married couple to carry on, is it?'

'That depends on the couple,' Michiko said wisely. 'Who's to say what's right and what's wrong. If it works for you then all well and good.'

Lisa gave an anguished groan. 'Yes, but that's the whole point. I don't think it will work for me. If I'm not happy with it now, how can I expect to change my outlook six months, or even six years down the line?' With a deep sigh she added, 'Whichever way I look at it, I can't see me and Akira lasting the course. If I do throw caution to the wind and accept his proposal, I can just imagine us petitioning for divorce within a year.'

There was silence from the other end of the phone for a moment, during which time Lisa could hear Michiko breathing softly. Then the young woman said, 'So you are planning to turn him down.'

'No,' Lisa said. 'Oh, I don't know. I feel as confused about it now as I did when he asked me. I honestly don't know what to do.'

'Then do nothing,' Michiko advised. 'You have to be certain. Marriage is a big step. For myself and Chun it seems obvious but for you and Akira – well, things are obviously not quite so cut and dried.'

All at once, as though her young friend had managed to clear through the mists of confusion, Lisa realised that she was right. A momentous decision like marriage should either come naturally or be made after careful consideration. She wished she had been able to throw herself into Akira's arms and say, 'Yes, yes, oh, darling, yes,' without hesitation. But she hadn't and wasn't sure if she ever would accept his proposal.

'Thanks, Michiko,' she said, deliberately playing down the gratitude she felt. 'You know you have a very wise head on those young shoulders of yours?'

'So everyone tells me,' Michiko said sagely. 'Now then, back to business. I'd like to arrange a meeting next time you're in New York—'

Thankful for Michiko's deft about-turn, Lisa readily agreed to a date and time that would suit them both. Then, after exchanging a few brief pleasantries, she concluded the conversation with an offer to take her and Chun out to dinner sometime which Michiko accepted happily. That done, she turned her attention back to the arrangements for the orgy.

* * *

Despite Lisa's disinterest in everything sexual she set about recruiting some new 'boys' to add to the Flights of Fancy team. Treating this aspect of her job purely as work, she put each candidate through his paces and was relieved when she had managed to recruit another six, plus a couple of stand-ins for emergencies. Deciding to come clean for once, she also approached the agencies she had used and made bookings for thirty or so extra men to be present at the orgy.

She was in her office, having just made the last of her calls for the day and was looking forward to going home for a nice long soak in the bath, when she was surprised to hear a knock at the door. Seconds later, Rio's familiar dark curly head appeared around the door.

'Someone around here works too hard,' he said, crossing the room to perch on the edge of her desk.

Reclining in her chair, Lisa gazed up at him with a fond expression. 'I have to,' she said, 'there's always so much to do and what with the orgy to plan and everything, well—' She gestured helplessly and stared at the young man as his face creased into a broad grin.

'You look as though you've forgotten how to relax,' he murmured.

Standing up, he walked around the desk and, to her surprise, fell to his knees in front of her.

'I think I have,' she admitted, gazing down at his dark, silky curls and fighting the urge to reach out and stroke her hand over them.

Rio gazed back but said nothing. Instead he began to remove her shoes. 'Take off your stockings,' he said quietly.

Lisa felt her heart begin to hammer. 'Why?'

'Because I'm going to fuck you silly,' he growled, then laughed and added, 'because I want to give you a foot massage. You look as though you could do with it.'

Lisa was surprised by the sudden dart of arousal that pierced her when he spoke about fucking and then the immediate pang of disappointment she felt when told his true intentions. Reaching under her skirt, she rolled the pale grey hold-up stockings down her legs and placed them in a neat, gauzy pile on the desk top.

'Now, sit back and try to relax,' he said. 'Close your eyes. Fall asleep if you want to. I'll still be here when you wake up.'

As she did as he asked, Lisa realised how much she trusted the young man who knelt at her feet and now took one of them in his strong hands. His fingers began to deftly massage each toe in turn, his thumbs rotating firmly on the soft pads underneath. An unbidden sigh escaped her lips and she allowed her eyelids to slowly close, her mind to drift.

She was on a desert island. Completely naked, she lay basking under the relentless heat of the sun which shimmered high up in a cloudless blue sky. Somewhere in the near distance she could hear the sound of waves breaking on the sandy beach and the soft rustle of leaves as palm trees wavered in the slight but welcome breeze.

Natives were there to attend to her every whim. Natives with long, dark, curly hair.

In her fantasy she closed her eyes and simply gave herself up to the sensation of being pampered to. Soft fruit was crushed against her lips, the pulp sliding down her throat, the juice running down her chin and trickling between her breasts. A tongue lapped it up at once, then moved to her nipples where it circled around and around.

Lisa sighed. Someone else was massaging her feet, the light touch sending small tingles of pleasure coursing the length of her strong, brown limbs to caress her naked sex. Other light caresses stimulated her body – the faintest of touches, like silk, upon her inner thighs, her breasts, her belly. Every part of her was being touched at once, or so it seemed and in real life she felt the tension slide slowly out of her to be replaced by the heat of desire.

Allowing her eyelids to flicker open, Lisa was first of all surprised to see that outside dusk had fallen and next to realise that her button-through dress had been undone. Her front-fastening bra had been opened and her knickers removed. To all intents and purposes she was completely naked, just as she had been in her fantasy.

The handful of natives were not there in her office of course but Rio was and she instantly noticed that he was using his long hair to good effect. The soft ends trickled over her belly and upper thighs like water, lighting small flames of arousal as they caressed her bare flesh.

Before she had the opportunity to say anything at all, she felt her labia being gently parted and the soft insistent lapping of a tongue.

'Ah, oh God, that's wonderful!' she cried out, spreading her thighs wider in unashamed abandon.

Rio didn't stop what he was doing to her. Even when the heat in her pelvis grew and she began to squirm, he continued to lap and suck at her exposed flesh. She felt him take her soft, hairless labia between his lips and suck gently. She felt him swirl the end of his tongue around her burgeoning clitoris. She felt his hair tickle her belly and thighs, her soft inner flesh. In moments she came.

It took a while for the waves of her climax to subside and the trembling in her limbs to die down to a slight shudder. She had been forcing her pelvis up towards him and now her thigh muscles quivered with the after-effects of their unaccustomed usage. It had been weeks since she had taken an active role in sex. Each time she had interviewed a potential candidate for the team she had simply lain there and let them get on with it.

'How did you know?' she said softly, putting out a hand to stroke his hair.

Raising his head from between her thighs he smiled at her. 'I know you, Lisa. I believe I know what you need, when you need it.'

'I think you're right.' She tried to laugh but couldn't. There was neither the energy nor the breath left in her lungs. It seemed the power of her orgasm had drained her of every vestige of strength.

Gazing down at his upturned face, she noticed, with a fresh surge of arousal, how her own juices glistened around his mouth and how soft and gentle his expression seemed.

For ages it seemed they stared into each other's eyes in

silence and when Rio finally spoke, his words shocked her and yet set her confused mind straight once and for all.

Chapter Fifteen

'I love you, Lisa,' Rio said softly, clasping her free hand between his. He glanced down as his fingers entwined with hers. 'I know I'm taking a risk telling you this. I've never been in love with any woman before but you do things to me. I can't explain. It's the way you look: your eyes, your body, your face, everything about you. And the way you move. The way you are. Like I said, everything.'

'Rio, look—' Lisa leaned forward, trying to interrupt but for once he wouldn't let her.

'No, Lisa, hear me out. Please.'

There was real anguish in his tone and so she sat back and gave him a look that said, 'Go on.'

'I don't know when I first realised it. Probably the first time we met. I thought you were a special lady then and I do now. Only more so. I would like us to be together forever, Lisa. I hope you feel the same way, I really do.'

'I don't know if I'm ready for marriage,' Lisa said quietly.

'Marriage. *Marriage!*' Rio almost spat the word out. 'I'm not talking about marriage necessarily, unless that's what you decide you want. *You*, Lisa. Not me. Marriage is just a piece of paper as far as I'm concerned. I don't need that, or a ring on your finger, to prove how much I love you.'

Lisa exhaled slowly. The way he spoke echoed her feelings exactly. It made her realise that the words 'marry me' had jarred with her when they came from Akira's mouth because she knew deep down that marriage to him would be the same as bondage. And she didn't want to feel bound to any man other than by love itself.

To her surprise Rio stood up and began to pace the room.

'Shit! I've blown it haven't I?' he said. 'I should never have said anything. I should have kept it to myself. I've managed all these months to keep quiet about it and then I go and give the game away. Why am I so stupid?' He clapped his palm against his forehead in a dramatic gesture that made Lisa laugh aloud, despite the seriousness of the moment.

She had never felt so certain of anything in her life as she stood up and went over to him. Standing directly in front of him to stop him pacing anymore, she reached out and cupped his face in her hands. As she stared directly into his eyes she said, 'I love you too, Rio. Perhaps I've only just realised it but it's true. I love you too.'

For a moment his expression remained serious then, it seemed, realisation slowly dawned and an exultant smile lit up his face. In fact, to Lisa, it appeared as though a bright light had just been switched on inside him. It shone through the burnt-almond translucence of his skin. It radiated in his broad smile and twinkled on the surface of his strong, white teeth. Most of all, it illuminated his eyes.

The brilliance of his gaze captivated her and she found herself staring into the depths of his eyes, searching for something that she quickly realized didn't exist – some vestige of doubt perhaps. It was true, she realised happily, when her visual search proved fruitless. He really did love her and for all the right reasons.

All at once, as though a cloud passed over her happiness, she remembered Akira again. Things would not, could not, be straightforward. All personal considerations aside, she and Akira were business partners. Flights of Fancy was doing well but not well enough to suffer the consequences of Akira's withdrawal of financial support.

'You're thinking about your business partner,' Rio prompted astutely. 'What is his name – Akira?'

Lisa nodded.

'There is more than just business between you two, isn't there, Lisa?' he said. 'You are lovers as well?'

Knowing it was pointless to deny the truth, Lisa whispered, 'Yes.'

Suddenly, everything that had seemed bright and hopeful a moment before was overshadowed by regret. Akira's existence hung over them both like an invisible cloud – a storm cloud. Lisa could feel the darkness gathering around her, obliterating her joy.

She opened her mouth to speak but Rio interrupted her. Reaching out to her he pulled her into his arms, nestled her head in the crook of his shoulder and began to stroke her hair.

'It doesn't matter,' he murmured.

'But it does.' Lisa raised her head and gave him an anguished look. 'You see, the last time we were together he asked me to marry him too.'

If Rio was surprised by her disclosure he didn't show it. 'And are you planning to accept?' he asked softly.

Lisa shook her head and buried her face once again in his shoulder. For a moment she allowed herself to luxuriate in the smell of him: his aftershave, warm and spicy, the clean, soapy scent of his freshly washed hair. And his arms around her felt good. Too good. There was no point in trying to deny her true feelings, she realised, she loved Rio as much as he obviously loved her.

'No. I couldn't then and I can't now,' she said. 'But I know my refusal is likely to cause problems.'

'With the business?'

'Yes, mainly with the business but I'm also worried about other things. Akira can behave very strangely at times. I'm not sure that I trust him.'

'In what way?'

The concern showed in his voice and Lisa hesitated about telling him why she was worried. But if they were on the brink of a permanent relationship, she knew she had to start as she meant to go on – by being totally honest with him.

Straightening up she led him by the hand to a low, two-seater sofa that stood under the window. They sat and then she cleared her throat. Hesitantly at first but becoming bolder, she told Rio everything that had transpired between her and Akira – from the day they first met to their last encounter.

'I wondered where your hair had gone,' Rio said,

when she had finished. To her relief there was laughter in his voice as he glanced down at her denuded mound.

It hadn't occurred to her that she was still wearing her dress unbuttoned. There had been nothing sexual about Rio's mannerisms since he had made her come. All he had shown her was kindness and understanding. Now though, she blushed hotly.

'I didn't want that,' she whispered in a voice that cracked under the overwhelming surge of emotion that she felt.

'But you let it happen?'

'Yes.' She glanced down at herself and unconsciously began to draw the edges of her dress together.

Rio put out a hand to stop her. 'Don't, Lisa,' he said. 'Don't be embarrassed with me. I quite like your new look.'

He laughed softly and Lisa glanced up at his face. The tenderness and love in his eyes was still there. As well as something else, she realised, something she recognised as desire. The familiar look kindled a tiny flame of arousal inside her.

'Do you really?' she said. 'I didn't intend to keep it like this. I was going to let the hair grow back. Though God knows how long that will take.'

He shrugged. 'It's up to you. I love you with or without hair.' A wolfish grin touched his lips and eyes. 'But while you are so – shall we say? – uniquely exposed. I think it is only right that I make the most of it.'

Urging her gently back against the arm of the sofa, he lifted one of her legs so that it lay flat upon the cushions. The other leg he bent at the knee, placing her foot flat on the floor.

In that position Lisa felt that her sex was supremely

displayed to him but the realisation didn't fill her with shame. This time, with Rio, she felt a mixture of emotions – all of them positive. Extreme desire coursed through her as he leaned forward and carefully perused her denuded flesh. And when he reached out to part the soft folds of her labia with gentle fingers, she couldn't help gasping out a whimper of excitement.

'I'm grateful to Akira,' Rio said, without looking up. 'Now I get to see all of you. Every tiny morsel. And touch you. And taste you—'

Lisa trembled as his fingers caressed her and then she groaned aloud with passion as he bent his head and lightly ran his tongue over every portion of her most intimate flesh. The sensations he created were delicate and yet intense. Her clitoris responded immediately, hardening under the teasing caress of his tongue. Time and again he skimmed over it lightly before gently lapping at the swollen folds of her labia.

As he moved his head, his hair tickled her inner thighs. Tingles of excitement stimulated her lower body, making her moist and open for him. His tongue circled the rim of her vagina and she groaned as he thrust it inside her, probing her hot, eager flesh and lapping up her juices.

'Oh God, Rio. It's too much, too much!' she cried as he continued to tongue her sex remorselessly.

She felt herself falling and floating, drifting on a cloud of sheer bliss. She was so close to coming, yet not quite there. Her arousal grew and grew until she clutched at his head and begged him to stop teasing her.

'Just let it go, Lisa,' Rio said softly. 'Let it all go.'

He bent his head and went back to the delicious torment his tongue created and, as though his words were all she needed, she felt herself slowly rise to the point of no return.

When she came it was with a vengeance, the power of her orgasm almost painful in its intensity. She tried to cry out but found her throat had closed up tight. Every part of her body other than her sex, it seemed, had contracted in on itself. Her muscles screamed, her whole body shuddering with unleashed tension and then, as her climax began to abate, she became aware of a slowly spreading lassitude. The relief she felt was too much. To her surprise she began to cry.

Rio was there beside her at once, stroking her hair, her face, kissing her wet cheeks. 'It's okay, Lisa,' he murmured. 'It's all going to be okay.'

'Are you sure?' Lisa blinked back the tears that glistened on her eyelashes as she gazed back at him. All at once she felt like a young child in need of his protection and reassurance.

'Of course,' he said. 'Have I ever lied to you?'

She shook her head dumbly, knowing that Rio was as straight as they came.

'Well then.' He sat back on his heels and took her hands instead.

For a while he simply held her hands, squeezing them gently and gazing into her face until she finally felt able to return his smile.

'Make love to me, Rio,' she whispered hoarsely.

He bowed his head solemnly. 'Whatever madam's heart desires.' When he looked up, she noticed the twinkle in his eyes and her smile broadened.

'In that case,' she said. 'Take your clothes off and come here.' Shifting to the back of the sofa, she patted the space next to her.

The laughter bubbled up inside her as he began to move swiftly, almost ripping his clothes off in a deliberate parody of a desperate man. His comical actions and facial expressions as he pretended to become entangled in his shirt and then have difficulty removing his trousers, soon had her in hysterics.

'Oh God, Rio,' she cried, 'you are too much. This is supposed to be a serious moment.'

'Is it?' He glanced at her and winked. 'I always prefer sex with a good sprinkling of humour myself.'

Lisa sighed happily as she realised just how much she loved him and how much they had to look forward to together.

'So do I,' she said, 'but I'm getting desperate. For God's sake just get those things off and fuck me.' Reaching down she deliberately slid her fingers across her moist sex and began to rub softly. 'See,' she said, 'I've had to start without you now.'

Pretending to groan with frustration, Rio quickly removed the rest of his clothes and stretched out beside her so that they faced each other. Straight away he reached down and grasped her wrist.

'Stop that,' he growled with mock ferocity. 'I'm here now.' So saying he moved her hand then thrust a couple of fingers inside her before hooking her top leg over his hip and replacing his fingers with his hard cock instead.

Instinctively, Lisa moved with him, urging her pelvis forward to meet his thrusts. Hell! It felt so wonderful –

and so right – to have him inside her. To her mind they fitted together with the precision of two halves of a jigsaw – physically, mentally and spiritually.

For once, it seemed, neither of them could bear to hold out for too long. Their passion for each other was overwhelmingly strong and they both rose quickly to climax within seconds of each other.

Lisa came suddenly – her orgasm apparently descending on her from nowhere in a cloud of dark, heat-filled lust. Moments later, she heard Rio groan and felt him thrust hard a couple of times. She stared straight into his eyes, watching as they seemed to glaze over. A blissful smile touched his lips and she smiled to herself, loving him for loving her in such an obvious way.

For a while they simply lay together, each gently stroking the other's shoulders, back and buttocks. Then Rio kissed her. A loving, lingering kiss that left her wanting him all over again. In a hushed whisper she told him and moved her body gently against his to emphasise her desire.

'You know you're insatiable don't you?' he murmured with humour in his tone.

Pretending to give a resigned sigh, Lisa nodded and kissed him again. 'I can't help it. I'm just a wanton woman,' she said.

He laughed. 'Lucky me.'

'No,' Lisa corrected him, 'lucky *me*.'

'Lucky us then,' he said, attempting a shrug. 'Now, where would you like me to fuck you next? I'm a bit bored with this sofa.'

* * *

Lisa moved in with Rio that night. When he asked her she agreed readily, although she wasn't sure if she could get used to living with a man after so many years of single-dom. However, his flat came as a pleasant surprise: a spacious Dockland apartment in a luxury building which housed a fully-equipped gym on the ground floor.

'Bloody hell!' she exclaimed as she walked into his huge bathroom and instantly spotted the white marble jaccuzzi which matched the rest of the fittings. 'I didn't realise you lived like this. Somehow, I imagined you in a scruffy little bachelor pad in Vauxhall or somewhere similar.'

'Oh, thanks a lot.' He pretended to sound aggrieved but his broad grin gave him away. 'Didn't you know us ex-escorts are used to making pots of money.'

She laughed, instantly remembering the circumstances under which they had first met. 'I should have realised.'

Leading her out of the bathroom, he took her into the equally luxurious kitchen and opened the fridge. 'Wine or beer?' he offered.

'Wine please,' Lisa said, watching as he poured her a large glassful and then opened a bottle of beer for himself.

They walked back into the lounge which was starkly modern, done out mainly in shades of black, grey and cream but with the odd splash of vibrant colour here and there. Plumping up a bright blue cushion, Lisa settled back into the corner of one of the two four-seater sofas that dominated the room and gazed thoughtfully at him over the rim of her glass.

'If I'm going to move in here permanently, you've got to let me pay my share,' she said.

Rio shrugged. 'That's up to you. I don't need the money.'

'How come? You don't exactly earn a fortune working for Flights of Fancy.' She pursed her lips, immediately wondering if he had been moonlighting – still doing a bit of escort work on the side perhaps – and was surprised to find that the possibility bothered her a great deal and not from any professional angle.

Crossing the room to sit beside her, Rio took the glass from her hands, kissed her hard on the lips and then sat back.

'I'm rich,' he said simply. 'A couple of years ago a regular client of mine died and left me a small fortune.' He sighed and a pained expression crossed his face for a moment. 'She knew she was dying. Being a widow and childless she lacked companionship and booked me one day. We just went out, to the theatre and then supper afterwards, and had a bloody good time. I must admit I was surprised,' he added. 'She was in her late fifties and I'd never escorted anyone as old as her before but she had a terrific personality. It was easy to be her friend.'

'Is that all you were to her – her friend?' Lisa hated herself for asking the question but couldn't help it.

'Yes,' he said, the smile returning to his face. 'Being an escort isn't always about sex, you know? Lots of women – in fact most women – who hire escorts are simply looking for someone they can go out with. Someone who they can trust to treat them well and not put any demands on them. Sheila was like that.'

'And so she left you all her money?' Lisa said, sounding as amazed as she felt.

Rio nodded. 'I was all she had,' he murmured softly. 'She often used to tell me what a difference I made to her life but I didn't really realise until it was too late.' He paused and glanced down at his beer, his brow creasing into a frown. 'The authorities forced her to go into a hospice in the end. Of course, I visited her a lot. Free of charge. But she seemed to give up then. She only lived for another two weeks.'

Lisa felt stunned. 'That's awful,' she said. Reaching out to him, she took him in her arms and held him as he sobbed quietly into her hair.

'I can't claim you are the only woman I've ever loved, Lisa,' he said in a broken voice, 'because I loved Sheila. I really did. She was never my lover in the physical sense but she was my best friend.'

That night they made love tenderly until dawn broke. When she heard the birds singing outside the bedroom window, Lisa snuggled closer to Rio and smiled happily.

'You're going to feel like shit today,' he said, fondly stroking her hair.

'No, I won't,' she contradicted him, 'I'll feel wonderful. I feel that way now and knowing that we're going to be together tonight and every night from now on will keep me walking on air.'

'You old romantic you,' Rio laughed. 'I never would have suspected that you were so soft inside.'

Reaching down and clasping his burgeoning erection, she grinned cheekily. 'And you're hard on the outside. It's a match made in heaven.'

* * *

Finally, they had to concede to the pressures of work and get up. Lisa was longing to try out the jacuzzi but there wasn't time. They were both scheduled to fly to New York in less than two hours.

They drove to the airport in Rio's Porsche – another surprise for Lisa. Her hair, which had still been wet from the shower, dried in no time as they sped along the M4 with the top down. As they pulled into the car park outside the building that housed the Flights of Fancy offices, Rio suddenly looked downcast.

'What's up?' Lisa asked.

For a moment it looked as though he hesitated about saying anything but then he said, 'I hope no one has booked me today.'

Suddenly, Lisa felt her stomach turn to water. Oh, God! For a few blissful hours she'd forgotten what he did for a living and it was all her doing. Fighting hard against herself, she conceded to the realisation that she didn't want Rio to fuck anyone else. Possessiveness or sexual jealousy were not usually among her failings but for once she felt completely different about a man. But then he wasn't just any man, he was Rio and it seemed the possibility bothered him as much as it did her.

Thinking fast, she came to a quick decision. 'It's up to you,' she said slowly, turning in the passenger seat to gaze directly into his eyes. 'But I do have an alternative.'

'Go on.'

She noted he looked relieved as well as intrigued.

'Take on a managerial role,' she said. 'I asked Michiko to become my deputy but I am planning to launch a second Flights of Fancy service. She can't be on two planes at once and as she's just about to get married she wouldn't want to work all the flights anyway.'

A slow smile spread across Rio's face 'It's a deal,' he said, 'at least until I can sort things things out properly.'

'What do you mean?' Now it was her turn to look intrigued.

'What I mean is, I'm happy to be your manager until I can become your partner.'

'How – what?' Lisa was certain her confusion showed as her brain whirled. What on earth was he talking about?

'It's simple,' he said. 'You're anticipating problems with Akira aren't you?'

She nodded and waited for him to continue.

'Well, as I said, I've got a small fortune sitting in the bank. I've been wondering what to do with it and now I know. I'm going to buy Akira out.'

Lisa felt stunned. 'But what if he won't agree to it?' she said. Knowing Akira as she did, she was certain that he would dig in his heels.

'He'll have to,' Rio said simply. 'Flights of Fancy is nothing without you. In fact, it *is* you. If you threaten to walk away from it he'll be left with next to nothing.'

As realisation slowly dawned, Lisa found her heart hammering with excitement.

The ensuing week was as busy as all the others. In between the usual scheduled flights Lisa still had the celebration orgy to plan. Deciding to keep things as hassle-free as possible she booked a firm of party planners. Although that in itself was a mini nightmare. Everyone was eager for the business until, it seemed, they got to a certain point – as soon as she mentioned the exact nature of the party most companies baulked at the idea and turned her down flat. A small firm run by two Sloanies who claimed to be ex-models, however, were delighted to take up the challenge.

'An orgy,' the one called Arabella crowed, 'how absolutely marvellous. I can't wait to get started.'

The other one, Sacha, cut in. 'Will it be themed – with everyone wearing togas and suchlike – what a hoot?'

'I hadn't really thought about it,' Lisa said honestly, turning the suggestion over in her mind, 'but now you come to mention it, I think a theme is a good idea. But not Romans,' she added. 'How about the nineteen twenties – you know, with flappers and the tango playing in the background, that sort of thing?'

'Fabulous!' Arabella said, warming to the topic. 'We can make the place look like an opium den. Get in a few of those hubble-bubble pipes and things.'

'Well, okay,' Lisa concurred, the slight doubt she felt showing in her voice. 'But I don't want any real drugs at this party. We're likely to be targets for a police raid as it is.'

'Trust us,' Sacha said soothingly. 'We know exactly how to approach this. I promise you the best orgy the nineteen nineties have ever seen.'

With that out of the way, all that was left for Lisa and her office staff to tackle was the guest list. Two days later, fifty invitations were dispatched by first-class post.

While all this was going on, Lisa had debated long and hard about exactly how and when to approach Akira. In the end – despairing of her own cowardice and finding herself with an evening at home on her own – she picked up the phone and ended up chasing him half way around the world. Finally, she tracked him down at a hotel in Detroit.

'Lisa, lovely to hear from you. How are you, darling?' There was a surprising amount of warmth in his voice which Lisa found disconcerting. This wasn't going to be easy.

'I'm fine,' she said cautiously. 'How are you?'

'On top of the world,' he purred back, 'but I'd feel a whole lot better if you were here right now.'

Lisa gulped and clasped the phone to her chest for a moment, fighting to regain control of her heartbeat which seemed to have gone haywire.

'Akira,' she said, deciding to come straight to the point, 'I need to talk to you urgently.'

His response was swift, cutting across the rest of what she was about to say. 'Fire away, darling.'

'Well—' Now she had his attention she hesitated and then crumbled. 'I don't really want to talk about it on the phone. How soon could we schedule a meeting?'

'Oh, a meeting?' He sounded amused. 'This does sound important. Let me see.' She heard the distinctive sound of him flicking through his diary. 'I'm touring the States for the next couple of weeks. Then I'm back in London.' He paused. 'I wasn't going to tell you this but I am aiming to attend the party.'

'Why weren't you going to tell me?' Lisa said, instantly suspicious.

'Because I wanted to surprise you, darling girl. I

planned to just turn up and make an entrance.'

'Oh.' Lisa didn't know what else to say. It was just as well she rang him, she thought. The idea of Akira suddenly turning up and her having to face him in the middle of one of the most important events of her life was too awful to contemplate. 'Can't we meet before then?'

'No can do,' Akira said. 'I told you. My schedule is packed solid until then.'

'Well, I can't discuss this in the middle of a party,' she said. 'It's, er, well, it's business.'

'Okay, Lisa, okay. Let me think for a minute.'

She heard him turn pages again and then she thought she detected the sound of him tapping a pen against his teeth. All at once she imagined him seated behind a big, powerful desk and her stomach turned to water. This was not going to be easy at all.

'Right,' he said finally, 'the party starts at nine o'clock, yes?'

'Yes,' Lisa said, 'but there's the press conference first and I need to be there early to make sure everything's set up properly. Really, I should arrive at the hotel at seven at the latest.'

She heard him hum a little as he pondered the dilemma. Then he said, 'Okay, that's no problem. Can you be at my London flat at five.'

Feeling relieved, Lisa said she could and felt a small wave of relief start to lap at her taut nerve endings. Then, just as she started to feel better, Akira – behaving true to form – totally shattered her composure.

'I know you want to discuss our marriage plans, darling,' he said smoothly. 'Of course I'd make time for that.

Oh, and by the way, I've already taken the liberty of booking a temple.'

'A—a temple?' Lisa gasped weakly.

'Yes,' Akira said, 'a very secluded place at the foot of Mount Fuji. I thought you'd get a real kick out of a proper Shinto wedding.'

Ten minutes later, after listening to a frighteningly graphic description of the plans that he had already put into motion – the least of them being verbal invitations to about a thousand friends, family members and business associates – Lisa managed to hang up on him. In fact, she'd used the hoary old excuse of someone coming to the door. But thankfully, Akira had bought it.

Sitting alone, in the twilight-laden silence that filled Rio's flat, she fought against the myriad thoughts that crowded her head and tried to make her mind go blank. It was a futile exercise and as soon as she let herself think again, she felt the distinct sensation of the walls slowly caving in on her.

Chapter Sixteen

Lisa came slowly awake to the sound of Rio's voice in her ear and the sensation of his warm body pressed against hers. Still feeling disoriented, she struggled to sit up on the sofa where she had finally dozed off and gazed at him wordlessly for a few moments before flinging her arms around him.

'Oh, thank God you're back,' she said. 'How did the meeting go?'

Rio had taken his bank manager out on the town that evening in an attempt to sweeten him up, in case he didn't have enough of his own money to buy Akira out.

'Fine, I think.' Rio put his finger under his chin and tipped her head back so that he could look at her properly. 'But never mind me. You look awful. Why didn't you go to bed? I told you I would be late coming back.'

Speaking slowly, as though the story were too painful to relate, Lisa told him all about her phone call to Akira.

'Why didn't you just tell him outright that you don't want to marry him?' he said, looking nonplussed.

Lisa sighed, wishing for the first time in her life that she smoked. 'Because he didn't really give me the chance to say anything. Because I wanted to be able to look him in the face and tell him. Because—' She was forced to break off as Rio kissed her lingeringly on the lips.

'Shush, okay, I understand,' he said, stroking her hair. Reclining against the back of the sofa, he pulled her against him.

Lisa gazed up at his profile, thinking how marvellous it was that he managed to look so young and yet so mature all at the same time. His strong chin had just the faintest coating of stubble on it and his wonderful, thickly-lashed eyes were staring straight ahead. She had seen this look before and knew he was thinking hard about something – a subject that he didn't much care to broach.

'What is it?' she urged gently. 'I know you want to say something.'

As he glanced down at her, she noticed the way love softened his eyes for just a moment before his expression became enigmatic again.

'I don't want you to go and see Akira alone,' he said.

'What?' Lisa pulled away from him slightly and stared at him in amazement. 'Do you think I'm going to jump into bed with him the minute I get there?'

He couldn't help smiling at her response and she felt an instant surge of relief.

'No, of course not,' he said softly. 'I'm worried about his reaction. He might turn violent. He might—'

Lisa interrupted him hastily. 'Akira may be many things but I don't believe he would try to hurt me physically,' she replied with conviction.

'Good, I'm glad about that. But I still don't feel happy about letting you go alone.'

'I have to, Rio,' she said. 'I can't risk taking you or

anyone else in with me, it might just tip the balance.'

During the course of the next few days, Lisa's determination to go and see Akira alone seemed to become a mute point between herself and Rio. But she wouldn't back down. No way. This was important – possibly the most important thing she had ever done in her life – next to starting up Flights of Fancy in the first place, that was. There was no way she was going to risk everything now. She was a big girl and could stand on her own two feet.

On the plus side – to her surprise and delight – positive responses to the invitations had already started trickling in and by the end of the week she had received acceptances from all but about twelve names on the guest list. Arabella and Sacha came in to see her and reported that everything was in hand. And to cap it all, she found the perfect outfit for herself to wear to the party, in a little secondhand dress shop next to Camden Lock.

The manager of the shop, a dark, elegant woman in her mid-thirties, assured her that the dress was an original by a little known French designer of the period. The colour was a rich, leafy green which suited her complexion perfectly. And the watered-silk under-dress was topped by a layer of sheer eau-de-nil chiffon, which felt as fine as a cobweb and came with a matching belt that draped loosely around the hips. A cloche hat, trimmed with green feathers and dotted with real pearls, completed the outfit. The whole ensemble wasn't cheap by any means but it was absolutely perfect and Lisa handed over her credit card with an eagerness which even she found astonishing.

* * *

As the day of the orgy drew nearer, she found herself rapidly approaching a state of blind panic which no amount of reassurance from Arabella and Sacha, or even Rio, could assuage. Thankfully, she still had two more flights to make before the big day arrived and it was the necessity of business as usual, coupled with endless blissful hours of lovemaking with Rio, that kept her sane.

Finally, the big day arrived. Forty-four women had promised to attend and in the morning Lisa went to the hotel to check on the suite. The sight that met her eyes as she walked through the door was astonishing. It seemed as though she had stepped straight into a Parisian opium den, of the type which had been frequented by the Left Bank bohemians and intellectuals of the period.

The high ceilings were draped with generous swathes of richly patterned silk in sultry shades of red, brown and ochre. And all the furniture in the sitting room had been cleared to make way for heaps of cushions covered with matching silk, satin and brocade. On small side tables stood groups of candles, incense burners and the promised hubble-bubble pipes – their curvaceous, smoked-glass bodies jostling with reproduction figurines of sinuous, scantily-clad ladies in graceful poses.

As she gazed around in awe, Lisa silently applauded Arabella and Sacha for their good taste and efficiency and tried to imagine the scene later that night, when the cushions would be smothered by a heaving mass of naked bodies. She had to admit, the thought turned her on a great deal and all of a sudden she couldn't wait to get back to Rio's flat.

* * *

As usual he was overjoyed to see her. 'I thought you were going to be tied up at the office all day,' he said, his face beaming.

'I thought I'd rather be tied up here, with you,' she joked. Since she'd moved in with him they had both played around with mild bondage and other sado-masochistic games.

Going into the kitchen to get herself a glass of wine and a bottle of beer for Rio, she called over her shoulder, 'I popped in to the hotel. The suite looks fabulous. Arabella and Sacha have done a brilliant job.'

To her surprise, Rio sneaked up behind her and grabbed her around the waist. 'Great,' he enthused, 'but we do have a teeny-weeny problem.'

'What's that?' Turning around in his arms, she held the bottle of beer to his lips and waited until he tipped his head back before pouring a little of the beer down his throat.

Smiling, he released her and took the bottle. 'Come on, let's go in the other room and sit down,' he suggested.

With a vague sense of unease, Lisa followed him. 'Akira knows you're living here with me now,' he said flatly as they sat down side by side on one of the sofas.

She whirled her head round to stare at him aghast. 'How does he know?'

Rio shrugged. 'Someone at the office said something perhaps. Who knows? It's not exactly the secret of the century at Flights of Fancy is it?'

Slowly, the implications of Akira knowing about her and Rio began to dawn on her. Shit! Now he had a head start on her. It would make things even more difficult when she had her meeting with him later that afternoon. On the other hand, she reasoned, at least now he already knew that she wouldn't be accepting his marriage proposal. Still, it wasn't really the way she would have chosen for him to find out. Although she didn't trust him, she still liked Akira and had intended to try and limit the hurt as much as possible.

While she and Rio made love, she managed to blot out her confused thoughts but when she glanced at the digital clock by the side of the bed and saw that it was almost four o'clock she began to panic again.

'That's it, I'm coming with you,' Rio said firmly as soon as he saw the way she suddenly jumped out of bed and began to rush around, getting dressed in her party outfit.

'No!' She was bent forward from the waist, just stepping into a pair of cream satin and lace camiknickers when he spoke. Dragging them up her legs and over her hips, she straightened up and stared at him. 'I must do this on my own.' She thrust her arms into the delicate shoestring straps and drew them up over her shoulders.

Rio still lounged on the double bed, naked, tanned and looking totally gorgeous – and for a moment her heart seemed to stop dead as she gazed at him. Then she felt the rhythmic beating against her ribs again. She was in a no-win situation. If she took Rio with her, there was no telling how Akira would react. But by refusing Rio's support, she knew she was hurting him.

'I'm not going to argue with you about this,' he said finally, looking downcast.

'Oh, Rio, don't,' she pleaded. 'You know why I'm going through with this. Let's face it, if all goes to plan we could be celebrating our new partnership in a couple of months. Won't that be worth it?'

'I don't trust him,' Rio said. 'I've been doing a little asking around and most people who have had dealings with him say he is just as capable of using his wealth and power to the bad, as well as the good.'

'All people in a position of power have to be ruthless sometimes,' Lisa argued, hoping she sounded more convincing than she felt. Ignoring his silence, she opened the top drawer behind her and took out a brand new pair of silk stockings.

Having rolled them up her legs and clipped them to the suspenders that dangled from her camiknickers, she turned around to look at him, a deliberate smile on her face.

'Now, do I look like the sort of person who could be ruthless?' She said, opening her arms wide and posing for him. 'Because I have been, you know. You can't run a successful business on kindness alone. I've had to hire and fire, be tough with suppliers and reprimand staff.'

'But you haven't ever had someone permanently terminated, have you?' he asked, crooking his fingers as he said the word *terminated*.

Lisa looked aghast. 'Are you saying Akira has?'

To her mounting panic, Rio shrugged. 'There have been rumours,' he said, 'but no one is prepared to point the finger for certain.'

She tried to laugh off his claim. 'That's just rubbish. It has to be. Akira isn't a killer.'

Instead of replying, Rio just looked at her. A long, steady gaze that shook her to the very core.

* * *

Despite everything Rio had intimated, Lisa continued to dress and apply her make-up as though nothing out of the ordinary was happening. In a few short hours she would be attending the most important event of her life but in the meantime she had to have a quick business meeting with her business partner. It was that simple. Oh hell! She wished she felt as calm as she was trying to appear.

Rio gave her a lift into the centre of London and there she insisted they part company. He was to go to the hotel where the orgy was to be held and check all the last minute details. She would get a taxi to Akira's and then meet Rio at the hotel by seven at the latest.

She knew he still wasn't convinced but at least he had accepted that she had to do things her way. They kissed briefly and then he was gone, caught up in a snarl of Kensington traffic. Raising her hand, Lisa flagged down a passing taxi.

Two hours later, Rio glanced at his watch and wondered for the twentieth time what was keeping Lisa. Although it wasn't yet seven he was worried. Well, to be truthful, he'd been worried ever since she refused his offer to go with her to see Akira. But Lisa was headstrong and, infuriating though her behaviour could be at times, it was a part of her that he loved. That and a million other character traits, he thought to himself, feeling an inner glow.

It had come as a shock to him, falling in love with Lisa. He was so used to being independent, footloose and fancy-free, that to suddenly find himself wanting to be linked body and soul with one particular person scared him a little at first. But it all felt so right. The way they

were together – thinking identical things and then simultaneously blurting out exactly the same, sometimes
totally ridiculous, words – proved to him that they were on
corresponding wavelengths.

Moreover, he couldn't get over the feeling of pure joy
every time she walked through the door, or simply glanced up and looked at him. He knew he had a soft,
sensitive streak but he never realised how ridiculously
romantic he was capable of being. Love songs on the
radio, the sight of a couple holding hands, babies in
prams, even tear-jerking films, all caused his heart to
melt.

I'll have to get a grip, he thought periodically, and then
instantly wondered why when he was enjoying this new-
found facet of his personality. He glanced at his watch
again. It was now only a few minutes to seven. Glancing
out of the window of the hotel suite, which afforded a
view of the street at the front of the hotel, he found
himself urging a black cab to draw up. Suddenly, his
longing to see Lisa again was like a physical pain and he
was suffering. His only hope was that Lisa wasn't suffering
too.

By eight o'clock, Lisa still hadn't put in an appearance and
now Rio was so worried he seriously considered ringing
the police. It frustrated him to realise that he wasn't sure
of Akira's exact address and so he couldn't even go round
there himself and rescue her from whatever terrible
situation he was certain she was in. Although he had
mentioned it, he had deliberately downplayed the
rumours that he had heard about Akira. Now he wished to

God he hadn't. Perhaps Lisa wouldn't have been so hell-bent on going to see him alone.

It was too late now, he realised. And yet too early to ring the police. Knowing them of old, he was certain they would simply laugh off his fears and insist that he wait until Lisa had been missing for twenty four hours. But if he did that, she could be found floating face down in the Thames by then. It was a chilling thought and one which wouldn't leave him.

By eight thirty the first of the press had started to arrive. According to Lisa's instructions – 'just in case', she had said airily – he let them into the suite and stood patiently to one side while the photographers went mad, pointing their cameras at everything in sight. One of the reporters tried to pump him on the exact nature of the party but Rio, refusing to be drawn into a difficult situation, simply insisted that he wait until the press conference at nine o'clock. He just hoped and prayed that Lisa would have arrived by then.

His hopes proved fruitless and by ten past nine, he had to concede defeat and go downstairs to the conference room that had been set up especially for the press conference.

'I'm sorry Miss Swift is late,' he began, putting up his hands as though to ward off the inevitable angry response.

A trickle of grumbles and irritated sighs greeted his words and several of the reporters looked pointedly at their watches. Some turned their heads to look at the door, as though they expected Lisa to come bursting through it full of apologies.

Rio also stared at the door and willed the same thing

but nothing happened. Trying to quell his feelings of panic, which had slowly mounted to an unbelievable degree, he picked up Lisa's briefcase which she had left with him, opened it and took out her speech and the notes she had made for the question-and-answer session afterwards.

'Ladies and gentlemen of the press,' Rio said loudly. 'I cannot apologise enough for Miss Swift's unfortunate absence. But perhaps you would be good enough to bear with me while I outline the original concept and subsequent success of Flights of Fancy.' So saying he glanced down at the sheaf of papers in his hands and began to recite Lisa's words aloud.

For almost forty minutes, Rio managed to put his fears to the back of his mind while he read out the short but erudite speech and then parried the questions that the assembled throng threw at him from all angles. With a scant ten minutes to spare he wished everyone a curt but pleasant goodbye and raced upstairs to the suite where some of the guests had already started to arrive.

Thankfully, being the troopers that they were, the team leaders Shane, Curtis, Jake and Tom had everything under control. A small bar had been set up and a couple of traditionally-clad waitresses wandered around with silver trays laden with glasses of champagne. Of the six guests that had already arrived, all had a drink of some description and a couple were starting to remove vital parts of their clothing.

More guests arrived and he found himself acting as mine host, greeting each woman as she stepped through the door with a strong handshake and then a kiss on the cheek.

Feeling pleased on Lisa's behalf, he noticed that everyone had taken the trouble to dress in twenties' costume and some looked quite stunning. He envied in passing the men who would be servicing them that evening but didn't feel any compunction whatsoever to join in the fun which was beginning to get underway in earnest.

By ten thirty the vast room was full to the gills. Some of the guests remained dressed and danced smoochily with their chosen partners. While the majority were in various states of undress and copulating with wild abandon upon the huge mounds of cushions.

This is just how Lisa dreamed the orgy would go, he found himself thinking. But why the hell wasn't she there to witness her success for herself?

For some obscure reason he found himself wandering into one of the suite's two bedrooms, where more naked bodies cavorted shamelessly on the king-sized beds. Walking over to the window, he drew back the curtain and stared out. Unusually for central London, the street outside was deserted and after looking anxiously up and down the road for about ten minutes he felt a profound sense of despair. Lisa was dead, he thought sadly, at the very least she was in serious danger.

Why? Why? Why? The word kept reverberating around in his head and then he realised he could hear a strange noise – like wings beating, only louder. All at once he realised it was the sound of a helicopter and he found himself straining to see where it was in the dense, black sky. It was no good, he could hear it but he couldn't see anything, although it sounded as though it was right overhead.

All of a sudden he was gripped by an irrational feeling of elation, which quickly turned to doubt. Nevertheless, he found himself walking quickly out of the room, negotiating the sprawl of bodies on the floor as he crossed the sitting room and stepping out into the corridor. From that moment he started to run.

Sprinting down the corridors and up flights of stairs, taking them two or three at a time, he suddenly found himself confronted by another small flight of stairs at the top of which was a door which obviously opened out onto the hotel roof. Ignoring the red and white notices which warned him not to open the door at any cost, he turned the handle and stepped out into the cool night air.

It took a few moments for his eyes to adjust to the darkness and then, glancing to his right, he noticed a large fluorescent 'H' painted on the concrete. All at once he heard the distinctive sound of the helicopter again and he watched with nervous trepidation as the small black aircraft emerged from the dark blanket of sky and hovered over him, looking for all the word like an outsized bluebottle.

As he watched, the craft dipped to one side, turned and made a perfect landing on the 'H'. Heedless of the rotors, Rio rushed forward. Someone was emerging from the helicopter, a dark, diminutive figure. For a moment his heart leaped as he thought: Lisa! But in the next moment his joy was shattered as he realised the passenger was Akira.

Rio waited with bated breath, watching the helicopter with one eye, hoping against hope that the next person to emerge would be Lisa herself. The other eye he kept firmly fixed on the Japanese businessman who now approached him with small but confident strides. As Akira came to stand in front of him, Rio turned his head to face him squarely.

'Where's Lisa?' he asked bluntly, unable to contain the panic and aggression in his tone.

To his frustration Akira ignored his question and instead stretched out a hand. 'Señor Fernandez?'

'*Mr* Fernandez,' Rio said, 'I was born and raised in England. I've never even visited Mexico City where all my relatives are.'

For a brief moment he couldn't help wondering why he was bothering to offer any kind of explanation to this man. Akira was the enemy. He had humiliated Lisa in the past and had done God knows what to her that very evening. Surprised by the overwhelming anger which suddenly erupted inside him, Rio ignored the proffered hand and instead landed the inscrutable Japanese man a good right hook on the jaw.

He watched as Akira staggered backwards with a mystified look on his face and then crumpled into a heap on the concrete roof. Walking up to the fallen man, Rio stood over him and fixed him with a contemptuous glare.

'Where the hell is she?' he repeated through clenched teeth. 'Where's Lisa?'

All at once he heard a voice. For one crazy moment it sounded like Lisa calling his name. Although he tried to dismiss the sound as simply wishful thinking, he glanced up and it was then he saw her. Dressed as she had been earlier that afternoon, in the green dress, cloche hat and low-heeled cream shoes which had made him laugh at their quaintness, Lisa stepped down from the helicopter and began to run towards him.

'Lisa?' His voice was suddenly thick with emotion and as he stepped quickly forward he felt the flesh and blood reality of her as she hurled herself into his outstretched arms. 'I thought you were dead,' he said hoarsely. 'I thought he had killed you.'

'Now there's a novel claim. I must remember to include it in my autobiography.'

As the amused voice spoke, Rio whirled around, taking Lisa with him. He stared at Akira who had got to his feet and now seemed more concerned about brushing the creases out of his immaculate suit than anything else.

'What else was I supposed to think?' Rio demanded, glaring at Akira. 'Lisa goes off to see you at five o'clock, promising to return by seven, and then four hours later she still hasn't returned.'

'So you naturally assumed that I'd killed her?' Akira said, still sounding amused, much to Rio's continued annoyance. 'There are other more feasible explanations you know. You could have tried one or two of those first before jumping to wild conclusions.'

Ignoring his sarcasm, Rio said, 'Such as?'

'Such as a bomb scare,' Akira replied calmly. 'The whole building was evacuated and we weren't allowed back in until they were certain the incident was just a hoax.' Smiling across at Lisa, he added. 'After an hour of standing around in the freezing car park, Lisa and I decided to go for a drink instead.'

'Oh, so while I was going out of my mind with worry, you were sitting in some cosy bar having a romantic tête-à-tête?' Rio now directed his accusation at Lisa who looked as though she was trying not to laugh.

'There was nothing romantic about it, I can assure you,' Akira cut in. 'Lisa said she had business to discuss and so that's what we did. We discussed business.'

For a moment Rio felt as though the wind had been taken out of his sails, then he felt Lisa's lips pressing against his and he allowed himself to simply drown in the wonder of her kiss.

'By the way, I believe congratulations are in order,' Akira continued, when the couple had finally broken apart. 'I hear you and Lisa are a serious item, as the Americans would say.'

Rio glanced at him in surprise. 'You don't mind?'

To his relief, Akira shook his head. 'No, of course not. Thanks to company gossip, I knew all about the two of you. And when I saw the look in Lisa's eyes when she began to tell me about you tonight I had to concede defeat. You're a lucky man, Mr Fernandez, she's quite the loveliest woman I've ever known.'

It look a few minutes for Rio to register that Akira, the man he had loathed and feared in equal measure, was giving them his blessing.

'Rio, please, call me Rio,' he said, looking non-plussed.

At this point the two men finally shook hands and then Lisa suggested that they join the party before it ended.

On the way back down to the suite, Lisa briefly explained the discussion that had taken place between her and Akira. With baited breath, Rio waited for her to tell him the outcome. To his surprise, it was Akira who replied to his unasked question.

'If you want to buy my share, in Flights of Fancy, Mr – er – Rio. I want you to know I have no problem with that.' He paused. 'I'll get my people on to it first thing in the morning.'

Rio couldn't help an inward smile at the Japanese man's use of a typical Americanism 'my people'. 'Okay, great,' he said. 'Let's shake on it now.'

'But you don't know how much I want for my share of the business,' Akira said, clearly not used to a situation where he didn't have to negotiate.

Rio shrugged. 'I couldn't really care less. Lisa and Flights of Fancy are all I am concerned about. Money is just money.'

'Then you must have a fair amount of it,' Akira said astutely. 'Perhaps I should think about revising my original figure.'

'Don't you dare,' Lisa cut in, laughing. 'We have a deal remember?'

To Rio and Lisa's surprise, Akira smiled broadly. 'Yes, we have a deal.' He mentioned a figure which Rio was surprised to find was much less than he had anticipated. He could afford it easily.

'Done,' Rio said quickly and the two men shook hands once again.

When they arrived at the party it was still in full swing and it was difficult for Lisa to make out who was who among the seething mass of naked, or near-naked, bodies.

'Oh, I missed all the costumes,' she wailed regretfully.

Rio laughed. 'Don't worry, darling. You'll get to see them when everyone gets dressed to go home.

As Rio put his arm around her and squeezed her hard against him, Lisa laughed happily. 'Go home? It doesn't look to me as though anyone's planning to go home tonight. Thank goodness the suite is booked until tomorrow lunchtime.'

There was a small area of vacant space just in front of the bar and Rio managed to unearth three chairs for them to sit on. With no sign of the barman employed by Arabella and Sacha, Lisa elected to pour drinks for the three of them.

It was actually five thirty in the morning when the last guest finally left. Apologising profusely for being a party-pooper, Akira had conceded defeat at around four o'clock, explaining that in a couple of hours' time he had to catch a flight to New York.

Relieved that they were alone at long last, Lisa turned to Rio and smiled warmly. 'It seems as though the orgy was a hit,' she said. 'Every one of the guests thanked me for the best time of their lives.'

'And poor little Lisa never got to join in the fun,' Rio joked, his eyes twinkling.

Lisa glanced at her watch and then gave him a suggestive smile. 'The suite's still good for another six hours. Why don't we have an orgy of our own?'

'Just the two of us?' Rio teased. 'That's not much of an orgy.'

Pretending to growl at him, Lisa pulled him off his chair and across to a pile of cushions. 'Believe me, darling,' she said suggestively as she fell back and pulled him down on top of her, 'I'm going to make sure you discover for once and for all that I'm all the woman you can handle.'

A Message from the Publisher

Headline Liaison is a new concept in erotic fiction: a list of books designed for the reading pleasure of both men and women, to be read alone – or together with your lover. As such, we would be most interested to hear from our readers.

Did you read the book with your partner? Did it fire your imagination? Did it turn you on – or off? Did you like the story, the characters, the setting? What did you think of the cover presentation? In short, what's your opinion? If you care to offer it, please write to:

> The Editor
> Headline Liaison
> 338 Euston Road
> London NW1 3BH

Or maybe you think you could do better if you wrote an erotic novel yourself. We are always on the look-out for new authors. If you'd like to try your hand at writing a book for possible inclusion in the Liaison list, here are our basic guidelines: We are looking for novels of approximately 80,000 words in which the erotic content should aim to please both men and women and should not describe illegal sexual activity (pedophilia, for example). The novel should contain sympathetic and interesting characters, pace, atmosphere and an intriguing plotline.

If you'd like to have a go, please submit to the Editor a sample of at least 10,000 words, clearly typed on one side of the paper only, together with a short resumé of the storyline. Should you wish your material returned to you please include a stamped addressed envelope. If we like it sufficiently, we will offer you a contract for publication.

More Erotic Fiction from Headline Liaison

VOLUPTUOUS VOYAGE

Lacey Carlyle

The stranger came up behind her and slid a hand round her waist while the other glided over her breasts. Lucy stared out into the darkness as he fondled her. She knew she should be outraged but somehow she wasn't . . .

Fleeing from her American fiancé, the bloodless Boyd, after discovering he's more interested in her bank account than her body, Lucy meets an enigmatic stranger on the train to New York. Their brief sensual encounter leaves her wanting more, so with her passions on fire Lucy embarks for England accompanied by her schoolfriend, Faye.

They sail on a luxurious ocean liner, the *SS Aphrodite*, whose passenger list includes some of the most glamorous socialites of the 1930s. Among them are the exiled White Russians, Count Andrei and Princess Sonya, and the two friends are soon drawn into a dark and decadent world of bizarre eroticism . . .

0 7472 5145 2

More Erotic Fiction from Headline Liaison

SEVEN DAYS

Adult Fiction for Lovers

J J Duke

Erica's arms were spread apart and she pulled against the silk bonds – not because she wanted to escape but to savour the experience. As the silk bit into her wrists, a surge of pure pleasure shot through her, so intense that the darkness behind the blindfold turned crimson . . .

Erica is not exactly an innocent abroad. On the other hand, she's never been in New York before. This trip could make or break her career in the fashion business. It could also free her from the inhibitions that prevent her exploring her sensual needs.

She has a week for her work commitments – and a week to take her pleasure in the world's wildest city. Now's her chance to make her most daring dreams come true. She's on a voyage of erotic discovery and she doesn't care if things get a little crazy. After all, it can only last seven days . . .

0 7472 5094 4

More Erotic Fiction from Headline Liaison

Vermilion Gates

Lucinda Chester

Rob trailed a finger over Rowena's knee, letting it drift upwards. She slapped his hand. 'Get off me,' she hissed, 'or I'll have you for sexual harassment.' Nevertheless, part of her wanted him to carry on and stroke the soft white skin above her lacy stocking-tops . . .

Rowena Fletcher's not having much fun these days. She's a stressed-out female executive with a workload more jealous than any lover and no time, in any case, to track one down.

Then she is referred to Vermilion Gates, a discreet clinic in the Sussex countryside which specialises in relaxation therapy. There, in the expert hands of trained professionals, Rowena discovers there's more than one way to relieve her personal stress . . .

0 7472 5210 6

Adult Fiction for Lovers from Headline LIAISON